COVENTRY CALVERT

Mario Martinez was born in New York. After university and military service he studied at the American Academy of Dramatic Arts. Several years followed in film production. From films he switched to fundraising for the Catholic Church.

Little did he know what lay ahead while working for an order of Belfast Priests; it was an era when sectarian killings were common in Northern Ireland. Despite killings near the Falls Road where he worked, he raised a fortune in weeks. This led to fundraising in Ireland for 14 years.

No longer active in fundraising, Mario now lives in London. Coventry Calvert is his first work of fiction; his other books are 'Lady's Men' and 'Hell, Fire and Damnation'.

Many experiences give Mario much to draw on in his writing. To mention but a few, he's been questioned by the FBI and followed by the KGB, acted with Robert Redford, socialised with Salvador Dali, been taken for 'Carlos The Jackal' in Kenya and questioned, produced a film in Sudan for UNICEF, and was behind the Iron Curtain back when Americans in Russia often disappeared.

In 'Coventry Calvert' Mario blends a fictitious character with historical facts and people from recent history, and he weaves a story that may, in parts, seem closer to the truth than fiction. Often the stitch is so tight and plausible that it's hard to tell where the facts end and the yarn begins. Readers will judge for themselves.

COVENTRY CALVERT

Mario Martinez

COVENTRY CALVERT

Olympia Publishers
London

www.olympiapublishers.com
OLYMPIA PAPERBACK EDITION

A CIP catalogue record for this title is
available from the British Library.

ISBN: 978-1-905513-54-3

This is a work of fiction.
Names, characters, places and incidents originate from the writer's
imagination. Any resemblance to actual persons, living or dead, is
purely coincidental.

First Published in 2009

Olympia Publishers
60 Cannon Street
London
EC4N 6NP

Printed in Great Britain

Acknowledgments

New York New York
by Leonard Bernstein, Betty Comden and Adolph Green

My thanks to Gordon Cave and Brian Nobbs for solving my computer problems and assisting in other ways. Thanks also to Marion Parry and Joe Masefield for proof reading help, and to the eye specialist Dr. Joe Toddonio for his many contributions.

ONE

December 7th, 1951 was a day Coventry Calvert would never forget. It was her tenth birthday, someone she admired had escaped from jail and a snowstorm was raging in New York. The blizzard was the backdrop for the daring jailbreak of Willie Sutton – a villain whose career had been jewellery thefts and bank robberies in the states of New York and Pennsylvania. A pistol-packing threat he may have been, but not once had violence been his style. He had never physically hurt anyone. He was – for most people – the likeable face of criminality. The day before the blizzard, everyone who had followed his career knew that Willie was in jail. But now, again, he had outfoxed his jailers and escaped. The cops in New York and Pennsylvania hated him. In or out of jail, he kept slipping through their fingers, but his fans in America had warm feelings for Willie. Millions admired him and thought he was great. They chuckled and wished him luck in his quest for freedom. After all, he had never harmed them. Indeed, over the years he had only given them reason to smile. His tricky style of larceny that gave a finger to the cops was most attractive to hosts of Americans who liked creative enterprise. They knew that to be a great villain, industry and dedication were required – qualities that Sutton had in abundance. By the same token Willie was no Robin Hood. Whatever he robbed, he kept. Then, after a taste of freedom – during which he would stick up banks and loot more jewellery stores – he would get caught, locked up, and then bust out of jail. The press, especially in his hometown of New York, loved the pint-sized crook they dubbed 'Slick Willie'. Newspapers telling of his antics would fly off the stands when Willie was thieving in his prime.

That snowy morning in December America awoke to learn that the legendary Willie had escaped again from jail, this time from the Philadelphia County Prison in Pennsylvania. As usual, crafty Willie had done it with a plan, and when its elements converged, he seized the moment and fled. He didn't have much schooling, but in a way he embodied all that was American – a person never discouraged and held back by obstacles. Willie's daring escape was the lead story on many radios and newspapers.

Coventry Calvert was the most unlikely of Sutton fans – she was a brilliant convent pupil from Manhattan. Influenced by her wealthy parents' zeal for Sutton's deeds, by the age of ten, Coventry knew just about all there was to know about the thief – he beguiled her. She had seen him in the movies and up on the screen in the newsreels. He was little, yet big as life, his hands cuffed behind his back, clothes ruffled and being led away by the cops. His dancing eyes captivated her. For Coventry, Willie's eyes were like bees buzzing round a honey-pot, but in his case, the honey-pots were usually banks because, as he was quoted as saying, 'That's where the money was'.

Eyes were a human feature Coventry noticed in people. No Peter Pan, lollypop kid was young Miss Calvert. She was deep. The focus of her mind was different from other girls, or even boys her own age. She was miles ahead of them in maturity and self-confidence, and she viewed Sutton not so much as a criminal, but like a Scarlet Pimpernel. In her active, vivid mind, 'he wandered here, he wandered there, he wandered almost everywhere', and hard as they tried, the law could never really hold him. He was the 'genie' the cops could never bottle, now you see him, now you don't. She liked the way he would change his appearance, dye his hair, alter his silhouette, expand his nostrils, wear lifts in his shoes and crook in many different uniforms.

The backdrop Sutton used to escape from jail was the snowstorm that paralysed the east coast of America, closed schools and caused streets to vanish under blankets of snow. Was Coventry's birthday what she and her family were celebrating that morning? Not a chance! They were celebrating Willie – the crook that didn't care for other crooks – who felt they were untrustworthy hoodlums of bad habits and filthy language. The Calvert family loved the contradictions of Willie's nature and his cunning ways. For Coventry's clan and countless others, Willie was special – he was an example of how the human spirit can overcome great odds. The fact that he was a villain was irrelevant. Crime was his game; he was willing to pay the price, to lead a life on the run, and even go to jail; what was there not to like about Willie Sutton? That's how Coventry and her parents felt, along with scores of people in New York and America.

Coventry was special. She was so outstanding that she was beyond the comprehension of many. She was the brightest pupil in Mother Cabrini Convent – a school in upper Manhattan with scenic views of the Hudson River, the George Washington Bridge and the palisades of New Jersey. When she was nine, her IQ was found to be amazingly high. Outstanding too were the hints of the body to come. She had a beautifully chiselled face and it was clear that one day her frame would be willowy. Her most striking feature was her vivid, rich eyes – her right eye was blue, the other brown.

Some people considered her eyes to be a punishment of nature – something eerie – something very odd. A pious Catholic lady who never missed mass called her a freak. But even at her tender age, Coventry was at ease regarding her eyes – they were the way they were, and if people chose to whisper about them so be it. She was shockingly mature for one so young and Paula, Coventry's mother, had a lot to do with this maturity. She once told Coventry: 'Despite appearances, most people are insecure – remember that. When someone stares at you, look him or her in the eye. They will wither – you will have struck at the soul of their insecurities'.

Coventry was nine years old when these words were spoken. 'You're special in many ways', said Paula. When, by the age of nineteen, Coventry's figure had fully blossomed, she became a magnet for men's eyes and despite nature's blemish, she was the envy of many women. She could easily be mistaken for a young Greta Garbo. It was then that Coventry's Godfather whispered to Paula that

Coventry's body was created by the devil to tempt men and that her eyes were a beautiful enigma, but all this is skipping ahead of our story, so let's return to the morning of the blizzard and the day Willie Sutton escaped from his Pennsylvania Prison.

T W O

Sutton was forty-six when he escaped. It was the third maximum-security prison he had broken out of and the Governor of Pennsylvania was fit to be tied. Like so many of his exploits, Sutton's escape was a work of art. The media loved his brass and skill he employed in carrying it out. His escape was doubly outrageous, since it had taken place under the noses of prison guards. Due to the blizzard and darkness, the guards in the gun-tower couldn't make out who the figures with the ladder were at the bottom of the courtyard wall. "We're from the electricity company," Willie called up to the guard. "There's a cable down, we're going up." Willie, the first to climb the ladder was soon over the wall and into the back of a milk van that happened to be passing in the street outside the prison walls. Lady Luck was with Willie that night, and when the guards finally copped on that an escape was under way, the only thing left of Sutton was his footprints in the snow. The elements needed to execute his escape were night and snow, and for them to coincide, Sutton and his chums had waited for several years, all of Sutton's fellow escapees were quickly apprehended. Already hated by the New York and Pennsylvania cops, the latter now thoroughly despised him. Years later, when Willie was nearly seventy years old – with the help of another lady – Sutton would again escape from jail for a final time.

With the snow falling hard, Sutton had been on the run for twenty-four hours. Hungry, cold and skimpily dressed, he had battled the elements across the Pennsylvania state line and was now up to his knees in snow – he was in a wooded area of 'Palisades', New Jersey, near the city of New York. In all that time, the only thing in his stomach was milk he had lifted from the van Lady Luck had sent his way. It was now night again; he had struggled to keep going and was very near the George Washington Bridge. His aim was to reach the borough of Brooklyn, where he had a pal with a flat and money Willie had hidden in his flat. The money was from a bank heist Willie had pulled years before. First he had to cross the GW into Manhattan where, not far from the bridge stood Mother Cabrini, the convent school Coventry Calvert attended. Willie didn't have a penny in his pocket, so obstacles had to be jumped before he was safe, and he had to be watchful because the cops were hopping mad. They had guns ready to be drawn if they saw him. Given half a chance they would fill him full of holes, and then they would claim that Willie had a weapon – which he didn't have – so they would conveniently provide one near his body. Best to lay low and rest, thought Willie and, with the snow still falling, he sheltered in a derelict shed.

That night, Willie's mind raced wildly because he knew steps must be taken to alter his facial appearance. Dead or alive his face would again be all over the newspapers. He recalled hearing from a fellow crook about a surgeon who was once legit but had lost his license to practice because he was a crook and had been found out. That night, Willie searched his mind for the name of the surgeon and when it finally came to him he thought, That's it, Dr. Brandywine.

When morning arrived, the starving, frozen Willie stood by the road and hitched a ride across the bridge on a truck driven by a chatty, well-spoken black man in his twenties, who didn't let on that he knew who was sitting next to him. But he knew who it was. Sutton's escape was big news, reported on the radio and in all the newspapers. He knew that it was Willie, but he didn't let on. He was not going to report Willie to the police. The black man – who had the noble name of Vincent Erwin Benjamin Yearwood – put Willie at ease and spoke only of the snow and baseball and those damned New York Yankees. Willie's mind was not on baseball – it was on hot stew and the fifty grand he had stashed in his pal's Brooklyn flat. He wasn't worried about the cops right now; he was worried about his money because he had secretly hidden the loot under the kitchen floorboards. His pal was a crook, and Willie didn't like crooks because he could never trust them. When all was said and done they were just a bunch of crooks.

Once across the bridge, the driver stopped to let Willie out and the grateful Sutton thanked and shook the driver's big black hand with his little white one. The well-featured Negro could see that Willie was starving, so he reached in his pocket and gave him a five-dollar bill. "Here buddy," he said, "get something to eat."

The black man couldn't afford the money. He was a full-time student who worked part-time to supplement his income. A decorated US Marine, he had fought in the battle of Iwo Jima and was now studying Journalism at New York's City College with the financial help offered under the American GI Bill Of Rights. "God bless you," said Willie, then he headed for the subway station, through pyramids of snow, while the black man drove off through the streets of Manhattan and never said a word to anyone. Whatever his race or views at the time, this black man was unusual – just the way Coventry and Willie Sutton were unusual.

Two hours later, Willie was safe in Brooklyn and so was his money. Naturally his pal knew about Willie's escape and was ready with stew from a can, bagels from a Jewish bakery and a fifth of whiskey from a liquor store run by a guy named Vito – a fellow who had once been a fulltime crook, but was now only crooking on a part-time basis.

Willie had again outfoxed and mortified authority. No one knew where he was and his fans all across the nation were chuckling. The newspapers – especially in New York – had a whale of a time and youthful Coventry read them all with laughter, rolling around the living room floor.

With the snow nearly cleared, New York returned to normal and Coventry was back in school. World War II had been over for six years and just beyond the GW, looking north and set against the shores of New Jersey, a parade of rusting Liberty Ships lay anchored in the Hudson as far as the eye could see. Between classes, Coventry would look out at the bridge and think that maybe, just maybe, Willie had slipped into New York that way. New York was his natural habitat and he was brazen enough to start thieving where least expected. The little man had balls the size of Texas. This thought had not escaped the cops, who prowled the city, pressing the underworld for the whereabouts of 'that little Irish bastard' who once again had made them look like shit. No one knew about Willie's links with his Brooklyn pal and that the pal had digs in the basement of 231 President Street – an Italian neighbourhood where names like Amalfatana Scupelleti; Dominica Chiamonte and Angelo Benedito were common. It was a district where the boys from the Mafia were in charge and it was a neighbourhood where the cops seldom ventured. Here the Mafia ruled and God help the black man that entered their turf and lingered too long. It was a good place for crooks, so long as they were white, knew their place and were respectful to the local Godfather.

Coventry was unique in many ways. Her written compositions were near flawless, without any useless words in her writing. Verbs abounded, keeping thoughts alive and her typing skills were superb. She had skipped grades often and was destined for university at an early age. At a time when young girls dwelt on magazines, romance and other silliness, Coventry's interests were politics, journalism, world events, baseball and, of course, Willie Sutton. She had often compared Willie with Joe DiMaggio, the star player of the New York Yankees whose Italian roots and talent crafted play as smooth as live oil, which was how, in the mind of Coventry, Slick Willie plied his trade.

The Mother Cabrini Nuns stressed decorum and lady-like behaviour in preparation for a Catholic life whose ultimate reward would be heaven. "The tone of a woman's voice is important," Sister Margaret-Mary would say. "It should be soft, gentle and low." The girls listened and practiced the art of speaking softly when they moved with poise from class to class after the bell. It was only when Sister touched on the dangers attached to romance and sex – a word the nuns never used – that the girls giggled and glanced at one another. Young Coventry listened clinically in class. She was always eager to learn something new, when it came to matters of romance, lady-like behaviour and the proper preparation for a future married life – these things fired her mind very little. 'Girls', said Margaret-Mary, 'never cross your legs at the knees. Cross them at the ankles. God made legs for standing and walking not for displays that tempt Satan'.

Her Catholic schooling complete at fifteen, Coventry began university, where she majored in teaching, world history and journalism. Her virginity intact, she was a shining example of a convent girl with her legs properly crossed. By the seventeenth year of her life, her body reflected the feast yet to come and both men and boys found it hard to keep their hands or their eyes off her. But though she mixed easily with the male sex, never once did the impulses to mate concentrate her mind or loins. Nor was frigidity a reason for this, just her mind was open to penetration. Unlike the other convent girls, the thought of sex held no fear or guilt. She was her own person and she was in no rush. Her outlook on sexual matters was clinical. For her, God's message was clear – pass life on – and that entailed doing what her girl friends called 'the dirty'. What else was life's purpose but for life to continue? That's how pragmatic her view of sex was at seventeen. At the same time, she would heed the words and advice of her Jesuit priest Godfather. She would be on guard against Satan's Angel, who she believed was always standing to the left of her, always ready to recruit new disciples for his master.

In 1959 at the age of eighteen, Coventry gained her university degree and began her high school teaching career. She was a fine educator and her grasp of history, politics and world affairs were profound for one of eighteen. No one could ignore her flair for teaching. That was one thing. Another was the impact her appearance had on people, those eyes that pulled viewers in and a body that raced men's hormones.

By now, Willie Sutton had been captured and was serving 'life' in New York State's Attica Prison. He had spent his years of freedom working by day and living by night in a Staten Island nursing home helping elderly people. When caught, the staff and the old folks were amazed to discover who Willie was. Many felt honoured to have known the kind, gentle little man. Needless to say that on his days off 'kind, gentle Willie' would hop the Staten Island Ferry to downtown Manhattan and rob a jewellery store, sailing to and from his capers on the five cents a ride ferry. Willie would marvel at the sight of the Statue of Liberty – that American symbol of the free, brave, and of the crooks on the run from the law, like him.

When the gates of Attica Prison slammed on Sutton, he was fifty years old and Coventry was fourteen. When she was seventeen, and prompted by a vivid dream – one of many she was having about Sutton – she wrote to him and, to her great surprise he wrote back. One Saturday, a year after she was settled in her teaching post, an impulse drove her to visit Sutton, and again to her surprise, with no prior notice, she got in to see him. It was a visit neither she nor Sutton would ever regret, and not once – not even to her parents – did Coventry ever reveal this, or subsequent such visits to anyone. Two people from opposite ends of life's spectrum had joined together and forged an odd friendship.

The deaths of three people close to Coventry took place within two years of her twenty-sixth birthday. The last death carried a further shock – a deathbed confession. First her Godfather died, then her stepfather, and when Coventry was twenty-eight, her mother died of raging cancer at the age of fifty-one. Although her mother's death left her with a fortune, the independence that it brought did not overwhelm Coventry. She was now alone in the world. She had lost the three people that mattered most. No other relatives remained, except the man whose seed had given her life. It was then, in 1968, that Coventry altered the course of her life.

The year 1968 marked the final twelve months in the Presidency of LBJ – Lyndon B. Johnson. America was changing but not all for the good in Coventry's view. Liberal thinking was washing across the nation and drugs were ever present. The Vietnam War, student unrest and the results of new Liberal Immigration Laws were daily in evidence. It was not a time Coventry liked. She felt that her country was in decline and too liberal in outlook. Foreign faces from third world countries were more evident and, out of the blue, 'black was beautiful' a ridiculous notion to her, since all white people are anything but beautiful. Forces in the US agreed with Coventry that the nation was in social decline and to them, it was clear who, in the name of liberalism had helped trigger America's downward slide; LBJ's predecessor, John F. Kennedy, the rich, white boy from a family of bootleggers whose ultimate 'Camelot' was a bullet in the head. Coventry felt that LBJ was no better than JFK, so for these reasons, and because of her mother's deathbed revelation, she decided to leave America and move to Britain. London, she thought. There is something I must see in the Café De Paris.

THREE

Her mother's confession shook Coventry but she cast it from her mind. It was too much to deal with then. Her mother was dead and this was the greater blow. A raging cancer had reduced Paula to the size of a doll and killed her.

It was well after the funeral that Coventry's mind returned to her mother's final words, and back to the Café de Paris where it had taken place. Coventry had cringed when the words slipped from her mother's lips, but at the same time a tingle of excitement ran through her loins. It disturbed her to hear such a confession, and for the first time in her life Coventry wondered if her eyes were signals for people to decipher, or a reminder of the act that brought her into being. She had to take stock. The confession had thrown a twist into her life she now had to confront. She had to see the place where the deed took place, an act that shook her, yet aroused her curiosity. Suddenly her life seemed headed in one direction – London and the Café De Paris.

Coventry flew to London in January 1969 after the presidential inauguration of Richard Nixon. He was a Conservative and this was preferable to having a Democrat in the White House, but in her view, the rot in the social fabric of America had set in, and was brought about by the United States Supreme Court's liberal interpretation of laws. The 'Immigration and Nationality Act Amendment' of 1965, which did away with national origin, race, or ancestry as a basis for immigration to America was in Coventry's mind a mistake, an error that in time would lead to dire social consequences.

Coventry rented a Belgravia flat in one of London's very best districts. Although quite rich, she had a deep respect for money. Her stepfather had worked hard for his wealth and had invested wisely. She would not dishonour his memory by spending her legacy foolishly. She would use money like the tool that it was, not as an instrument to curry envy from others and make her life a meaningless charade.

Her Godfather had warned her to be aware of 'The Evil Eye'. 'Never encourage The Evil Eye', he said. She would not draw undue attention to herself with material displays. She would be guided by high standards. As for her personal presentation, she would be modern and modestly outstanding with the looks God had given her. She was in the flower of womanhood and wished to know what its buds had to offer.

Since she had an interest in the power of words, Coventry sought work in journalism – she felt she had to do something of value with her life that involved words carrying a message. She would not lead a life geared to pleasure like Aly Khan, Doris Duke and others. The world was a feast that lay at her feet, but its growing liberal menu was not to her liking. Given the chance, she would be a standard bearer of conservative ideals; she felt that there were values that had to be retained, not discarded for the sake of liberally inspired aims. She was happy to be away from America, with all its growing tensions, glad to be living in Belgravia with its atmosphere of solid, unshakable permanency. The Café De Paris lay in waiting and as she grew in courage, Coventry's new life started easing into place.

With her skills and fetching looks, it wasn't long before she found work as a reporter with a newspaper called *The London Evening View*. Her modest column would appear twice weekly and deal with all manner of subjects from an American perspective. The column would be called 'One Yank's View'.

Anxious and slightly shifty Trevor Tiplady – the man who hired her – and who was the newspaper's editor, had no doubts about Coventry's potential value to *The London Evening View*. Near the end of the interview, Coventry sat with her long legs crossed, wearing a skirt Sister Margaret-Mary would not have liked, but whose length Tiplady relished. In addition to her body, her eyes wove a web of wonder.

She passed his test with ease – her compositions and typing dazzled him – and as she uncrossed her legs and stood to leave, he drank her in with no attempt at concealment. Of average size and build, the well-dressed editor gave no hint of a sunny disposition. A smile was foreign to his lips, but on the whole, as far as Coventry could judge, he didn't seem a bad person. He appeared bedevilled by something and only he was privy to his demons.

In 1969, the Labour party ruled Britain and Jeremy Jones was Prime Minister. British troops were in Ulster, the Berlin Wall was up and the Cold War was at its height. The war in Vietnam raged on, Robert Kennedy and Martin Luther King had been shot, race riots abounded in America, oil was struck in Alaska, Holland had approved films of pornographic nature, and *The Pride of Miss Jean Brody* had reached the New York stage.

Educated woman that she was, Coventry knew the United Kingdom – or Great Britain as the nation was also known – was a political entity drawn together since the Norman Conquest, comprising England, Scotland, Wales and Northern Ireland. She wasn't in the country long before she realised that the UK was less than a nation living in total harmony – there were stresses at the fringes of the entity.

The Welsh thought they were unique. The Scots felt they were a race apart, they were Scots first, then British – and God help anyone that called them English – and the same applied to the Welsh. In Northern Ireland, Ulster Protestants were killing Irish-Catholics to retain their Britishness, even though most were transplanted Scots, and like the Catholics of Ulster, both were mostly born in Northern Ireland. The English felt they were superior to the lot but were increasingly shy about saying so, for fear of being attacked by the British press for being racist. The Welsh and Scots both looked forward to beating their snooty, English neighbours senseless on the super-charged, nationalistic battlegrounds of football and rugby, and in addition to all this, parts of Cornwall were grumbling for freedom from the whole lot. Nevertheless, on its own unique and laid-back way, the entity jogged along in the present with much to be proud of in its past. Then, of course, there was the matter of the British Monarchy.

Queen Elizabeth II, who was part Scot, part German was married to a chap whose bloodlines were not that British. Born in Greece of Danish-German parents, his surname had conveniently changed from Battenberg to Mountbatten and then to Windsor – the Queen's chosen name. Even Coventry's hero, Churchill, who had saved Britain in the war, and was booted out of office by the British electorate weeks after the V-E Day, was born of an American mother – Jenny Jerome –- who was a well-known adulteress one-quarter Iroquois Indian and years ahead of her time. Maybe, thought Coventry, that's where Winston's grit and cunning came from. Jenny Jacobson/ Jerome was a spunky Jewess who had a tattoo of a snake around her left wrist. She was born in 1854 and died in 1926. Grit certainly wasn't in the makeup of Mr. Chamberlain, the Prime Minister in the thirties, or in the soul of the British Nation when for years, Hitler's intentions were clear. Coventry thought it interesting that in 1940, the Conservative Lady Astor, an American from Virginia, the second elected female member of the British Parliament, who like Chamberlain was a first rate appeaser eventually saw the light and voted against her party, thereby helping to bring to power Winston Churchill's wartime government. Coventry was also well aware of another common thread, that the wartime leaders Churchill, Roosevelt, Stalin and even General Eisenhower, all had Jewish blood.

With August nearing, Coventry was ready for a visit to the Café De Paris. She had written cryptic pieces about Richard Nixon and how the Democratic Party had urged Democrats in Chicago to vote more than once, thereby robbing Nixon of the presidency in 1960 in favour of JFK.

She had also written a piece about Willie Sutton who by now had served seventeen years of his life sentence in Attica State Prison. But her story about Willie was, of necessity, incomplete. She had held

27

something back. She and Sutton had kept in touch. Something was on the brink of happening that she could not divulge.

Saturday night and Coventry is ready for the Café De Paris. She's looking like a rose, wearing a short blue dress moulded to a body that any man would love to pluck. With her hair swept back and her eyes like magnets, she's primed for what awaits her at the Café de Paris. Her stomach quivers. This visit was unavoidable – she's drawn to it with fears – but drawn to it she is. She hails a taxi, slithers in and heads for the dancehall. Out comes her mirror for a quick facial check. Fine! So far so good!

She arrives at the entrance of the Café de Paris with eyes the size of saucers and a rush of blood to the face. The narrow West End streets are crowded with taxis, buses and tourists from near and far. Piccadilly Circus is but a stone's throw away, as is Leicester Square. Café de Paris sits between the two. The Café entrance has little to boast about. Gone are the days when Princess Margaret would arrive with a cluster of friends. Gone are the days when the Café's code of dress was formal. It's on the seedy side now, giving the impression that the inside, like the outside, is rundown at the heels and that its best days are in the past. Gone are the days when the crest above the name, 'Café de Paris', symbolised the royalty and high society status of its patrons.

She enters the Café, descends a few steps and eases her way to the ticket booth. She pays, and little by little drifts into a world of strange-looking people, most with their best years behind them. She moves like a cat along the balcony, looking the Café over. Men spot her and instincts swing into play at the sight of her cleaved breasts and a body that lifts their spirits. Signs of the Victorian era are everywhere Coventry looks, but no longer is the little basement dancehall a venue of bygone Champagne and Chandeliers. She stops at the balcony railings and looks down. The main dance floor is below, deep beneath street level. The Café's shape is like the inside of a hollowed out egg. It pulls the eye down. Coventry's interest is the balcony's back staircase, that is hidden by closed double doors that swing both ways.

Not yet, thinks Coventry. First I must compose myself. Her heart is racing.

The balcony overhangs the two-tiered dancehall. She wandered around its perimeter, eyeing couples dancing on the tiny balcony dance floor near the closed double doors. She can see the intimacy between couples growing, and this Coventry finds compelling. Her eyes dilate. Her attention shifts below to the larger dance floor, then to the columns that support the balcony, and to the tables that encircles the floor. She looks all round, drinking everything in.

A host of sweaty guests are in the Café de Paris and others are drifting in on the hot, August evening. The atmosphere is pinched, on edge. Women were fanning themselves and most men shed their jackets and were down to shirtsleeves. Upstairs and down, the sexes were prowling. Looks of determinations are common. Nothing can disguise the patron's motives. They buy their tickets, take their chances, and whatever follows is or was not to be. If he or she clicks with a mate for the night, they click. If they don't, they move on to someone else. Coventry is drinking all of this in.

Old, middle-aged and youngish ladies with made up faces wait at tables, hoping for dance invitations. Men hover, stop, look, hate what they see and move on. Others like what they see and move in. Somehow in these rituals, strangers become friends – at least for the moment.

People are smoking and drinking. The smell of smoke, beer and whiskey hang heavy in the air – so too are people's spirits high with anticipation. Below, the dance floor reveals newly acquainted couples feeling each other out – a form of negotiation of short duration, leading to a friendship that may lead to sex and more.

A small band at the front of the dance floor plays The Windmills of Your Mind. The musty mix of perfumes and ladies with muzzled nests that perspire is everywhere. Most of the men are no better – shirts that cling to their torsos and their armpits are ringed with sweat. Coventry's eyes hop from couple to couple writhing slowly to the music down in the main dance floor. She dwells on a tall, dark man who's wooing the redhead in his arms. Smartly dressed, he is not down to shirtsleeves. With his left hand he strokes her hair, and with his right he draws her close, belly-to-belly to whisper in her ear. Coventry's back arches and her loins respond. All this is new and exciting to her. She stops to draw breath, then makes a mental note to keep the dark man in mind. She sits, digs for a cigarette and lights it. As the smoke streams from her nostrils she wonders about him. Who is he? What is he? Is he a gigolo? Shame steps in and she pushes the questions aside. She wonders what Margaret-Mary and her dead mother and Godfather would think of her, in the company of such people.

The band is playing on a low, elevated stage. On either side stairs rise to the front of the balcony, where people are prowling, looking and mingling. In its cabaret heyday – the 20s and 30s – it was down these stairs that stars like Noel Coward, Maurice Chevalier and Marlene Dietrich would make their entrance in the presence of royalty and high society that came to the Café to see them. On both sides of the stage, doors lead back to a bar and to a staircase that climbs to the balcony and to more people prowling, looking and mingling. Opposite the stage and across the dance floor there is still another set of doors leading to a final staircase. They in turn lead to the balcony and beyond. This staircase is the reason Coventry had come to the Café De Paris. This is the same staircase at the rear of the balcony by the closed doors. Coventry has a journey to make to the top it.

Due to its depth below street level, in World War II the Café de Paris billed itself as the safest place to dance in London. This is what Martin Paulson, the Dane who managed the Café said in 1941 – but he was wrong; on a night in early 1941, two bombs crashed, killing Paulsen and the black orchestra leader called was Ken Johnson. His Caribbean band was playing when the bombs struck the dancehall. Some eighty guests were killed in the Café that night and more died at the nearby 'Madrid' restaurant.

Coventry had politely refused dance invitations from men whose motives were obvious. Most of them stopped in their tracks when they fixed on her eyes. A huge black man beat a hasty retreat, but one request came from an unfazed, polite, green-eyed man in his thirties. "Not now, thanks, maybe later," Coventry replied in a pleasant voice. "See you later then," said the man as he backed away. Coventry was here for one reason – to climb those stairs – dancing would have to wait.

Still in the balcony, Coventry stared at the closed double doors, which are not far away. The time had come! She begins weaving her way in their direction, round and through the dancers on the balcony dance floor. She pushes the doors open and enters the spooky staircase, bent on climbing them. For a brief spell she stands motionless, as if gravity and inertia were against her in this dreary setting. After a pause, she begins to climb, thinking the stairwell leads up two flights. She creeps up the stairs. The stone steps, and walls, the old iron banisters are eerie and lead up to a bare exit level with a fire door and horizontal bar to push. The level is dark, damp and musty. A fat beetle runs over her shoes and Coventry recoils. She scans the surroundings. Everything is ugly. She pushes the horizontal bar and the fire door opens. It leads to Coventry Street. The smell of Piccadilly air hits her. This, her mind tells her, is where she was conceived the night before the bombs hit the Café De Paris. Coventry's mind races back to her prim and proper mother.

FOUR

Up to the point of her mother's death, Coventry knew little about her real father. Reference to him was seldom made nor were there any photographs. He was a closed subject. Clever girl that she was, Coventry suspected that there was much about her parent's past that remained unspoken for a reason, but, given that the only father she had known was her stepfather, her curiosity about her real father was a mild one.

Coventry didn't pry. She knew that there were always reasons for silence. When she was small she had been told that during the war her mother had worked for the US Embassy in London, and met an RAF Flying Officer; she had married him, and he had been killed in action. Her mother's deathbed confession set the record straight and went into details.

Friends had invited her to the Café de Paris where she met a soft-spoken RAF pilot in his early twenties. His name was John. Everyone had been having a nice evening when the air raid sirens began to sound. She and John were dancing on the tiny balcony dance floor. Her friends were below, dancing on the larger floor. John told her not to worry. He took her by the hand and said she should stay close to him. Paula went with him to the top of a staircase. By now bombs were exploding in the distance, but their sounds were getting louder and louder, getting closer to London's West End. People in the Café were calling out. She was terrified. Then the bombs began falling even closer, and stricken with fear she had fallen into his arms. They were alone in the staircase. John held her close and whispered in her ear and told her not to worry. His first kiss was on her forehead – then he drew her closer. He kissed her left cheek, then the other. Being in his arms made her feel safe and below she could feel the pulse of his growth. When bombs struck closer, passions started to erupt – who knew where the next bomb would strike? John kissed one of her ears and there his lips remained. Then, like a serpent, his tongue slipped into her lobe. His growth increased and so did her desires. They succumbed to each other as bombs fell because who knew where the next bomb would strike? Paula then said to Coventry, "Next to the moment you were born, that night was the most exciting event in my life. I never heard from John again." The brief encounter lay in the past, as did Paula's life, which slipped away immediately after making her confession. What was a mystery to Coventry was the man who fathered her. Perhaps, she thought, one day I will look into the matter of who he was.

Paula did not start life a Catholic. Her parents, Brian and Jane McComb had immigrated to New York from the town of Ballymena, in Northern Ireland before World War I. Although solid Presbyterians, they bore no malice to Catholics, which was not the view of their fellow Protestants in Northern Ireland. As far as Brian and Jane were concerned, America offered hope and distance from poverty and the madness of religious bigotry.

Coventry's stepfather, Ian Calvert, was a self made man and descended from Ulster Protestant stock as well. His parents came from Shankhill in West Belfast, and he was a splendid man. In 1913 they immigrated to Boston to escape the terrible social conditions of Ulster. He married Paula in 1945 and after his release from the US Navy he had put himself through university, graduating in record time with a degree in business. He then entered 'merchant banking', made a bit of money, and through clever investments he amassed a few million in twelve years. Although a fit man, he died at the age of fifty-three from a heart attack that devastated his family.

Paula McComb was four months pregnant when she returned to New York in 1941. Because of the war in Europe, sea-travel across the Atlantic was not only dangerous but hard to come by. It took weeks for her embassy to get her passage on a ship. Her voyage from England had been doubly arduous due to stormy seas and the threat posed to US ships by German U-Boats prowling the Atlantic. Although America was not yet at war, US ships crossing to and from Britain were under constant threat because of the aid they were carrying. It was on this voyage that Paula met Father Aiden McAvoy – a Jesuit priest who was returning to America after a two-year sabbatical in Scotland. He was returning home to a military post of Army Chaplain in a war America was soon to join. He and Paula forged a friendship during the rough sea voyage. His depth of understanding and kindness drew her very close to him, and his non-judgemental stance was a badly needed comfort to Paula who was pregnant. Her faith in the forty-year-old priest prompted her to confide everything leading to her pregnancy and the fears she held for the future, given that she would soon have a child out of wedlock – a child sired by a stranger whose whereabouts were unknown at a time when Britain was struggling to survive.

The Jesuit did not condemn. He followed no hard rules that lacked compassion. He spoke softly and asked if there was 'love in their hearts' the night her innocence had been lost. Given the circumstances, how could such a question be answered? When McAvoy asked the question an angry storm was howling. The ship was pitching from one side to the other. Huge waves were crashing against the side of the ship. The bow of the vessel was digging deep into the water, the wind howled and whistled, yet the Jesuit was rock-steady and held Paula's hand. "Oh yes," Paula replied. "On my side, and I think on his side too."

"Are you sorry?"

"Yes, and also fearful."

The Jesuit asked what happened next. Paula thought back.

"By then, the bombing had stopped, and the 'all clear' had sounded, so we pushed open the fire doors. It was misty. We were on Coventry Street. We walked to Victoria Station. John had a train to catch. He left, saying he would call."

"Did he?"

"No."

"Might something have happened to him?"

"Probably; each day was often the last for those flyers."

"Did you try finding him?"

"Yes."

"Any luck?"

"No, there was little to go by. I was so ashamed."

"Were you pure up to then?"

"Yes."

"Do you want this child?"

"Oh yes."

"Have it as God's gift then," said McAvoy. "I understand for I once fell from grace too." These confessions on turbulent seas, in a world on the brink of war forged a bond that led to Paula becoming a Catholic.

Coventry was born on Sunday, December 7th, 1941, the day Japan bombed Pearl Harbour and America entered the war. She was christened Coventry Victoria McComb. Her Godfather was The Very Rev. Aiden McAvoy S.J. Even though canon law forbided this for Jesuits, McAvoy, like most Jesuits, including their founder, Ignatius Loyola, viewed the rules of their Order flexibly.

Paula married when the war ended. She was twenty-seven; Ian was thirty-one; Coventry was four. Their first real home was a large apartment in Manhattan's Washington Heights. The Heights was where the well-to-do lived and after Ian gained his degree and joined his first Merchant Bank, the Calverts moved. The apartment offered a splendid view; the neighbourhood was wholesome; its people were good and this, coupled with Coventry's Catholic education, gave her deep, healthy roots. Ian remained Protestant for the rest of his life but supported his family's faith without reservations. In all respects his knowledge of Paula's past went with him to the grave. He adored the actress Bette Davis, but he could neither abide the sight, or the sound, of the liberal-minded Mrs. Eleanor Roosevelt, the wife of President Franklin D. Roosevelt.

FIVE

Coventry knew the way life was lived in wartime Britain at the time she was conceived. Day after day London was bombed. Any moment could be one's last. On reflection could anyone fault Paula for what she did? Not Coventry. Nor could she blame the man who fathered her. Day after day he and other pilots would scramble to the skies to battle scores of German aircraft. Day after day their chances of surviving grew less and less, and surviving that battle was only a reprieve. They soon had to zoom up and do battle again, often many times a day. Those flyers from Britain and other nations who defended Britain in her darkest hour would be dubbed 'One of the few', of whom Churchill once said, "Never was so much owed by so many to so few." Coventry's father had been one of them and she was quietly proud.

Still at the top of the staircase, Coventry shut the fire doors and turned to return to the balcony. By then, the fat beetle had scurried to the street just as Paula and John had scurried to the top of the stairwell when London was being bombed. One thing puzzled Coventry. Why they had chosen to shelter higher up in the dancehall, and not lower? But then, she thought, who knows what they were thinking at the time? It was easy to question their actions, but what was the reality for her parents? Coventry returned to the balcony.

On the way down the stairwell she felt as if a weight had been lifted. She felt inwardly free. The first person she spotted was the tall dark man she had earlier observed dancing with the red-headed woman. He was alone sitting in a corner by the balcony railing. The band was now playing swing and the temperature in the dancehall was rising. She noticed that some of the couples she had earlier observed had gone their separate ways and other friendships had replaced them. One couple locked in each other's arms on the balcony dance floor were oblivious to all around them. They were giving each other tongue at a furious rate. As Coventry watched them her pupils dilated.

The mood in the Café' was lighter than before; its guests were more at ease with themselves in their hunt for someone to be with for the night. The dancehall was uncomfortably hot. Upstairs and down, tall fans were spinning but with little cooling effect. All they did was shift hot air from one place to another. Downstairs, the Café was jumping with jiving dancing couples. Up in the balcony on the tiny dance floor the scene was different. There the couples were almost motionless, body to heated body grinding away. As Coventry worked her way through the balcony dancers, a friendly-faced, slightly tipsy lady in her fifties said to her, "Cheers, me beauty. I'm Margot."

"Hello! I'm Victoria", Coventry smilingly replied.

The tall dark man was in his early thirties; he was sitting at a small round table; there was an unoccupied chair nearby. With no other chair vacant, and with her heart beating quickly, Coventry drifted towards it. The man's pull was strong and despite the heat, Coventry's hands felt cold. When she reached the table he stood, smiled, and eased back the table, making room for her to slip into the chair. Coventry reacted with a smiling "Thank You." After sitting she avoided his eyes. In a matter-of-fact way she casually looked over the balcony railing at the couples on the dance floor. With her eyes on them but her mind on him, her pupils dilated. Even though his pull was erotically strong, there was something noble about the man.

She had no illusions; she knew he was on the hunt. She nonetheless hoped he would fix on her and not another woman – she was not the only woman thinking this thought. Other women were lurking and watching for a sign that he was picking up their signals. They could sense his nature, just as the redhead he was dancing with before could sense it, but the redhead's hopes had been dashed. Coventry could see her dancing below, but this time the lady had lowered her sights. The look on the face of the redhead said it all. Her new man was not a 'god' like the man Coventry sat opposite. He was a hyperactive chap who handled her roughly. What an odd-looking couple, Coventry thought. How could such a nice looking lady switch from caviar to curry so abruptly?

During one of her Attica Prison visits, Willie Sutton had spoken of his dancing days at Roseland Ballroom in New York, and how he rarely failed picking up a lady for the night, but that his passion for his pickups always faded by morning. Coventry wondered what the morning would bring for the newly acquainted couples around her, after their organs had locked and climaxed with a stranger they had met at the Café de Paris. Many Willie-Sutton types were in the Café this night, but the man opposite her was not that type. He wove an invisible web – a web that by his presence salivated women. Coventry fumbled in her handbag. She tapped out a cigarette and lit it. As the smoke streamed from her nostrils it drifted towards the man. Immediately embarrassed, she quickly reached across the table and brushed the smoke away. "Pardon me," she said, "it's a nasty habit, I know." As Coventry spoke, the man, who had been looking at the dancers below, turned his head in her direction. Their eyes locked, then released, and then locked again. "That's quite all right," he replied with a smile. Unlike most men in the dancehall, he looked cool and though Coventry detected an accent, she could not quite place it. He smiled again and said, "Excuse me. "It's hot here." Then he rose from his chair and left the table.

When he had gone, Coventry was disappointed but a little bit glad because the man had an unsettling effect on her. She was moist and could smell it; she needed to compose herself. He wasn't leaving the dancehall so maybe, their paths would cross again. She finished her cigarette, left the table and made her way to the front of the balcony, down the stairs and back to the bar. Along the way the rhythm of her gait drew attention from both men and women. Male eyes fixed on her lengthy legs and the short, snugly fitting dress she was wearing. The contour of her legs that rose to join her nest beckoned looks and whispers aplenty. No woman in the dancehall could match her looks and no woman who saw her could honestly disagree.

The Café de Paris was now full to overflowing. Both dance floors were packed with couples. Not a vacant table was on offer anywhere. When Coventry reached the bar the scene was one of mayhem, with thirsty people two rows deep jostling for position to buy drinks. With so many bodies close together the heat was terrific. Coventry wondered what would happen if a fire struck. It put her in mind of the Thanksgiving Day fire in Boston, USA when many people died in the bar of a dancehall like the Café de Paris.

Unescorted as she was, Coventry felt a little cheap, and realising that reaching the bar was hopeless, she thought it was time to head home. She had seen what she had come to see. To her happy surprise, leaving the Café just then was not to be. She turned and who should be behind her but the tall, dark man holding a drink in each hand – he was smiling in her direction. Coventry returned his smile and they moved towards each other through the mill of the crowd, until they were face to face. "Excuse me," he said. "Will you join me in a drink?" A rush of blood rose to Coventry's face. Now she placed the accent. It was Spanish. She liked his style.

Unlike other men he had not shed his jacket. With no attempt to disguise her interest, Coventry's eyes ran over the man's body. He wore a smart, cream coloured suit, tailored to a matador body. He was slim at the hips, broad at the shoulders and his trousers were snug at the crotch. Her eyes lifted to his handsome face and then to his beautiful deep, chocolate-brown eyes.

"Yes, thank you so much," Coventry said softly.

"I was being served when you entered the bar so I thought I'd save you the wait."

"How very thoughtful."

"With pleasure," said the man. "Shall we find seats?"

"Yes, maybe upstairs," replied Coventry, fanning her face with one hand. They made their way to the balcony and luckily an empty table appeared.

"I'm Juanito. (Little-John) - Juanito Mendez-Gomez."

"You're not so little," Coventry said, again looking the man up and down.

"Oh, but my father – he's also John – is taller."

"How tall are you?"

"Only six three, that's why I'm 'Little-John'." Their chat was suspended when Margot, now tipsier than before, swayed by in the company of an Asian-looking man. He's half Margot's age and wearing an obvious hairpiece. They drift to the small dance floor and slip into a clinch. Coventry and the Spaniard observe them, then their attention returns to each other.

"And what is your name?" asks Juanito.

"Victoria. Victoria Calvert."

"Are you American or Canadian?"

"American from New York. And you?"

"Spanish from Madrid."

With eyes fixed on hers, Juanito says, "May I say something personal?"

"Yes, of course."

"La Milagrosa, a Spanish saint, has eyes like yours."

"I didn't know that."

"She's also known as 'Ojos de dios' – 'Eyes of God'."

"Are you religious?" asked Coventry.

"No, but my parents are, and my brother is a Jesuit priest."

How interesting, thinks Coventry.

She was enjoying learning all about the Spaniard. The band was on a break and people were laughing and talking and couples who had earlier met were drifting out of the dancehall. With its break over, the band began to play, but now the music was slow. The lower dance floor was less crowded than before and Coventry was warming to the Spaniard.

When the band struck up, Juanito took Coventry by the hand and led her down the stairs to the dance floor. He took her in his arms and drew her close. She felt good in his arms. Cocooned. By now she knew that the Spaniard was Jesuit educated and that his English was good because of his schooling at Stoneyhurst College in the northwest of England. His studies had sharpened the English he needed to become the commercial pilot he now was. How ironic, thought Coventry, that her Godfather had been a Jesuit, that Juanito and his family had Jesuit links and that he, like her father, was a pilot. How ironic that her mother's innocence had flown with a flyer too.

The Spaniard danced with her smoothly and with each step and glide, the pace of her heartbeat rose. With their bodies snug together, she could smell the scent of man coming from his body. She felt the strength of his arms and legs that deftly found the gap between her legs as they danced. On and on went the dance, on and on went the evening at the Café de Paris, until its doors closed and all guests had departed.

Juanito hailed a taxi, helped Coventry in and bid her good night. He didn't ask for her number or make the slightly rude overture – he was a perfect gentleman.

"I hope to see you here again," he said.

"I do too," Coventry replied.

"We'll leave it in the hands of God."

"Indeed," Coventry replied from inside the taxi.

As the taxi pulled away, Juanito waved and said, "Adios, Ojos de Dios" – 'Goodbye, Eyes of God'.

That night Coventry dreamt. Her mother's past had drawn her to the Café de Paris and the Café de Paris would see her once again. As she tossed in bed she remembered Willie Sutton who, quoting Emerson, had said, "Living is the rarest thing in the world. Most people only exist. I've lived badly, but I have lived. Be sure, Coventry, you do the same."

SIX

COVENTRY IS SLEEPING AND DREAMING.

Sounds of night propel her flight to streams of dreams of heady heights. Tick, tick, tick. The clock by her bed is ticking. Raindrops are tapping on her half-opened window – tap, tap, and tap. A breeze like a cat creeps in; it springs on her bed then whiskers her with licks. Coventry dreams on.

CAROUSELS and rollercosters dancing in her head. Parachutes pop open, landing on her bed. Belgravia is quiet, Wilton Crescent too, daffodils are fast asleep 'till spring returns anew'. Tick, tick, tick. Splatter, splatter, splatter, thunderclouds orgasm on her windowpanes that shatter.

BREEZE, breeze, breeze, kin of the wind, slips through the window for a lick, lick, lick. Coventry responds, turning in her bed, shadows of a cat dancing in her head. Bubbles on the ceiling, banjos on the floor, rocking chairs are empty, rocking by the door. Tick, tick, tick. Tap, tap, and tap. Thunderclouds are empty, empty as her flat.

ENTER Juanito, naked as can be, stepped through the mirror like a hou-di-ni. Not an ounce of fat, tall as a tree, striding like a cat, cocky as can be. Cat sniffs her pillow, then licks her nose, alley cats are mating, and then begin to doze.

STRIDES on Juanito, God made of flesh, bronzed by the sun, getting kind of fresh. Closer to her bed, closing in on her, cocky as can be, loins begins to purr. Then he sits besides her, silent as a cat, rigid as a rock, milky as can be before he finds her slot. Still her eyes are closed, still the twitch in spots, smell of man besides her, more alive his rock. Then he reaches down, gathering her breasts, each of which he handles like a lady blessed. Then a hand he takes, in between a rest, sliding down her jelly belly to her spongy nest. Tick, tick, tick. Dream, dream, dream. Alley cats are at it. One begins to scream.

ENTER Willie Sutton, looking kind of silly. Enter Willie Sutton, feeling kind of chilly. Here comes Willie, looking like a waif. Here comes Willie, crooking for a safe. Out goes Willie, running with a slob, there goes Willie, having pulled a job. Here comes the law, looking for the breakers. There go crooks, all the money takers.

HERE comes Winston, posing like a saviour, there goes Churchill, oh what odd behaviour. Here comes the Queen, looking kind of Prussian, there goes the she, sitting on a cushion. There trots her carriage, stepping kind of skittish. There goes Queen, feeling kind of British.

HERE come Lords, lunch was kind of piggish, there go Peers, wobbling kind a wiggish. Here comes Father God, McAvoy's his name, priestly like a J, not an ounce of shame. Eyes on Juanito, then on her lips, back to Juanito, back to her tits. Never mind he says, put aside your doubts, time you had a splurge, time to turn her inside out and satisfy her urge. Go ahead Juanito, this God says to him, give her what she needs, don't be lean but dim. Alley cats are mating, one pair up a tree, lady cats are prowling, brazen as can be. Up jumps Juanito, cocky as can be, strides towards the J, kneels twixt his knees.

COVENTRY is shocked, sits up in her bed, can't believe her eyes, can't believe his head. Alley cats are mating, two begin to scream, dancers are mating, and then begin to cream. Mr. Cat is cruising, looking for a date, sniffing for a lady cat, so to penetrate.

HERE comes Paula, all done in pink, one hand on her belly, one hand on a drink. One step towards Juanito, then one towards the J, smile on her face as the two men play. Up again Juanito, cocky as can be, slips through the window for a tree to pee. Paula reaches down, off flies her crown, up comes her dress, down goes the rest.

McAVOY is looking, McAvoy is rocking, and McAvoy is getting, very very rocky. Paula is approaching, legs astride she comes, Coventry is looking, looking kind a glum. Tick, tick, tick. Dream, dream chair. This is now one long night-mare. Holy man is ready, ready with his staff, up hops Paula, eager for the shaft. Rockaby they go, creak, creak, and creak. Daughter is looking, looking very meek.

IN struts daddy, no one shot him down, hidden by a mask, ready for a spree, ready with his gun and Café de Paris. Meets a girl that night, she is nicely dressed, she is taken down by medals on his chest. Coventry is looking, bulging eyes that stare, new arrivals swell the room, adding to the creaky tune. Creak, creak, and creak. Thrust, thrust, thrust. Satan is smiling, happy with the lust.

IN zips a saint, stinging like a bee, goodness me her eyes are strange, strange as they can be. In strolls a new man, lingers for a while, back steps the same man, green eyes in his smile.

ENTER Juanito, wet from rain on he, in slips Juanito, did it on a tree. August leaves are falling, shaken from a tree, shaking by the mating cats, as if they numbered three. Jesus Christ is watching, Eyes of God too, Sister Margaret-Mary pops from out the loo. Shame, shame, shame. Hell, hell, hell. Just one sniff reveals the smell. In slips Margot, in from town, out drifts Margot, howling like a hound. In comes Shady, 'Hello there Tiplady', out goes Shady, didn't Tip the Lady.

IN comes a black man, cocky by the score, in bangs his Richard, crashed it through the door. Up floats Juanito, Coventry is reeling, gone is Juanito, vanished through the ceiling. Gone is Paula, done up all in red, gone is Paula, didn't need a bed. Back comes Margot, lays down on the floor, have a peep at Margot, spread out like a whore.

DOWN comes the rain, harder than before. Down goes the black man, also on the floor. On tick the clocks, tick, tick, tick. Down is the black man playing with his stick. Up flies the curtain, pricked by the wind. Up flies a bed, round goes the spin. Out goes the J; Margaret-Mary too, out go the pair, followed by the Jew. Out goes

Margot, looking like a mope, out goes cocky black man, lengthy as a rope. Tick, tick, tick. Tap, tap, and tap. Little Willie Sutton left behind his gat.

COVENTRY is turning, Coventry is itching, Coventry is twitching, Coventry is bitching, Coventry is moaning, Coventry is groaning, Coventry is waking, coming out from under. HERE COMES SHE, RUMBLING LIKE THE THUNDER.

SEVEN

It was early Sunday morning, stifling hot and Coventry lay in bed staring at the ceiling. She was thinking – turning the dream over in her mind. It was so real. It had powered her to a climax, the first she had ever known, an experience that left her staring at the ceiling with a buoyant sensation, but at the same time it had disturbed her.

She had produced the dream, not a beat of which she had missed with eyes that had leapt from one scene to the next. She had cast the players for their parts and even the cats. Now that the play was done, the curtain down and her eyelids up, Coventry had another production to deal with. She had to produce a review to try and judge what, if anything, the dream really meant. It was too powerful a dream to ignore, too symbolic to cast aside without reflection.

Was it a good or bad dream? Was it sinful? What did it say about her? These questions needed answers. What did it say about her mind, those alleys with conduits of slippery steps that fell further into slime; the slime that was so willingly travelled by people she knew, people of pure and elevated thoughts, people that didn't belong in her dream. People like her mother, McAvoy, and Sister Margaret-Mary.

Then there was the dream's consequence – she had to deal with that as well. It had two parts. One was real, the other surreal. Her orgasm was real. Its pungent aftermath lay scattered around her. That was one thing, then there was the other – the surreal – the words to describe the indescribable. There was something heavenly about the sensation, something crafted in another world by a cosmic goddess. It was a divine moment – what Italians call 'El Momento Divino'.

More than three thousand miles away, the beat of life went on for Willie Sutton just as it did for Coventry, but there the similarity ended. Willie was in his Attica cell in upstate New York, lying face down on his bunk. Coventry was in London, lying face up in her bed, her legs indecently apart, her dream, even with all its madness, still alive, willingly jailed in her mind. With one part of her mind she pushed it away, with another she held on tight, afraid it would slip away and rob her of the chance to examine it more closely.

Unlike her younger days, when her dreams were vividly rich, her dreams had been few and elusive since arriving in London, like the taste of ice cream that sits on the tongue and once gone cannot be described. Not this dream! This one was unique. She could almost taste it. "But why them?" she asked herself. "Why them?" Why had her mother appeared like a vamp and mounted her Godfather? What was the significance of the rocking chair? What behaviour could be more improbable in its conception – her mother, legs apart, mounted on McAvoy on a rocking chair? Why did Willie Sutton act so true to character while everyone else did not? Willie's face was clear. She knew it was him, yet his face was different. Maybe it was the new face he paid for after he broke out of jail that snowy night. He had told her the story on one of her visits to Attica. When he was safe in Brooklyn and the heat was off, he had gone to Dr. Brandywine to have his face altered. When the time came for the bandages and stitches to be removed, Willie had to do it himself because the law had locked up Brandywine. Willie had paid two thousand dollars for the job and the surgery was not good. It was the reason a tailor riding in a Brooklyn train had recognised Willie and turned him in for a reward. The informer was a Jewish fool named Schuster who later got his just reward. He had messed with the wrong crook. Someone shot him dead in a Brooklyn alley.

In her dream, Juanito had passed the test of her desires. He had swaggered through her dream like El Cid, brandishing an organ the likes of which was a tingling revelation and new to her in every respect. He had touched her like a woman blessed. She could still feel his probing fingers in her flower, a flower that was still alive with the residue of her eruption.

She recognised all the faces in her dream, but her real father wore a mask. Could he still be alive? Impossible, she thought. He died in the war. Why had he jumped from the broken pieces of his death into the jigsaw puzzle of her dream?

Why had carousels and roller coasters danced in her head? She hadn't thought about amusement rides for years. As a youngster she was never keen on them, but she recalled one incident on a ride because of a shoe. One summer, when she was eight, her mother took her to Coney Island. They had puttered round and decided to try a two-seater parachute ride. They were strapped to their seats and up they went inside what looked like a huge birdcage. She remembered that cables hoisted their seat to a great height until they reached the dome of the ride. She remembered that when they reached it, they dropped, the parachute filled with air and down they floated. This was when the shoe appeared. A woman in a ride above had lost a shoe, and Coventry recalled the shoe falling past her parachute, and remembered saying to her mother, "Look, a lady has lost a shoe."

Why had cats appeared in her dream? She was not crazy about cats either. A ginger cat had once bitten her. She understood why Satan had appeared in her dream. It was right up his alley. Lust was his kind of game – no wonder he was smiling. The creak from chairs and pelvic thrusts had prompted his jump from hell for a crafty look. Coventry thought that when Satan returned to hell to file his report, that he must have been a happy devil, but that the damned fool didn't realise he was part of a dream. Coventry's Good Angel – the one that always stood to her right – was also in her head helping her to review the dream. He wasn't happy. He didn't like the stains on her sheets, stains that were real and not a dream, and he was less than happy with the actions of her fingers, fingers that lingered round her nest even as her mind turned the dream over. She was losing points in the Good Angel's book, but on probed her fingers until they thrust deep into her nest, and with her back arched, she again reached rapture with the powerful exhale of a moan.

After she had recovered, Coventry thought what on earth was Margot doing in my dream? She didn't belong there. She didn't know

Margot; they had only exchanged a few words in the Café de Paris. Yes, thought Coventry, Margot seemed a friendly soul but she acted silly from too much drink, and was dressed in a manner inappropriate for her age. Her hairstyle was wrong, and for someone in her fifties, her skirt was too short, and yet, Coventry reflected, Margot appeared a nice soul who was only looking for a mate for the night.

Maybe this was also true of Tiplady. Editor of a newspaper he may have been, but the signals he flashed spoke of insecurity, of a lonely man. He would tap his fingers, bite his nails and when sitting, his knees would almost always knock. He didn't stay long in her dream. He was in and out like a shot. This was also true of the Spanish saint with eyes like hers. They glowed like beacons in a lighthouse on a foggy night. The saint zipped like a bee in and out of her dream. Coventry wished she had stayed longer for a better look. What was her name? Oh yes, La Milagrosa – Eyes of God. The Spanish nation seemed to hold her in esteem.

What was Margaret-Mary doing in a dream of such immorality? Its theme was the opposite of all her teachings, the ultimate in shame, ladies with open legs, the devil's playground. What was Margaret-Mary doing in the loo? Nuns were too close to divinity for such earthly functions.

Why did Churchill and the Queen appear in her dream. Where were the folk of the red, white and blue. Where was Jenny Jacobson/Jerome, Winston's American mother? Did she need an invitation? Where was Lady Astor? Even Jesus the Jew had dropped in – why not Jenny Jerome the Jew?

What about that business between McAvoy and Juanito? Where the hell did that come from?

Satan seemed to love it. What was a black man doing in her dream? He had made a big entrance with his hellish rope that burst through the door. Maybe he sprang from the buck that had asked her to dance and had swept away when he saw that her eyes didn't match. He didn't seem to think they were Eyes of God. They scared the hell out of him. If Margot and he had teamed up, she may have had the fear of God rammed into her, even though the black man didn't wear a collar. Madness, my dream, pure madness. Coventry thought. Could her father still be living? She knew that in 1941 he was twenty-two; his name was John, he was a pilot and had flown in the Battle of Britain. Not much to go on.

Coventry lay in bed staring at the ceiling, her hands now clasped behind her head. Her mind was on her father. Was he really still alive, or did he suddenly come to life only in her dream? Assuming he was still alive, how on earth would she go about finding him? The key to resolving the problem popped into her head in the form of a Jesuit priest she knew. He was a friend of her Godfather and was privy to the story of her conception. Cyril Powell was his name; he worked in Rome for Vatican Radio and was as near to St. Peter as anyone could be. As was the custom since the Counter Reformation, Powell was the latest in a long line of Jesuits to whom the Pope himself confesses. Coventry had met Powell when he was visiting in New York. She recalled that he had a good sense of humour and was very approachable. Yes, that's what she would do. She would call him and seek his help. He and other Jesuits were in powerful positions and many doors were open to them, through the offices of the Holy See. If anyone could help glean details about her father, Powell could do it. She would wait before calling him; she had other matters to attend to right now.

Over the next two months, Coventry's career raced ahead. She had written other fine pieces for her paper and was greatly enjoying the challenges her new profession offered. On a number of occasions she had visited the Café de Paris in the hope of meeting Juanito again, but, alas, the Spaniard was nowhere to be seen.

EIGHT

It was now a mid October Monday. The year was drawing to a close and this was the day she would call Father Powell. Her intention was to telephone from work but an envelope on her work desk that morning diverted her. Her call to Powell had been on her mind of late. She had been dreaming almost nightly, and in every dream her father had appeared in one scenario or the other. He was always wearing a mask. The dreams were telling her something, but she didn't know what. Assuming that the note in the envelope had to do with her next assignment, Coventry thought this to be odd. Since joining the paper all her assignments had come by way of the deputy editor, so the note aroused her curiosity. It said, 'I have a job for you to consider. It involves a trip to Eastern Europe. Please come to my office. And please, not a word to anyone. T.T'.

In the 1960s, The Cold War was at its height. By 1969 the Berlin Wall had been up for nearly ten years. Political espionage was the order of the day and spies from both sides of the Iron Curtain were beavering away undercover throughout Europe. By 1969 the British Civil Servants – Kim Philby, Guy Burgess and Donald Maclean – had been found to be spying for the Soviet Union and all three fled to Russia. Their treachery had devastated the British establishment and crippled British intelligence. Other spies of their ilk, mostly products of Cambridge University and often homosexuals, lurked in the British civil service. Russia was the country the West feared and the author John LeCarre was in his element with novels like 'The Spy Who Came In From The Cold'.

Tiplady had a job in mind for Coventry that would take her to Russia. It would be a difficult job and would court dangers. Reprisals could come from many directions. The shadowy world of political espionage was unrestrained by rules of law. There was little difference in the methods used by the KGB or the CIA. Their British equivalents MI5 and MI6 were no different. If the stakes were high enough and you stepped on the wrong toes, you could end up dead and your demise would be deemed to be suicide – assuming that your body was ever found. The job Coventry would be asked to consider would expose her to this dark, sinister world.

Tiplady felt that she was right for the job. Of all his reporters, she was his first choice. The fact that she was a Yank was an extra plus and very convenient because another American was involved and central to everything. Tiplady would not give Coventry the job unless she wanted it – unless he felt she had the grit to see it through.

The job required commitment and he would set the wheels in motion once the two of them had discussed the assignment and he was sure she was committed. Much was at stake, so he had to be sure. He was sticking out his neck and sailing the newspaper into dangerous waters, and yet the matter was too important to be ignored. Under whose flag was the Prime Minister of Great Britain sailing? That was the question. If the rumours were true, the British public had the right to know. It was the duty of the press to inform them.

It was clear to Tiplady that Coventry had something special. She was no ordinary reporter, nor was she just another clever person. He saw the cunning touches she displayed when dealing with her colleagues. Although new to the business, no one at the London Evening View could match her natural skills. Some were openly jealous of her, but Tiplady saw how Coventry rose above it all and handled these situations. If she disagreed with a colleague, there was never an edge to the view she held, and by her easy-going manner she never upset anyone. She could unpeel people like an onion, strike at the heart of an issue with the right question and all this appeared to come easily to her. She could be trusted. She was not a gossip. Her work was always in on time and not once had she tipped her hand about sensitive stories she was working on.

This was evident when she wrote about the Nixon/Kennedy election of 1960 and the seedy role played by Joe Kennedy, JFK's father. Her story told how Joe had engineered the theft of the presidency by getting scores of democrats in the states of Illinois and California to vote more than once for his son, and how he had arranged the stuffing of ballot boxes in key wards with the help of the Mafia – a contact provided by Frank Sinatra. The old rogue had used the Irish ploy of 'vote early and often' – which was the title of Coventry's piece. Given that he was of Irish extraction, no doubt Willie Sutton would have pulled the same stunt had he been a politician. But he wasn't. He was a crook in jail. He was paying for his crime, but not so for the Kennedys, who from the time of their arrival in America from Ireland had been the biggest of crooks. That's what Coventry's piece about JFK's election victory over Nixon had been about and no one other than Tiplady knew what she was working on, until the story appeared in the *London Evening View*.

Her piece had appeared in many foreign newspapers with favourable comments from global Conservatives. The Liberal political class fell silent. The manipulative and hypocritical side of the Kennedy Clan was not something about which they wanted to hear – nor did they want others to hear about the way the Kennedys operated.

Tiplady's office door was open when Coventry appeared. Smartly dressed, he was reading something and when he saw her at the threshold he waved her in.

"Good weekend?" he asked.

"Fine," she replied while handing him back his note. "It's best you have this back."

"Good thinking."

Tiplady tore the note into little pieces.

Coventry sat and Tiplady slid into the chair behind his desk. The moment he was sitting, his knees began to knock.

"Down to business." he said. Fingers laced, he leaned forward and quietly asked: "Have you heard anything unusual about the Prime Minister?"

Coventry turned the question over in her mind. "Yes, I think I know what you mean."

She had heard a rumour in New York from a Jesuit who taught politics at Fordham University, and had strong Vatican connections.

"Is it true?" she asked.

"Looks like it, but more proof is needed."

Tiplady took a key from his pocket, opened a drawer and pulled out a file. Slapping it on the palm of one hand, he said: "See this? It's all about his links with Russia and Robert Borasky."

Coventry's eyes widened.

Tiplady slid the file into an envelope, sealed it, and handed it to her. "Here, slip home quietly and study it."

"Shall do."

"Guard it with your life."

"Of course."

"We need to talk about this away from here."

"Of course," replied Coventry, "if it's true, this file could be dynamite."

"Indeed, but we need to know more. That's where you come in."

"I see." Coventry answered. "I see", but she really didn't know what she was supposed to consider, or what was expected of her.

"Do you know the restaurant in Piccadilly called Martinez?"

"No," said Coventry, "but I can find it."

"Meet me there tomorrow at 6:30."

"Will do."

Coventry rang Father Powell and the Jesuit was helpful. She learned that Westminster Cathedral displayed a list of flyers that had been killed in the Battle of Britain and that through a contact of Powell's in the Ministry of Defence, she could probably get a list of all the flyers that took part in the Battle, including those killed in subsequent action. She was to ring Adam Stewart of the MoD. His brother, a friend of Powell's, was a teacher at Stoneyhurst College. Powell would ring his friend and pave the way. How ironic, thought Coventry that Stoneyhurst was the school Juanito had attended. Before arriving in London, Coventry's life had been academic but now it was different. She was in touch with her sexuality, her reporting career was on the rise, and there was now a good chance that she might learn more about the man who fathered her. In addition to all this, more spice to her life was to follow at the Spanish restaurant.

On reaching home, another surprise was waiting – a letter from Willie Sutton. It had been written using a code she and Willie had devised if special news had to be conveyed. If the letter was coded, the salutation would begin with: 'My dear friend Coventry'. It was coded! Willie's message hinted that he would soon be released from Attica. Coventry knew that his release was in store and Willie's missive confirmed it. She smiled, and replied to Willie's letter two days later saying that she would be praying for his early release.

It was Tuesday, October 15th, the evening of the following day. Coventry had read the Prime Minister's file. It was almost time for her meeting with her boss at the Spanish restaurant. In 1968, the year before Coventry's arrival in London, Britain under Labour had devalued the pound and though London was swinging for the young, the country's finances were anything but buoyant. With Britain's finances hurting, other unsettling events were soon to take place and cast further doubts about the way the Labour Party was governing Britain. Civil Rights marches would soon erupt in Northern Ireland and lead to British troops patrolling the streets of Derry and Belfast. A scandal was poised to break out involving the government's National Coal Board. Their negligence had led to deaths in the Welsh mining village of Aberfan, and something else was rumbling beneath the surface of the political establishment, involving none other than Prime Minister Jeremy Jones.

Well before Coventry arrived in London, there were suspicions in the British Security Services that led to Downing Street and the Prime Minister. The file Coventry had been reading reflected these suspicions. The PM's links with Russia, and his friendship with Robert Borasky – a garment manufacturer of East European origins, who lived in Britain and who was thick with the KGB – was troubling people in high places. Although the suspicions were unknown to most people, those who did know in Britain and America were troubled. Concern throughout the US intelligence community was acute and the 'file' lent to Coventry by Tiplady strongly suggested that the PM was a communist and that like Philby, Burgess and Maclean, he too was a British turncoat.

The code name of the 'file's' source was 'Big Ben' – an American who worked in Moscow. Coventry knew that Tiplady had to be well connected to have access to such a file. He was. His connection was Big Ben and Tiplady told her so. Flattered though she was to be offered such a job, Coventry was uneasy and wondered how the evening at the Spanish restaurant would unfold – and exactly what kind of job her boss wanted her to consider.

Martinez Restaurant was situated behind Swan Edgar's store on Swallow Street in the heart of Piccadilly Circus. It was a popular restaurant whose origins in London went back many years. A Spanish waiter with snug black trousers and trim red waistcoat did a double take when Coventry arrived. He stripped her of her clothes with his eyes. Coventry's ensemble was a neat, blue dress that nicely showed off her legs. A necklace of pearls adorned her neck. She looked tasty and was worthy of any man's menu, he thought. A few men who were waiting for friends and talking to the waiter also undressed her with their eyes. The waiter strode over but stopped short when his eyes fixed on hers.

"Dios meo, La Milagrosa," he said softly to himself.

"Pardon?" said Coventry.

She knew what had unhinged him. The waiter pulled himself together and said his name.

"I'm Jesus," he said. "May I help you?"

Coventry smiled and thought, You're no Jesus, not with that display between your legs.

"Yes," she replied. "I'm to meet Mr. Tiplady."

"Oh yes, Mr. Tiplady," said the waiter. "Please, this way."

Coventry followed him up circular stairs, whose banisters were decorated with red plastic roses. In doing so she thought of the stairwell steps she had climbed in the Café de Paris. These stairs may have been different, but the same element of the unknown was waiting for Coventry at the top. As she went in the background an audiotape of Paco Pena was playing guitar music beneath the earthy singing voice of Carmella Ruiz, the Spanish diva with the sound of Gypsy in her voice and Moor in her blood.

Tiplady was sitting at the bar. The moment he saw Coventry he rose to his feet and joined her.

"How nice you look," he said.

"You too," Coventry replied. The waiter led Tiplady and Coventry to their reserved table.

Tiplady was wearing cavalry twill trousers and a smart blue blazer. He was pleased with the complement, a rare smile curled his lips. "Do you mind if I order?" he asked. "I've been here before, I know what's good here. Their food is almost as good as sex."

"By all means," replied Coventry. She ignored the remark. Her boss got the message. He ordered and they got down to the business.

"Did you read the file?"

"Yes, twice."

"What do you think?"

Coventry had to be careful with her reply. "It's hard to say."

Quick to realise that she was holding back, Tiplady altered his approach. "Do you think he's a Red?"

"The file suggests it."

Leaning towards her and speaking softly Tiplady said: "If it's true, it's the duty of the press to make it known. But more proof is needed. Big Ben has a lot more in his file. That's where you come in. Would you like a crack at the job?" Coventry decided to take up the challenge.

"Yes, with pleasure!"

"Great. You leave for Moscow this time next week. Of course, anything you write will need to be cleared by our lawyers."

"Of course."

They arranged to meet the following Friday. By then her tickets and travel documents would be ready. Tiplady would make all Coventry's travel arrangements, so as not to involve others at the newspaper. He had personally handled her visa application. In Moscow she would stay at the Ukraine Hotel – it was near the US embassy. The official but bogus reason for her trip would be to write about cultural matters, and to this end she would liaise with George Bolchakov, who was the director of the Soviet Press Agency Novasti. Her real mission would be to meet with Big Ben – he was the cultural attaché attached to the US embassy.

Tiplady had studied journalism in the US. In the course of his studies he had made a number of American friends.

One of his American friends was Big Ben.

NINE

By 1969 Willie Sutton had served seventeen years of his life sentence. He was eligible for parole from Attica but an obstacle stood in his way. He still owed one hundred and thirty-five more years to the state of New York for past crimes the courts had found him guilty of. If he could leap the hurdle of this debt, his parole would be his greatest escape. Unlike his other escapes however, this would be legal. He would leave Attica through its front gates, not over the wall or through a tunnel as he had from other jails in previous escapes. Brains and knowledge of the law would power this escape. His lady lawyer was a smart woman and he, was far from a fool. Both were au fait with the new, criminal-friendly laws sweeping through the American judicial system of the 1960s.

Willie was now sixty-seven, he had emphysema and needed leg surgery. A life of crime, of heavy smoking and of constantly looking over his shoulder had taken their toll, but his sight remained elevated. Unlike other 'lifers', he had not lost his spark. His urge for freedom was as strong as ever and his hopes were high that soon he would be free, away from prison bars, the sounds of rattling keys, guards whistles, from rotten food, dirty mice and the filthy language of his fellow inmates. Above all he didn't want to die in prison.

From the early 1960s, America was changing. Liberal thinking had taken hold when it came to the civil rights of defendants in criminal cases. The laws governing past criminal trials and legal procedures dealing with defendants in such cases were now leaning in favour of criminals and not society. If it could be proved that the judicial system had neglected the letter of the law in cases where the defendant had been found guilty, this omission was deemed to have been legally negligent and breached civil and human rights. Willie and his lawyer were counting on this new twist in the law – a loophole – to gain his freedom.

In most cases and trials in which Willie had been found guilty and for which he still owed jail-time, Willie was truly guilty, but that wasn't the point. The issue was whether or not the letter of the law had been followed by the courts in these past cases. Coventry knew about the changing laws and that Willie had appeals in motion, so when his letter arrived, the news came as no surprise. After serving seventeen years, the only thing standing in the way of Willie's freedom was the huge number of further years behind bars he owed to the State of New York. America's increasing liberal stance which Coventry so disliked, was now likely to be the vehicle that would help him gain freedom.

Sutton was in one of the worst US prisons. Its regime was brutal and he couldn't wait to get out. Not only was life in Attica appallingly hateful, but everyone around him including the guards were a bunch of thugs. Given his age, his state of health and his high profile image, Willie had been treated better than most inmates and this made life in Attica a little more tolerable. But only just a little. Too old now to withstand prison much longer, his hope was to be free and live out the remainder of his days with his sister in Florida.

In 1969 a sinister element was festering beneath the surface in Attica State Prison. A mood of rebellion was growing amongst the inmates, due to their inhumane treatment and Willie didn't want to be in Attica when the shit hit the fan.

He could see a riot coming, and with his appeal in motion, he hoped to be free from Attica when it took place. Eventually, in 1971, an ugly riot did occur that took the lives of eleven prison guards and twenty-eight inmates.

In a life of crime that began when he was nine, Willie had spent thirty-three of his sixty-seven years in one jail or another. One of five children, he was born in Brooklyn in 1901 and after leaving school early to work, he never held a job for long. Crime was more up his alley. He staged his first bank job in 1927. In the next twenty years, when he wasn't in jail, he staged many more. When asked why he robbed banks he was quoted as saying: 'Because I love the action. I am more alive when I'm inside a bank, robbing it, than at any other time in my life'.

For most of his adult life, until he last went to prison, Sutton was consumed by two ambitions. One was to make as many illegal withdrawals as possible from carefully selected banks. The other was to escape from the prisons in which he wound up. Over the years he had escaped from jail three times.

For Willie, banks were an irresistible challenge. In his years of such crimes he had stolen more than two million dollars and his style was so unique that other thieves copied it, and if they weren't caught, Willie got blame for sticking up the bank. Often, according to the police, he would leave a bank with a cheerful admonition to his frightened victims, 'Don't you worry', Willie would say as he was fleeing, 'the bank's insurance will cover this'.

He had married in 1929 but his wife divorced him when he attempted a robbery and was caught. He married again in 1933 from which a daughter Jean resulted. As the years passed and his fame grew, Sutton acquired two nicknames: 'Willie the Actor' and 'Slick Willie', for the multiple disguises he used while thieving. He would pose as bank guards, window cleaners, milkmen and furniture removers. He once posed as a diplomat. His most outrageous stunt was to impersonate a policeman. On his way to commit a robbery in Manhattan dressed as a cop, he deferred his robbery plans and stopped to direct traffic on Broadway and 145th Street. His duty as a traffic cop fulfilled, he then swept into a bank, pulled out a gun, and robbed it of eighty thousand dollars – much more money than he thought the bank had on hand that day. Sometimes, after a particular robbery, Willie would comment on his robbery. After this robbery he wrote; 'This caper was both an artistic and financial success'.

He was a nifty dresser and even though he was a crook, his reputation was of being a gentleman. People present at his robberies often said that Willie was most polite. One person said, 'Witnessing one of his robberies was like being at the movies, except that the usher had a gun'. When asked his reason for robbing banks, Willie is reported to have said, 'Because that's where the money is'. Willie, however, denied ever having said it, but the alleged answer was grist to the mill of the press. They loved the quote.

In 1933, Willie and two other crooks tried to rob the Corn Exchange Bank & Trust Company in Philadelphia. Disguised as a milkman, he entered the bank early in the morning, but the curiosity of a passer-by caused the robbery to be aborted. But that didn't stop Willie. The next year he and other villains entered the same bank through a skylight and robbed it clean.

Among his most celebrated robberies was a jewellery store theft in Manhattan during lunch hour. For this robbery he posed as a Western Union telegraph messenger. The heist was a masterpiece that required impeccable timing and Willie's comments in writing confirmed it. So popular was his image with the public that in 1953, after his final arrest, and at the suggestion of Quentin Reynolds – a popular journalist and broadcaster of the day – they co-authored a book titled, 'I, Willie Sutton'. The book sold well but Willie didn't get a penny because he was in jail.

Jailed in 1931 on robbery and assault charges, Willie was sentenced to thirty years, but he escaped in 1932 by scaling the prison wall on two ladders he had joined together. Locked up again in 1934, he was sentenced to twenty-five to fifty years in Pennsylvania's Eastern State Penitentiary, for the robbery by Machine-gun of the Corn Exchange Bank in that state.

In 1945, Sutton was one of twelve convicts who briefly escaped from a 'maximum security prison' through a tunnel they had started digging on the day of the Normandy Invasion, June 6th, 1944. They finished digging on V-E Day, May 8th, 1945 and tried to escape. However, Willie and his cohorts were quickly apprehended. As bad luck would have it, a cop was outside the prison grounds urinating behind his car when the escaping convicts popped out of the ground, almost under his feet. Sentenced to life imprisonment as a fourth time offender, Sutton was sent to the Philadelphia County Prison in Pennsylvania from which, late in 1951, he and other inmates dressed as guards, executed their famous escape under cover of blizzard which, even today in 1969, Coventry Calvert still recalled with a sense of satisfaction. With the snow streaking down, the convicts had carried two ladders across the prison courtyard to the wall and were poised to climb. When the searchlights hit them and the guard in the tower called down, Sutton yelled back: "It's okay. We're from the electricity company." No one stopped them!

In 1952, William Frances Sutton, who was better known as Willie, but who preferred to be called Bob, became a star of the underworld when the FBI named him one of the Ten Most Wanted crooks in America. His photo was now on display in post offices all across the nation, and because of his love for expensive clothes, his photo was given to tailors nationwide. This photograph was Willie's downfall, and the reason why in 1969, he was locked up in Attica State Prison.

During his years in Attica, thousands of letters had been written to Willie by fans all across America, but most had been withheld from him. Strangely, however, all of Coventry's letters reached him, and so did other letters from one particular person. The prison authorities never realised that the letters between Willie, Coventry and that one other person – which on the surface seemed bland – were in fact – coded.

TEN

Coventry was leaving for Moscow the following day. She was surprised and slightly thrown off balance when her eyes were compared to the Saint La Milagosa. Up to that point the fact that her eyes were the way they were hadn't bothered her. It was the way God had made her. When Juanito made the comparison that was too much. The last thing she wanted was comparisons to a saint. So she had done something about it. She made up her mind to look into the matter of lenses that would balance the colour of her eyes so that both looked the same. She consulted the yellow pages and found a Knightsbridge optician that was near her flat and opposite Harrods department store. His name had a thoroughly British sound – Leslie Rupert Hawkins-Goodfellow.

One Saturday she took the plunge and visited his place of business, and she was glad she did. She found him to be a decent and very obliging man, and despite a minor handicap, she learned that he had a distinguished record with the RAF. How he overcame his handicap left Coventry speechless but amused.

He was an ordinary looking man in his fifties with greying black hair, much the type and manner of Peter Falk, the actor that played the detective 'Columbo' on TV. To look at Goodfellow would not conjure images of a dashing RAF flyer in the Second World War.

He explained all about contact lenses, examined her eyes and found them to be fine. He warned her that contact lenses took time getting use to, that they should only be worn for short periods, and had to be cleaned after use, but that women adjusted to them better than men. He said that they should never be worn in dusty places, or when travelling, and that their use should be limited to social occasions.

He could have ordered the lenses himself, but he referred her to a colleague at the Moorfields Eye Hospital who was an expert on lenses that called for colour application. In 1969, contacts were hard plastic and could not be tinted. They had to be painted so it was best for her to deal with an expert. Goodfellow advised her to opt for brown, rather than blue lenses. Brown would more easily match the iris of her eyes and given her completion and hair colour, the eyes would look much the same. Brown was fine with Coventry. Goodfellow said that he had only known two people with eyes of different colours, David Bowie, and a pilot he had met in the war whom he thought had been killed in action. He had met him briefly at a mission briefing in 1940 but had never seen him again. He didn't know his name.

Goodfellow and Coventry hit it off from the start. From the moment she entered his shop and began to speak, Goodfellow responded warmly and was Coventry's to command. When she mentioned that her father had been an RAF pilot who had been killed in the war, that opened the floodgates of Hawkins-Goodfellow's RAF past. It was a fascinating story.

From childhood in Yorkshire he had been myopic – short-sighted. He could see little that was at a distance. When Britain went to war, he was hell-bent on fighting for his country, but due to his myopic condition, there was not the slightest chance that any of the British forces would accept him. He didn't just want to be a foot soldier. His ambition was to fly with the RAF. So determined was he to join the war and be a flyer that he memorised the optical eye charts, passed the eye test, and bluffed his way through training, ending up as an air gunner on a Lancaster bomber. That was not the end of his deception. There was more; he had covered every angle of his ploy with forethought and skill.

Prior to his training, he craftily sent his eye prescription to the American Optical Company in Boston, USA. They ground the prescription into Calobar, tinted sun lenses, which Goodfellow wore during daylight high-altitude bombing missions. No one was any the wiser. During night missions he would slip on his regular clear spectacles at the right time and again, no one seemed to notice. Pretending to just look cool, and irrespective of the weather, he would wear his tinted glasses on the ground and no one ever caught on that without them, the only thing he saw at a distance was a blur. The most amazing part of his story was that on his first mission over France, he aimed in the right direction and shot down two German aircraft, while the other gunners on his Lancaster didn't hit a thing. By the time the war ended and after fifty-four missions, he had shot down eight enemy aircraft. With a chuckle Goodfellow said, "I think I got a piece of another."

On leaving his shop, Coventry reached into her purse to pay but Goodfellow smiled and said, pointing to each of his cheeks, "A little kiss here and a little kiss there will be payment enough." Coventry obliged with the greatest of pleasure. What a team he and Willie Sutton would have made, she thought.

An hour later, a young lad from Harrods walked across the road and into Goodfellows place of business. He was delivering a bottle of the best champagne Harrods had to offer. It had a beautiful ribbon wrapped around its box.

"Mr. Hawkins-Goodfellow?" enquired the young man.

"Yes, that's me."

"For you, sir," he said, handing the optician the box. "It's from a young lady who said that you are a very lovely man."

A note with the gift said, 'Thank you for your kindness and for your wonderful story. Best wishes and God bless. Coventry V. Calvert'.

"That girl is a saint," said Goodfellow to the lad.

Within two weeks, Coventry had her lenses. Based on what Coventry had said about her family, Dr. David Corcoran, Goodfellow's colleague at Moorfields Hospital, was certain that the trait that caused her eye colour difference had to have come from her father's side of the family, since different eye colours had never been known on her mother's side. Since she never knew her father or his kin, the trait almost had to have come from him.

As Goodfellow had warned, the lenses were difficult to adjust to, but Coventry was coping with them well. She had worn them at home for brief periods to get the feel of them. When she finally ventured out, it was on a short walk to her optician. She wanted to know what he thought, and if they looked natural and not freakish. After a long look, Goodfellow said, "Smashing, my dear. Smashing."

Needless to say he was thrilled with the gift Coventry had sent him the day of her visit. He said it came at a good time because that day marked the third anniversary of his wife's death, and that his spirits were low.

"Our chat and the gift gave me a lift," he said.

"The visit gave me a lift too, sir."

"Please," said Goodfellow, "call me Leslie and I'll call you Coventry. What a beautiful and unusual name Coventry is. My city with your name was bombed to hell in the war. You wear it well and do it justice."

It was now the evening of Sunday, October 20th and Coventry was leaving for Moscow early the following morning. She had met with Tiplady for her final briefing and everything was in order. She was packed and ready to go. Her contacts were neatly secure in their little box in her handbag. Her flight from Heathrow was on Air France flight 666 leaving London at 7:45am. Not leaving it to her alarm clock to wake her, she had called the telephone company and arranged for them to ring her at 4:45am.

Her office had organised a taxi to pick her up at 6:00am and take her to the airport. She was set, ready to go. Tomorrow would be a day of adventure. She would embark on her mission, ostensibly to write pieces about cultural matters like the Russian ballet and circus – this was the ploy her newspaper used to acquire her visa – this was her cover story. The real purpose of her trip was to meet with Big Ben, the

American from the US Embassy who had more information in his file about Prime Minister's Jones' closeness with the Soviet Union. She knew nothing about Big Ben or what he looked like. He would contact her when she arrived in Moscow. Yes, tomorrow would be a big day, and Coventry had the nervous stomach to prove it. She doused her cigarette, slipped into bed, switched off the bedside light and slipped into a smoky pool of dreams.

ELEVEN

Coventry is sleeping and dreaming. She's breathing deeply, tossing and turning in her bed. Her dreams appear and then go, and then returns like a windmill in her mind.

She's packed, ready for her trip, but first she must jump the hurdle of this dream, a dream that's come to trouble her mind the night before a special day. After dousing her smoke and switching off the light, she almost instantly falls asleep and now she's in the dark, smoky gutters of a dream that begins with the numbers 666.

These are her flight numbers. She didn't like them from the start. Earlier in the year an Air France flight had crashed while landing in Panama City, so she disliked the numbers straightaway. She knew all about the three sixes and what they represent. Her Godfather had often spoken of them. Three sixes were the calling cards of Lucifer, Satan and the Devil, all the forces of evil and darkness. They were the other side of the Goodfellow's coin: the Father, Son and the Holy Spirit, all separate, yet one. When Coventry first saw the flight numbers on her ticket, a current of disquiet shot through her body. Though she brushed them from her mind at the time, they hadn't swept far enough away. They were still there, tucked away in a corner of her subconscious. Now here they were again, the wretched triples sixes, this time in a dream.

Satan kicked off the dream with a phone call. Ring ring, ring ring, ring ring. Coventry can hardly find the phone for all the smoke around her, but out of nowhere the phone suddenly appears in the

69

palm of her hand. She thinks the rings are from the telephone company.

"Hello, is it four-forty-five already?"

"No, bitch, it's me, Satan!"

"Who?"

"Satan, woman, Satan! Sins my game, you're my flame."

"What do you want?"

"You, bitch, you!"

"What do you mean?"

"I'm getting you like I got your mother! You're next."

"Am I next?"

"Hell yes, you're next." Coventry angrily turns in bed and tells Satan, Lucifer and the other spook to get lost. Satan hangs up, mumbling something about a 'mother of all dreams'. When Satan hangs up, Coventry tosses and turns again. She's now lying on her right side with her left arm limp across her body. The fingers of left hand are twitching.

The dream fades, and then returns. Coventry is now in the Café de Paris. The venue is streaked with layers of smoke that rise, expand, vanish, and then reappear, just like her dream. The Café is full with people who are smoking, but no one is dancing. The band is on a break. The people in the balcony are flush up against its railing. They are all looking down on the dance floor and the people below that encircle it. Coventry is standing in the centre of the dance floor and everyone in the Café has their eyes on her. A red brassiere and black panties are all she is wearing. Nothing else, except for a cigarette, which is brazenly placed in the corner of her mouth, smoke curling upwards. Everyone in the dancehall is devilishly happy. They like Coventry's ensemble. It's swaggeringly suggestive and it signals her eagerness to pick a man from the assembled for her first crack at sex.

"We must come here again," says a pimp to a Jewish lady in the crowd.

A black man yells down from the balcony, "Whatta 'bout me?"

"No way, black man, no way," Coventry calls back.

"Discrimination!" shouts the black man.

Now the band appears. It begins to play and everyone in the Café de Paris is poised for what Coventry has to offer. The song being played is 'Lady Be Good', a popular tune from the 1940s. The smoke from Coventry's cigarette curls up and up until it reaches the balcony, then suddenly it pops. The moment it pops the smoke turns into a bubble the size of a big, glass balloon, inside of which Willie Sutton is caged. Willie is angry as hell, he's trying to break free. He's looking down at Coventry on the dance floor. She's looking the men over, choosing the best. She's eager for her nest to be showered for the first time. She's looking for Juanito, but he's nowhere to be seen. His voice an echo from within the bubble, Willie calls down: "Don't do it, don't do it, what would the nuns think, 'lady', you better 'be good'. This is not the time or the place. This dump is full of creeps, the women are tramps, and the guys are crooks. I know 'because I'm a crook. That's why my soul is jailed in this bubble."

Tiplady suddenly appears at Coventry's side. He's dressed in a black tuxedo. "OK," says Coventry. "Juanito's not around, you'll do. Strip, get it up, you can be my first."

"What do you mean?" says Tiplady.

"Listen, need I draw you a picture, get it up – now!"

"You mean here, with all these people watching?"

"Yes!"

"What about your virginity?"

"SCREW IT!"

The viewers are chanting like a Greek Chorus, "Get it up! Get it up!"

71

The black man calls out, "No problem here, I'm up, I'm ready."

A lady as old as Methuselah with dyed hair, proclaims for all to hear that Lloyd George had no trouble getting it up, that he gave her a good seeing to back in 666. The gathering cheers and jeers!

Standing to her left, Coventry's bad angel is happily taking all this in and scribbling notes. The bad angel was listening to the phone conversation when Satan called Coventry and she told him off.

The bad angel is on the job, working like a demon on this 'mother of all dreams'. The pace of the dream quickens. Up to the balcony fly Coventry's bra and panties, and down to the floor she goes. Legs apart, open she be, her nest ready, oiled and in mint condition. The cheers grow louder and so does the tune 'Lady Be Good'. Responding to all this, Tiplady stiffens. Up in a flash to the balcony flies his tuxedo. He's finally got it up! "Thank God," screams Coventry, as she looks up at his growth. "Don't thank God," says the bad angel, "thank me." Coventry twitches. She can see, she can hear, she can smell the action unfolding in her dream. She and her boss are at it. At it fast, at it hard, at it on the dance floor. Her legs are wrapped tightly around Tiplady, who is well and truly dipping into her. Smoke in the dream ebbs and flows. The crowd are cheering – all except Willie Sutton. He's even madder than before. "Screw this shit," he cries. "I want out of this cage; I want a piece of this action. I want to be next!" he bellows.

Juanito appears dressed as a matador. He's standing in the middle of the dance. He's looking down at Coventry and her boss, who are at it like dogs. Coventry is looking up at Juanito. She's looking up at him but she doesn't miss a beat. She and Tiplady are thrusting as one. Juanito says, "May I be next please?"

"Willie is next," replies Coventry between grunts. "And where the hell have you been? You could have given me my first drilling."

"Sorry," says Juanito. "I've been away. I'm now flying from Madrid to Lima and back every eight days– it's long, long haul."

"Tough," replies Coventry. "You'll need to wait. First is this guy who's doing me, then Willie, and then it's your turn. They get it free, you pay 666 for getting me hot and making me wait. But I need to see VISA 'causes I only take credit cards. You get to do me in private, up the stairs where my mother gave it for free."

"It's a deal," says Juanito.

"And who's that cocky guy next to you playing with himself?" asks Coventry.

"It's me, Coventry, Goodfellow. I came to check your lenses. May I follow Juanito?"

"Hell yes, didn't think you had such a big gun – no wonder you screwed the Luftwaffe. You did me for free; I'll do you for free."

Goodfellow says, "There's a queue of men waiting to be next. A guy with a mask named Ben is at the end. Who the hell is he? And what are Russians doing here?"

"Don't know," says Coventry, "or care." Ring ring, ring ring, ring ring. "Hello," says Coventry, barely awake.

"Good morning, Miss. It's four-forty-five."

"Good morning and thank you," says Coventry.

The morning is bad for travelling. It's misty. It's also raining hard. Coventry must now get to the Heathrow Airport. Then she must board flight 666 to Moscow.

TWELVE

The sky was a blanket of lead. The air was raw. It was misty, and on her way to Heathrow, rain was drumming on the roof of Coventry's taxi. Sherlock Holmes and Dr. Watson would have said the morning was 'filthy'. It was an ideal morning for Holmes and Watson to sip tea by the fire in Sherlock's Baker Street flat. Then, at some point, Holmes would say 'Elementary, my dear Watson', after a brilliant deduction that brought him closer to catching not Willie Sutton, but another villain – the fiendish mastermind outlaw professor Moriarity. It was the perfect backdrop for the forensic mind of Holmes and ideal for Watson to mumble as he lit his pipe. In the mind of their creator, Sir Arthur Conan Doyle, the two sleuths never journeyed to Moscow and Coventry was headed there for real. This thought tickled her mind as her taxi crept towards the airport. She liked the fictional detective who caught crooks, just as she liked Willie Sutton, a real crook, who was in jail planning a real but legal escape. These thoughts sat comfortably in Coventry's mind, nicely in tune with the tan, London raincoat she wore so well.

On radio that morning the BBC's Brian Redhead had said that the mist would lift and the rain would stop by nine o'clock, but that no flights would be moving in or out of Heathrow until then, so Coventry wasn't concerned about missing her plane. "Not to worry," said Angus, her taxi driver.

"Yes, no worries," replied Coventry as she sat back comfortably and lit a cigarette. The driver, a Scot, was well versed in 'The Knowledge' – the test of London's streets and byways all Black

Cab drivers must pass. Coventry leaned forward and asked, "Where are we now Angus? I can hardly see for the mist."

"Park Lane, miss, Park Lane – then Bayswater, Notting Hill, Chiswick and the A4 motorway – the A4 takes us right to Heathrow. No worries miss, we have buckets of time."

What a smashing looking woman, thought Angus, and those eyes. They had jumped out at him through the mist when Coventry swung open her door at six o'clock in answer to his ring and told her his name. He couldn't craft words like Juanito who called them Eyes of God. But as Angus drove to Heathrow, he wasn't lost for words about the Jaguar close behind him. "That bloody Jag's been on my tail since we left Belgravia."

Since she would only be away ten days, Coventry was travelling light. She carried a single brown suitcase and a large brown handbag that had a shoulder strap. She had purchased the gear in Harrods, on each of which her C.V.C initials was embossed in red. Her travelling outfit was smart-casual: dark slacks, a red pullover and a beautifully fitting tan raincoat with a belt. Her shoes were black loafers. Her hair was swept back and her chiselled features, just like her eyes, were in a mood to overpower any onlookers; the same reaction would have been the case years before for anyone who laid eyes on a young Greta Garbo or Katherine Hepburn.

After cleverly manoeuvring through the inner city, Angus reached the A4 and twenty minutes later he arrived at Heathrow's terminal Three. The journey had taken ninety minutes. The mist was as thick as ever, the rain kept falling, and travellers were checking in for flights that were grounded due to the weather.

Coventry was travelling First Class so checking in with Air France was swift. Unlike Economy Class people, she didn't have to join a queue. She could see that her flight would be full and that seemed a bit unusual because the Cold War was at its height and Moscow was behind the Iron Curtain.

Something else struck her as very unusual. About two thirds of the passengers on her flight were Chinese nationals. They were

75

clustered in bunches, chattering loudly in Chinese, oblivious to the other people around them – people they were annoying. Their world, it seemed, was limited to the one in which they existed. At this point the plot thickened when Coventry remembered something Angus had said: 'That bloody Jag's been on my tail since we left Belgravia'. Now it connected with something she was now very much aware.

Shortly after entering Terminal Three, Coventry had the feeling that two well-dressed men in black raincoats were looking her over – and it wasn't with looks of admiration. Every time she turned round, there they were, looking. They were tall and in their thirties, well-built and each carried a black attaché case. They didn't invade her space. They stood away, but now, after recalling Angus' comment, Coventry was certain she was the object of the men's special attention and that they might be connected with the Jaguar vehicle he had complained about.

The men were James Bond types. Their eyes kept darting to her handbag and the embossed C. V. C. letters.

Something strange was brewing. Who are they? she wondered. They were thirty feet away, near the WH Smith newsagent pretending to read the morning's papers headlines. The answer to her question lay in a meeting Tiplady hadn't revealed to her. The two men had paid him a visit following a phone call he had received from British Intelligence.

Her departure gate was 27A, which was near the end of a long passageway in Terminal Three. It was now close to eight o'clock. As a First Class passenger, Coventry could use the Air France hospitality room, an added perk for flying First Class. During check-in, Coventry had been told about the room and given a leaflet showing where it was located in the terminal. It was only now, while reading it carefully, that she noticed the room's name: Café de Paris. She fixed the room's location and headed that way via a very long passageway at the far end of which was gate 27A. She willed herself not to look back, just head for the hospitality room. With her handbag slung over her shoulder and her heart beating quickly, Coventry walked up the passageway in a seemingly casual manner looking for the door marked Café de Paris.

Normally the passageway would be a beehive of activity, with people going to, or coming from arriving flights, but this was not the case as Coventry made her way along the empty passageway. Hardly a soul was to be seen other than cleaning ladies whose origins were in the Middle East. They were pushing trolleys with equipment or tidying tall, round ashtrays next to seats that ran along the passageway. Outside on the tarmac, rows of jets sat waiting for the rain to stop and the mist to lift before taking to the sky. Not far behind, in pace with her strides, the two men had Coventry in their sights. Who were they?

They were agents of the Central Intelligence Agency – the CIA. The reason they had given for their visit to Tiplady was to enquire about Coventry's trip to Moscow. They were also curious as to why her visa application had been approved so quickly by the Soviet Embassy in London. They told Tiplady that the latter was unusual. What the agents did not say was the real reason for their visit. They cautioned him not to say anything to anyone about their visit. The caution was followed by a second visit, this time from an operative of British Intelligence, a tall, thin man with a slim moustache with the double-barrelled name of Smirthwaith-Cave.

At long last to her right was the hospitality room entrance door baring the name Café de Paris. Having only had coffee that morning, Coventry was ready for more. The room's motif was geared to put guests in a French state of mind, with wall-to-wall murals of French scenes and piped accordion music. The room and the dancehall shared the same name but there the similarity ended, except that both fell short of expectations. The room was large, its furniture comprising soft chairs of no particular acclaim and a long buffet table, set with fruit juice and cereals as well as bacon, eggs and the usual breakfast spread. The room offered a degree of comfort and except for a staff member or two, only three other travellers were there. Coventry picked her breakfast and dug in. She was under suspicion and though the men who shadowed her were out of sight, they were nonetheless near. In fact they were yards away in the passageway, poised to enter the Café de Paris hospitality room. So what was the CIA suspicious about and how did this all come to be? Their suspicions concerned the matter of Coventry's identity and the real motives for her trip to Moscow. Her Visa application stated that the reason for her trip was to write articles on Russian cultural affairs and that she would be doing this with the help of the Soviet Press Agency Novasti. The reason the agents gave to Tiplady for their visit was to confirm these facts, but their real motive was to enquire about Coventry herself. Her initials had the CIA in a jumpy mood. They didn't want a Russian leader shot by anyone, especially not by someone claiming to be American. The Russians, who were privy to all this, didn't want it either. None of this scenario seemed very likely, but neither the Russians nor Americans were taking any chances. As far as both were concerned, a political assassin was on the loose whose identity was unknown and the killer, be it he or she, might be this woman named Coventry Victoria Calvert. The world of political intrigue in the Cold War was throwing up the most unlikely equations and this female with C.V.C. initials had to be carefully scrutinised.

Given that in 1969, spying, intrigue and defections were the order of the day between East and West, all visa applications to Russia by US citizens first had to be vetted by their local embassy before being sent to the Russian Embassy for approval. In the course of this vetting, Coventry's initials had been noticed and brought to the attention of the CIA. The US Central Intelligence Agency had agents in Britain, due to the number of British civil servants who were revealing military and other British and American secrets to the Soviet Union. Three British turncoats, two of them homosexuals, had long since been found out. They had fled to Russia and were living in Moscow. Other suspects – one of them in charge of the Queen's art collection – was being watched closely.

Unbeknownst to all but a few at the highest levels of global intelligence, the assassin known as The Jackal, who had already made an attempt on the life of President Charles DeGaulle, was strongly suspected of being a female whose profile fit Coventry's. They suspected that she, along with Lee Harvey Oswald, was one of three snipers involved in the killing of John F. Kennedy, and that she was the one who fired from the grassy knoll near Dealey Plaza in Dallas, Texas. This information had come to the CIA from the FBI who had received it from an unlikely source. When the FBI investigated, the claim appeared to have merit for the following reasons.

In the autumn of 1968, after the assassinations that year of Martin Luther King Jr. in April, and Robert Kennedy in June, the FBI received word from Sinn Fein – the political wing of the IRA – that the real Jackal was almost certainly an Ulster born Protestant female who originated from Limavady, Northern Ireland and whose name was Joyce Elizabeth Esler.

Sinn Fein claimed that in the early 1960s, Elser was a student in her last year of study at a US university. They said that as a youngster she was highly proficient in the use of every type of firearm. According to Sinn Fein, she operated under bogus names, each of which began with the letters C. V. C. They claimed that she travelled on the passports of many nations and that three of the names she used were Camilla V. Connors, Constance V. Collier and Catherine V. Caton. They said that in all cases, the middle name she used was Victoria. Sinn Fein further claimed that Esler was the assassin who had shot dead the Presidents of Panama and Ecuador, and that she had made an attempt on the life of the Pope – an attempt the Vatican had kept secret but that had nearly succeeded when a bullet passed through the left sleeve of the Pontiff's cassock on Easter Sunday. Although Sinn Fein had no photographs of Esler, the description and age they gave were similar to that of Coventry's. Sinn Fein was not sure, but they thought the colour of Esler's eyes were almost certainly blue.

Sinn Fein's tip to the FBI had come from a protestant cleric from Belfast who knew Esler as a child. The cleric said that in her final university year in America, persons unknown doused her Limavady family home with paraffin in the dead of night, then torched it, and that all her kin had perished in the blaze. The cleric said he heard that she blamed the IRA and all Catholics, that she was now in her late twenties, but that he had not seen her since she was a youngster.

When the FBI looked into the claims, they found that a Joyce Elizabeth Esler had graduated from the University of Salina, Utah, in 1963, and that her major courses of study were journalism and history. After graduation, no one from the university had seen or heard from her again. Her scholastic records showed that she was bright, that she had flair for acting and that she had been active in the University's Drama Society. The FBI discovered that a Constance V. Collier was registered at the Dixie Motel in Memphis, Tennessee, on April 4th 1968, and that a Camilla V. Connors had been registered at the Ambassador Hotel in Los Angeles, on June 5th 1968. Martin Luther King Jr. was shot and killed on April 4th 1968. He was shot while standing on the balcony of the Lorraine Hotel in Memphis, Tennessee. The Dixie Motel was directly across the street. Robert Kennedy was shot and killed at the Ambassador Hotel in Los Angeles, California, on June 5th 1968. He was shot by a Palestinian named Sirhan Ali who had studied at the University of Salina at the same time as Joyce Elizabeth Esler.

The two CIA agents had this in mind as they prepared to enter the Café de Paris hospitality room. Once inside they flashed credentials, helped themselves to coffee and sat in a corner of the room, well away from Coventry. They didn't have the slightest notion that she was on to them. They had no idea that she knew a crook named Willie Sutton who knew when he was being tailed and had told her what signs to look for. When Coventry saw the agents, her heart skipped a beat and since the real purpose of her trip was to see Big Ben about the Prime Minister's chumminess with Russia, many possibilities ran through her mind. With coffee in one hand and a cigarette in the other, her brain ticked away and the pupils of Coventry's eyes expanded.

When the mist and rain lifted and her flight had been called, Coventry headed up the passageway to gate 27A. Her mind was on the men who were behind her. She could see 27A ahead and could see and hear the clusters of Chinese people rushing past her and running towards the gate, carryon bags flopping at their sides.

The men were not far behind and Coventry knew it. She could feel their presence just as Willie Sutton could always sense the law's presence throughout his criminal career. What would Willie do, she thought. He would make an unexpected move and this is what Coventry did. She stopped in her tracks, turned round, threw back her shoulders and waited for the men to reach her. Her blood was boiling and she was suddenly in a filthy mood. She would say nothing to the men. She would fix their eyes with hers. She would take them to the cliff edge and see who first would flinch.

THIRTEEN

Her eyes on fire, Coventry waited to face the stalkers to reach her. As the men drew near, they immediately spotted her demeanour. They could see she was on the warpath. For an instant they were thrown off balance, but they reacted swiftly, swept past her and made for Gate 27A. Coventry thought they'll be on my flight, I must compose myself! At the gate the agents threaded their way through the clusters of Oriental people who were making their usual noisy racket. The men disappeared through the caterpillar tunnel leading to the aircraft, leaving the other passengers behind to pass the boarding formalities, which they had not undergone. Nor had the Air France staff at the gate stopped them.

At the boarding gate the Orientals were out of control. They were pushing and shoving, waving their boarding passes at the Air France staff, all but demanding to be boarded first. The few Caucasian passengers around them were giving way. Coventry's eyes were fixed on the Orientals. Her mind was diverted from her stalkers. She was not always Christian when it came to people. She didn't care for Orientals. Her nose was well and truly in the air when it came to some people and she often wondered why God had bothered to create them in the first place. She was an 'a'la carte' Catholic. She chose selectively from life's menu of humanity. She had little tolerance for races that were not white. She respected her fellow man, but to her way of thinking, she felt under no obligation to also draw them all to her bosom. That was a leap too far and she didn't feel guilty about it either. Loud, pushy Orientals with bechive behaviour were not her cup of noodles. God, she believed, had given her a brain to use, not a harness within whose bounds anyone was welcomed. That's how she felt. Her circle of human acceptance was reserved for West European stock, and even there she was selective. She cared little for the French, thinking them to be a slippery bunch with overblown opinions of themselves, their language and culture.

As far as East Europeans were concerned, she had no special feelings. They were behind the Iron Curtain and that, to her mind, was not so bad. As far as she was concerned, they were just about where they belonged, within the orbit of the Soviet Union. She had nothing whatever against Israel or Jewish people. Yes, Judas was a Jew, but so was Simon of Cyrene, the only one who had helped Jesus carry the cross, and so was Joseph of Arimathea, in whose tomb the body of Christ lay before resurrection. Who wiped the face of Jesus? Veronica, another Jew. So Jews were OK by Coventry. Of all the European people, Coventry liked Italians most. She liked their elastic view of life, their approach to Catholic dictates, and their natural disposition to the arts. About the Germans, Coventry had no particular feelings except that she always remembered how one of her teaching nuns, Sister Edith, described their dining habits. The nun said; 'They are the only people who, rather than raising food to their mouths, bring their mouths down to their food'.

As for Orientals, as a youngster Coventry had taken on board Napoleon's words – even though he was French. 'Let the sleeping giant sleep' – leave them to their opium. Let them slumber on their pillows of powdery dreams because if they ever got together and march west, the weight of their numbers would be consuming to all in their path.

Neither did the US escape Coventry's scorn. The country had much to answer for from the presidency of JFK forward, for the Liberalism that he, from his privileged background had let loose in America. Liberalism in which almost everybody had rights – but no one seemed to have responsibilities. Above all, she hated America's new immigration laws – laws that allowed the steady intake of people from Korea.

Now, as Coventry waited to board her jet with the flight numbers she so disliked, her mind returned to the two men who she was certain were already on board. With her handbag slung over her shoulder, she boarded her plane, not knowing what lay ahead, but with a chain of Christ dangling from her neck, she was travelling hopefully and made the sign of the Cross.

Coventry was different in ways beyond the mismatch of her eyes. She had flown to London in January economy class. It wasn't out of frugalness that she had flown economy. Travelling First Class hadn't occurred to her. Her mind was never set on seeking special comforts. Other things were on her mind when she flew to London – the death of her mother, the Café De Paris, the new life ahead of her, the changes occurring in America and perhaps even with the hope of discovering who her real father was.

There were two gay attendants working First Class. One drew back when he fixed on her eyes, but not in horror. Smiling, he led Coventry to her seat and took her coat. Her eyes took his breath away and he responded by nearly melting. Just like her optician Goodfellow, he was hers to command. "Coffee, madam?"

"Please," replied Coventry, as she slipped into her front row seat near the cockpit and crossed her legs. The other attendant, taking an instant dislike to Coventry, swung his head sharply to the left, fussed with his hair and wiggled his rear towards a motioning passenger. He cared little for the magnetism Coventry held for his colleague.

The First Class section had sixteen seats. It was isolated from the passengers behind First Class by a drawn curtain. With the two men on her mind, Coventry's eyes jumped from seat to seat but the men were not in First Class. Everyone was now on board. The mist had lifted, the rain had stopped and the plane's doors had been shut. There were only five other First Class passengers. One was Maurice Chevalier who, like many other stars, had entertained at the Café de Paris back in the dancehall's heyday. Everyone in First Class could hear the Chinese at the back of the aircraft chattering in loud voices, like monkeys in a cage and Coventry was happy to be away from the little Eastern people who bred like rabbits and behaved like bees.

Her flight would stop in Paris before proceeding to Moscow and this leg of her journey would not take long. From Paris to Moscow was another matter as two thousand miles had to be flown, which would take four hours. The captain, a tall, slightly bent man near retirement age began an ambling tour up the aisle of his plane's cabins and the passengers he was carrying, but for no apparent reason he lingered too long in Coventry's vicinity. When their eyes met he looked away quickly. This was not the normal behaviour of pilots whose similar tours aimed to make passengers feel that they were in safe hands.

Her coffee arrived and still there was no sign of the men. They're probably in economy with those wretched Orientals, thought Coventry. When we're off the ground, I'll wander up the aisle and see where they are. This was her plan. On the heel of this thought, the captain returned from his tour and entered the cockpit. He was nothing like Juanito and this drew her thoughts to the Spaniard. Within minutes the jet was under way and fifteen minutes later Flight 666 was above the murky weather and into sunny skies, on its way to Paris.

As her jet roared upwards, Coventry's mind was not on the men but on Juanito. Her eyes were closed, there was a smile on her face and she began to re-live the night they met, when he danced his leg between hers and when, in her dream, his behaviour was so erotic. She wondered where he was and what he was doing. Had she known, she would have been fearful for Juanito and for herself, because she was in the air, high up above the ground, flying in a plane. Little did she know that he too was in the air, but flying above the Irish Sea near the Isle of Man, and was struggling to keep his damaged plane in the air. Some three hundred souls were on board his plane and everyone was in trouble. His jet was rocking and creaking. People were yelling, and those not harnessed to their seats were being knocked about. Injuries were plenty. Sweat was pouring off the faces of Juanito and his co-pilot. A female cabin crew had broken her neck and lay spastically in the aisle. Her eyes were open and she was sliding forward and back as the ship fishtailed in rollercoaster style.

ETA, the Spanish separatist group, had planted a bomb in Juanito's plane. It had detonated over Northern Ireland and the Jumbo seemed doomed. There was a huge hole on the portside of the aircraft near the cargo section. "Holy Mary, Mother of God, save us," prayed a Mercy Nun on board. Coventry snapped out of her daydream and made her way to the rear of the plane. As discreetly as possible, her eyes scanned all the seats. The men were nowhere to be seen. If she caught the eye of someone, there was always a reaction from them. People whispered to their neighbours and heads turned. To cover every angle, Coventry checked the toilets at the back of the plane but the men weren't there. Where can they be? she thought. The only other place was the cockpit. She returned to her seat and minutes later the captain announced that they would soon be landing at Charles DeGaulle Airport, and shortly thereafter they did. Coventry kept her eyes on the exit door – the men did not leave the aircraft.

When the exiting passengers had left, a handful of Moscow-bound people boarded the plane and soon after landing in Paris, Flight 666 was up and away, headed for the Russian capital. The weather had been brutal in Paris – rain, rain, rain – but now the jet was above the clouds, streaking though the sky towards Russia. The flight path was over Germany, Czechoslovakia and Poland.

There came a twist to the tale of this flight. Over Czechoslovakia the captain made a strange and unexpected announcement that alarmed everyone. The plane was to make an unscheduled stop at Warsaw, Poland. There was loud chatter from the Chinese when they heard about the detour. What's this all about? was the thinking of passengers throughout the aircraft. The closer she got to Moscow, the more Coventry's mind fixed on her mission to the Russian capital. George Bolchekov, Big Ben and Prime Minister Jones were at the centre of her thinking. Her mind was also fixed on the two men still on the plane.

After landing in Warsaw, the plane taxied to the airport's perimeter. For Coventry, this twist was taking on the cloak-and-dagger hallmarks of the Cold War. The crew could offer no explanation as to why the plane had landed in Warsaw. They didn't know and Coventry had no reason not to believe them.

When the jet came to rest, it stopped near a large, rectangular, single-story building. From her window, Coventry thought the building had a military look and she could see a tall stair platform being wheeled towards her plane's left front door. Next came an announcement that someone would soon board the plane and that all passengers should follow that person down the stairs and into the building. Everyone was to do as ordered. When the stairs were in place and the ship's door opened, a stocky, Slavic-looking woman in uniform led everyone on board the plane, except the crew, to the building.

The interior of the building was bare, save for long wooden benches that hugged the four walls. Two tall, strapping looking soldiers with oriental looks motioned the Chinese people to enter a room the soldiers were pointing to. Everyone else – all of them Caucasians – was motioned to remain where they were and sit. Thirty minutes later the Caucasians were motioned to follow the uniformed lady and return to their aircraft. When Flight 666 took off for Moscow, not one of the Chinese passengers were back on board the plane. None of the remaining passengers dared ask questions and the CIA men were still nowhere to be seen.

FOURTEEN

The arrangement was that someone would meet her flight, and after Coventry had cleared customs she would be driven to the Ukraine Hotel. The Ukraine was near the Moscow River, Red Square, St. Basil's Cathedral and the US Embassy. Soon after reaching Moscow, Coventry was required to report to the embassy and fill out some forms. This was normal procedure for visiting Americans to the city and it was very convenient, because Big Ben worked there. He was the cultural attaché.

Coventry knew what to expect when she arrived in Moscow. Tiplady had briefed her well. The person or persons meeting her would be KGB operatives, (the committee for state security) but she should not be concerned. KGB involvement in every walk of life was normal in the USSR.

No one was above suspicion. Tiplady said, "The state's power is ruthlessly applied in Russia." In 1969 the General Secretary Of The Communist Party of the Soviet Union was Leonid Brezhnev and he, like his predecessors since Stalin, ruled with an 'Iron Fist', and their grip was the fist of the KGB.

As her flight neared Moscow, New York, Belgravia and the Café de Paris seemed a long way off. The memory of her dreams were now tucked away in a corner of her mind and her friend Willie Sutton was still in Attica prison – prison was also the fate of others in jail in Russia that KGB didn't like. Some had simply vanished, never to be seen again, and much of this was courtesy of the KGB, so Coventry was aware that she had better watch her step.

An hour before landing, incomprehensible customs declarations were distributed to everyone on board. Nothing in French or English, just Russian, so few on Coventry's flight could fill them out. She had been warned that airport officials were often deliberately awkward when it came to dealing with foreigners. The flight was full of non-Russian, mostly men travelling to Moscow on business. Among them were a small group who were almost certainly Cuban. Few, if any of the people on her plane appeared to be tourists. The disappearance in Warsaw of the Moscow-bound Chinese had reduced the plane's numbers greatly.

As the aircraft started its descent through the cloud, terrible vibrations began. The cloud the plane was passing through was a powerhouse of rain and gusts. It was a jarring ride for the Air France passengers and they all hated the experience. The same filthy weather that had gripped London and Paris was also battering Eastern Europe and Russia. The jet creaked and shuddered but it was nothing like the sounds that were coming from Juanito's injured ship a few hours earlier. He was, however, alive and so were his passengers – but only with God's help. Or perhaps the blessing had simply come from Lady Luck – the same Lady Luck that sent a milk van to aid Willie Sutton the night of the snowstorm and his escape from his Pennsylvania prison.

When the bomb blew a hole in his plane, the weather was terrible. Destined for London, Juanito had already started his descent when the bang came and he was now struggling to control his plane while flying in and out of windy cloud – the same type cloud Coventry's jet was battling now. The explosion had damaged the ship's rudder and electrical system, so the Spaniard didn't know if his distress calls were being heard. No response was coming from his Mayday calls. Juanito and his cockpit crew thought they were over the Irish Sea, near the Isle of Man, but they weren't sure. Even at low altitude there was too much cloud. Three hundred lives were at risk.

Despite his efforts to steady the Jumbo and keep it up, the aircraft kept going down. Then, what must have been 'The Eyes of God' spotted the stricken craft and God must have said, 'Let There be light'. And there was light! What luck! The cloud vanished, the sun shone and before Juanito, a mile ahead and perfectly lined up, was a runway on what had to be the Isle of Man. It was 'Jurby', on the northwest corner of the island, where a disused RAF airfield from World War II stood. God or Luck had done their part. Juanito and his co-pilot had to do theirs, but was the runway long enough for a Jumbo to land? Would the wheels lower and lock? God only knew!

The Jumbo was a thousand feet up and hard to handle, but the air speed was low enough to drop wheels. This was no time for fiddling. It was time to go for broke. There was no other option. On Juanito's command of 'gear down', the co-pilot pressed the 'gear down' lever. Three green lights appeared on the panel before them, as the wheels lowered and locked with a thud. Then, as if God himself was at the controls, Juanito landed the Jumbo as if it were child's play – and at no time did the wings touch the ground. That could have meant disaster.

Unbelievably the old runway was just about long enough due to a pasture that joined it. With his heart thumping, Juanito used the pasture to touch down. He then aimed his bumping jet towards the runway. His airspeed was just about low enough to allow this treacherous manoeuvre. When the Jumbo came to rest at the end of the runway, the nose of the plane just short of the wings had stopped between two aircraft hangars once used by Spitfires. Cheers abounded and it was then that three hundred 'prayers of thanks' began, and only then the sun vanished and the mist returned. Soon after, a lone policeman on a bicycle appeared and said that help was on the way, and soon after that, some of the island's good folk began to gather for a look at the Jumbo with a big, jagged hole in its side.

Within sixty minutes the news was on BBC Radio. Then it circled the world. Later, one headline in a Spanish newspaper cried out – 'Bravo Juanito!' Another said – 'Gracias-a-Dios'. Still another said, 'Viva Juanito!' God, luck, or pre-destination had provided the light and earth for the Spaniard to land his plane on the Isle of Man; a tiny island of seventy thousand souls who's southern-most stretch is called Spanish Head.

Coventry's jet was on its final approach to Moscow Airport. The ship was fishtailing, swinging from one side to the other all at once. The winds were severe and rain was slapping on the windows. Everyone was tense. Bump after bump, thump after thump, the aircraft soldiered downward. When the wheels hit the runway, the plane's touchdown was less of a landing and more of a controlled crash, not quite on a par with Juanito's landing but good enough. When Coventry's plane rolled to a stop and the pilot switched off the engines, the only sounds that rippled through the plane were the words 'Thank God'. The look on the faces of the crew said it all. Two months earlier an Air France Boeing had crashed in South America while landing in similar conditions. Half of all on board had been killed.

Like all other passengers, Coventry was on her feet, quietly waiting for the exit door to be opened. Shaken by the landing but outwardly poised, she stood near the door. Her raincoat was on and her handbag with her C.V.C. initials slung over her shoulder. The bitchy gay attendant was standing by the door. He was waiting for the captain's signal to unlock and swing them open. When the signal came, he responded with the gestures of an irksome female. There was, however, more to him than met the eye. He had survived the air crash in South America without a scratch and he was still flying.

Two, big, potato-faced men with glaring eyes stood waiting to lead new arrivals to the customs area of the airport. They worked for the KGB. Waiting also were two burly, middle-aged women. They too had glaring eyes. One of them was a redhead with long hair. They were waiting for Coventry. The redhead held a sign bearing the name: 'Miss C.V. Calvert'.

Dressed in sad, dark clothes, they were waiting for the American to make herself known. Coventry fingered the crucifix round her neck, stepped out of the aircraft and when she saw her name, she waved in the women's direction. She was smiling. When the women spied her wave, they smiled and as Coventry approached, they drank her in head to toe. When their gaze fixed on her eyes, their stern demeanour came slightly off the rails and their expressions

91

changed. "Welcome to Moscow," said the redhead in surprisingly good English. "My name is Tina," and turning to her colleague, Tina said, "this is Tanya."

Both women wore swaggering hats with slouching brims much like the hat Ingrid Bergman wore in the film 'Casablanca' near the end. The women were powerfully built and when they shook Coventry's hand, the clash between their femininity and Coventry came sharply into focus. Tanya's eyes were all over her handbag and its C.V.C. initials. Neither did the stylish belted raincoat Coventry was wearing escape her notice. No such attire was available in Russia. "So sorry to greet you with bad weather," said Tanya in even better English than Tina.

"Not to worry," Coventry replied, giving the weather little importance, "It was the same in London and Paris."

"Yes, we know," said Tina.

"How was it when you left New York?" inquired Tanya. It was a strange question – it did not escape Coventry's notice. It put her on guard. She had left New York in January, not today, as Tanya's question implied. Tanya – clearly a lesbian – was up to a KGB trick intended to trip-up the unsuspecting. "Oh," answered Coventry with a smile of innocence, "when I left New York in January, I seem to recall it was cold." Tanya got the message that Coventry was no fool.

"Do you speak Russian?" she asked.

Coventry said, "No – and I could use help filling in my customs forms."

"Yes, for sure," said Tanya. It was obvious that Tina and Tanya worked for the KGB.

With the small talk over, Tina informed Coventry that she would be her driver during her stay in Moscow. Tanya would be her translator when required. The women then led Coventry along a maze of passageways to the baggage claim area, where after an endless wait with other passengers, Coventry's luggage appeared. It tumbled down the shoot of the carousel amid other luggage. She immediately noticed that her luggage had been tampered with because some of her garments were slightly exposed, which was not the case at the start of her journey. Coventry said nothing and pretended not to notice, but Tina and Tanya did. They knew that Coventry had spotted the exposed garments.

In the customs area, Tanya asked Coventry an array of questions posed by the declaration forms, and in the proper spaces, Coventry filled in the answers in English, not really knowing if her answers matched the questions. She then signed other forms, again not knowing what she was signing. Without help, most of the other passengers from her flight were lost filling in their forms and no one from customs seemed inclined to help them. In the meantime, officials in grey uniforms were keeping their eyes on everyone and in the background, soldiers hovered. Some of the soldiers were oriental in appearance, like the soldiers in Warsaw where the Chinese had vanished.

At the customs checkpoint there were half a dozen tables, each with two stern-looking male attendants. They were waiting for passengers with luggage to approach. Flanked by Tina and Tanya, Coventry was one of few to do so. The Cubans on her flight had been met and their forms had already been filled in. The other passengers were still struggling with their paperwork. In addition to her customs forms, Coventry had her passport, visa and all other documents ready for inspection. When the attendants at her table saw her eyes, they looked at one another. Coventry spotted their reaction but pretended not to notice. Having placed her luggage and handbag on the table, one officer motioned to her for both to be opened, while the other dealt with her passport and documents. Coventry opened everything and Tina and Tanya stepped to one side. The attendants began doing their job. The one dealing with her documents looked up from her passport, stared into Coventry's eyes and asked, "What is your business here?" Coventry looked into his and was taken aback. One of his eyes was pale blue, the other pale grey. He was quite handsome, in a vulgar sort of way.

"I'm a journalist," Coventry replied. "Here to see Mr. Bolchekov of the Soviet Press Agency Novasti. Copies of his letters to my editor are among my papers." The attendant started pouring over everything, while his colleague went through her luggage.

When the latter came across her contacts, he asked, "What is this please?"

"They're contact lenses for my eyes," answered Coventry. The questioning officer showed them to his partner, who made no comment.

"How much foreign currency do you have?" asked the handsome Russian.

"One thousand Sterling."

"US dollars?"

"Yes."

"How much?"

"Not sure, about one thousand."

"How long will you be staying?"

"Ten days."

"Have you ever been to Russia before?"

"No."

"You were born in New York?"

"Yes."

"Why is an American working for a British newspaper?"

"Why not?"

"Have you anything to declare?"

"No."

"Do you like Russians?"

"I like you," Coventry replied suggestively.

The customs man did not react, asked no further questions and stamped her passport. As he handed it back, he said that it would be taken and held at her hotel, but that it would be returned to her when she was leaving Moscow.

"That's fine," said Coventry.

She knew all about this procedure. After careful perusal of her luggage the men said, "Everything is in order, you can go." Her luggage was zipped up; her handbag was closed and off to the city went Coventry with her minders.

On the way into Moscow, a twenty mile drive, there was a steady downpour of rain and a hint in the air that winter was on its way. It was the same miserable weather with which Coventry had begun her journey, only colder. There was little to interest the eye on route, until they reached the inner city and even then the weather did little to improve Coventry's first impressions of Moscow. The cars were mostly Russian Ladas, grey or black, square-shaped frames on wheels made for A to B travel only.

Coventry was tired. It had been a long, stressful day. She couldn't wait to reach her destination and have a shower and rest. As they neared the Ukraine, Tanya pointed to it in the distance and said it had been built in the 1950s when Stalin was in power. Like everything, Coventry had seen to this point, the Ukraine looked grey and uninviting – a tall structure of twenty-nine storeys shaped like the Empire State Building in New York. Ten minutes later they were there.

In order to enter the hotel. sixteen stone steps had to be climbed. As the three women mounted the steps under two black umbrellas, six men were descending on their way to a black sedan parked and waiting at the kerbside. They were speaking Spanish. One of the men was Fidel Castro. The women then entered the Ukraine's lobby where Coventry's passport was taken, and without warning, Coventry was taken a-back! This time it had nothing to do with the eyes or a handsome Russian. There, sitting in the Ukraine's lobby were two individuals – the men from Heathrow Airport.

FIFTEEN

A friendly letter from George Bolchekov was waiting for Coventry at the Ukraine's lobby desk. It welcomed her to Moscow and said that Tina and Tanya would bring her to his office the following morning. After she had registered and surrendered her passport, Tina shook Coventry's hand and left. Tanya then led the way across the lobby to the elevator. Coventry's room was on the third floor, and if she didn't like her flight number, she liked her room number even less – No. eighteen – the three sixes again. Hell!

On the way to the elevator, the two agents eyeballed Coventry. She returned their looks with one of her own. No one said a word. From the time Coventry entered the lobby and spotted the men, she sensed that Tina and Tanya were somehow in league with them. Their lack of recognition to their presence was unmistakeable. The men were conspicuous in countless ways, sticking out like two sore thumbs. America was written all over them and yet Tina and Tanya, who were trained to spot such things, acted as if they weren't there.

The agents had flown to Moscow on an Aeroflot jet that was parked beyond Coventry's Air France carrier. The Aeroflot had left Heathrow before her plane, had flown directly to Moscow and had arrived an hour before her flight. Tina and Tanya had met the Aeroflot and had huddled with the men about the impending arrival of Miss Coventry Calvert – the lady with the C.V.C. initials – the suspected assassin.

The CIA and KGB were closer to the real assassin than they knew. He was in Moscow, but it was not to kill a Russian. He was on

Coventry's flight. He was the most unlikely looking killer imaginable – a tallish, slim, brown haired Cuban in his thirties, of fair complexion and piercing blue eyes, whose impersonations of a woman were remarkable. To look at him it was easy to see why. He was beautiful in a manly way, and he was that – all man. With an IQ of 177, he was a brazen, slick Willie Sutton type of character with upper class credentials whose focus was political. He was neither homosexual, transvestite or a deviant. Women were his candy and his tooth for them was sweet. His identity was unknown to the KGB, the CIA, the FBI or Interpol. He was a blank sheet; he did not exist. Coventry with her C.V.C initials did exist, and she was here in Moscow at the same time as him. He was not, as thought, a killer for hire. He was an enigma, a rich man. He was a globe- trotting vigilante, a Latin whose mission was to kill people in high places whom he felt were bent on pushing liberal agendas, like his womanising and hypocritical victims Jack and Robert Kennedy and Martin Luther King. He could have left Cuba at anytime. He had the means and knew the ways, but because he was Cuban to the core, he had chosen to stay.

He followed the Jesuit rule of 'influencing the influential', and when called for he had bullets ready for the ultimate influence. In past killings he had worked alone, except in the shootings of the Kennedy brothers. The killing of Jack he had plied with kin, Caesar – a younger brother, his only sibling. Caesar was the sniper who fired from the grassy knoll and missed, but our marksman didn't miss. It was his two bullets and not those of Lee Harvey Oswald that drilled JFK and it was the second of his bullets that blew open the president's head. Guilt ridden, Caesar had killed himself two days later, but his mastermind brother showed no remorse. He was icy as Dracula and ready for more liberal blood.

In the killing of Robert Kennedy, the Cuban was in league with someone who got to RFK first. He had acted alone in the killing of Martin Luther King and would do so again in the slaying of Castro. He decided that in future, except in the case of Castro, he would continue as before, posing as a woman. The disguise had been the key in the killing of the Kennedys. He knew a female would never be suspected. She could get close to a target. The ploy could open doors otherwise closed, and for him, it had. Others took the blame for the killings of RFK and King but he was the brains and instigator, a Cuban intellectual with splendid legs, posing as a woman. He had played female roles in school productions and performed them convincingly with legs most women would have killed for. He was one of the Cubans on the plane whom Coventry had noticed, one of eight men on a tobacco and sugar trade delegation to Moscow. After years of waiting, the chance to kill Castro had come, but this time bullets were not on his menu. His weapon would be a cigar from a box of cigars that would be given to Fidel at a Kremlin dinner hosted by Leonid Brezhnev. The assassin was familiar to Castro. He had Fidel's confidence and could get close to him. He was one of the chosen, an old comrade who in the old days had fought with Fidel in the hills of Santiago. He had been tough when the revolution needed men with grit and this was why Castro trusted him.

Because of his links with Fidel, he, as chairman of the Cuban Trade Board, enjoyed unusual freedoms in post revolutionary Cuba. Under false names and passports, he could enter America with ease from counties in central and South America friendly with Castro's regime. Fidel's death, which would occur within hours of lighting the cigar, would appear to be caused by heart failure. Few would question his death or suspect foul play. Castro was known to have a bad heart and to be a heavy smoker. In the mind of the would-be assassin, his death would atone for all Fidel had done to Cuba and perhaps stop the nation's rot. Castro was known to be possessive about his cigars. He would never give one away. He would always pick them from their box, starting from the left. That's where the poison cigar in the box would be placed. So where did this killer spring from? What made him tick? What triggered his attitude and behaviour?

His name was Dr. Jose Del Valle de la Rosa. A Jesuit educated lawyer, the son of the wealthy, deceased, Oscar Del Valle de la Rosa, and a judge from Santiago de Cuba in the Oriente Province of the island near Guantanamo Bay. The judge had been a farsighted man. He had never kept most of his wealth in Cuba. It was invested in Swiss, New York and Miami banks. Over the years, his friends thought that in the past his kin were Jews, due to his monetary skills, and because his blood could be traced to Toledo, Spain, which was once a Jewish centre. That was only conjecture. 'Tengo nada de Judeo', he would say – 'I have nothing of a Jew'.

The Judge's parents, Caesar and Carmella, had arrived in Cuba in 1899, a year after the Spanish American war. Both were issues of rich Galician parents that were prominent in commerce and Spanish society. When settled in Cuba, the couple eventually had six sons. The eldest, Oscar, became a lawyer in 1930 and a very rich man from investments in America. Jose, Oscar's son was born in 1933.

All de la Rosa's sons were educated to the teeth and they studied with the Jesuits in Santiago de Cuba. From there they progressed to El Colejio Belen in Havana where they gained PhDs in Law. This was the same educational Jesuit route followed by Fidel Castro, who had gained his Doctorate aged twenty-four in 1950.

Fidel and the Jesuits were close; one was always at his side. Like his father and uncles before him, Jose was Jesuit educated and in 1954 he gained a PhD from El Colejio Belen. It was there, soon after, at a school reunion, that Jose met Fidel Castro, a man with whom he had much in common.

In 1952, Fulgencio Battista toppled Carlos Socarra in a palace military coup. Contrary to his promises, he had suspended the Cuban constitution, thereby continuing the country's military rule. Nothing had changed. America's involvement in Cuban affairs went on and so did the mass impoverishment of the Cuban people. Fidel had enough, so he began his drive to rid Cuba of Battista. The blatant suspension of the Cuban constitution appalled Jose and was the reason why, in 1954, after he gained his Doctorate in Law, he took up arms with Castro against Battista.

Together with Fidel and others, Jose had taken part in raids against Cuban military barracks and had killed at least a dozen of his countrymen from distance. He was a deadly shot. Fortunately, unlike many of his comrades, including Castro, Jose had never been captured, tortured or imprisoned, as Fidel had been before being exiled to Mexico. This was when Castro began to change politically and when Jose's drift from Castro began. Before his exile, Fidel was not a Marxist. His political change began in Mexico when he met the Argentinean Che Guevara, who was also in exile there. Part of the Che clique in Mexico was a man of great influence, a former Cuban Jesuit named Ignacio Mendez-Gomez y Ruiz. He was not a Jesuit like McAvoy, Coventry's Godfather. He was quite different – dark and sinister in demeanour – there was something of the night about him.

Between 1955 – the year Fidel met Che – and 1959, when Battista fled Cuba and Castro came to power, Jose cared little for Fidel's growing Marxist leanings. In the years that followed he liked it even less when in the name of 'La Revulucion', Fidel stripped the assets of the Cuban middle class, froze American assets, and turned Cuba into a banana republic, whose primary market was Russia. The American market and everything that went with it was gone, and Cubans, most of them Caucasians, were fleeing to Miami through shark-infested waters on anything that would float.

The exodus appalled Jose. In 1962, when it was discovered that in exchange for aid, Castro had allowed Russian missiles into Cuba, and the Missile Crisis occurred, Jose decided that 'enough was enough'. Something had to be done about Fidel and JFK.

Kennedy became a de la Rosa target for his last minute withdrawal of support to the Cuban exiles active in the CIA- led Bay of Pigs invasion. Jose had yearned for its success. He also had another bone to pick with Kennedy. He did not agree with his liberal stance. The first person on his 'hit list' would be JFK and eventually, when the chance came, he would also kill Fidel. Between the two, others with whom Jose had issues would fall. And they did!

Now, on this rainy Moscow day in October 1969, Jose and the Cuban Trade Delegation were in the Metropole Hotel in the heart of the city. In three days they would attend a dinner hosted by Leonid Brezhnev in honour of Castro. At this function, and when the time was right, Jose would embrace Fidel and hand him a box of Cuban Cigars, the best in the world. When Fidel was dead and buried, his Jesuit sidekick would give soothing reasons for his tragic death, but Jose and only Jose would know the truth about Castro's demise.

When the Ukraine's third floor elevator door slid open, in the corridor behind a desk with powerful square legs sat the burly, round-faced Olga. She was chewing brown bread with her yellow teeth. Her face was a landslide of sadness. On her desk sat a large silver ring holding Mortice lock keys of the skeleton type variety with two jagged teeth. "You must report to her. She has charge of the floor," whispered Tanya to Coventry.

Olga got to her feet. She was a huge woman in height and width. Wrapped around her waist hung a black apron with two pockets bulging from the items they held. With a scowling look on her face, Olga moved from the desk to meet the oncoming Coventry and Tanya. Although Olga knew Tanya, she did not address her. "Your name?" she asked Coventry.

"Coventry Calvert."

"I Olga. Your key!" she said, coldly holding out a big, grasping hand. Coventry handed her the key and Olga blinked and was slightly thrown back when her eyes locked on Coventry's. Olga then made the sign of the cross on her chest the orthodox way. "You come," said Olga.

The key to room eighteen was made of iron. It was heavy and measured five inches long. The only similar keys Coventry had seen were those to dungeons at the Spanish Museum in New York. The lock on the door of room eighteen was the double tumble type. Olga slipped in the key, turned it twice and the locks tumbled to unlock. The sound was something like the one Willie Sutton had described when he was cracking a jewellery store safe, only louder. Olga swung open the door and the women stepped in. Coventry's room was small, Spartan but neat. A narrow bed hugged a wall. In the centre of the room there was a round table that held a silver tray. On it were a bottle of water, a bottle of vodka and a single drinking glass. A brown bureau stood against another wall and off to one side was a small inlet that led to a door-less bathroom. By a window on a desk sat a radio with a round canvas face, but no dials. Next to it stood a bulbous shaped telephone, also with no dials. "Your room," said Olga, as she handed Coventry the key. With her eyes fixed on the key she added,

101

"Give to me back when you leave room. I bring breakfast at eight." Then she left.

Coventry looked at Tanya with a weary expression. "I hope I sleep tonight," she said. "I'm very tired."

"Good food on the plane?" asked Tanya.

"Yes, and plenty." Tanya placed Coventry's bag on the dresser and prepared to leave.

"You rest," she said. "Tomorrow you see Bolchekov. You will like him. Women fall at his feet."

"How's his English?"

"Not so good."

"Is he married?"

"No, he is free. Will see you in the morning."

"Yes, see you then," said Coventry as Tanya closed the room door behind her. There was much to do tomorrow and Big Ben was on Coventry's mind.

A thousand yards away, atop a sloping street in an office of the American Embassy, Big Ben stood at a window. He was a black man but not of the street type variety. The rain was pouring down. He could see Coventry's Hotel. He knew she had arrived. He was tall, clean-cut, and smartly dressed. He was similar in appearance to the singer Harry Bellafonte. He was Vincent Irwin Benjamin Yearwood, the former US Marine, who as a student after the war, had given Willie Sutton a lift across the George Washington Bridge. He and Coventry had more in common than being fellow Americans, more in common than the real reason for her Moscow visit, but neither knew the link the other had with Willie Sutton.

Coventry stood at her window, looking out. In the distance she could see the drenched American flag hanging limply at the crest of the American Embassy. To the left she could see the narrow, winding Moscow River and recalled what she had learned about Russian history after the Bolshevik Revolution. She recalled the dead bodies floating in the river when Stalin was purging dissidents. She was too weary to recall any more. She had to rest. She had to close what Juanito had called her 'Eyes of God'.

SIXTEEN

The rain was relentless. It beat hard on her room window. Her eyes closed, shoeless but dressed, Coventry lay stretched out. In London, her bed was spacious but not the one she was in now. This one was narrow, short and hard. She felt clammy after her trip. She would rest for a while and then shower.

There was a feeling of sadness in the room – one that had never known joy. There was something else, the unreality to her situation; a sinking feeling in her stomach that made her wonder where on earth she was, what she was doing and how this trip to Moscow would unfold.

Geographically she was fifty-five degrees, forty-five minutes north of the Equator, thirty-seven degrees, and thirty-five minutes east of the Meridian. The time in Moscow was 4.10pm. In Britain it was 1.10pm, in New York 8.10am. At this moment in these places, many wheels were turning that Coventry was not to know about – nor were they hers to know. It was the big picture of simultaneous events known only to God. He knew the present, dwelled little on the past and knew the future. The future was his ace in the hole. The future was his dangling carrot designed to keep us in suspense, keep us on our toes, and give us dreams to strive for while filling in the unknown number of days remaining in our lives. The future was his game of Russian roulette, whose chambers housed that one inevitable moment when the grim reaper would call.

Half a mile away from Coventry and also stretched out, Jose del valle de la Rosa knew exactly where he was and what the outcome of his journey to Moscow would be. His bed at the Metropole Hotel was also narrow, short and hard and he too was tired and clammy. The trip from Havana had been hard, even for the youngish man he was. He and his Trade Delegation had flown economy to Moscow via Caracas, London and Paris. No one in Castro's Cuba was free to fly First Class. It was a symbol of capitalist decadence, but this rule didn't apply for Fidel and his entourage. They had flown on a private Russian jet. They were Brezhnev's guests in a palace on the outskirts of the city.

There, Fidel, the Cuban chief, lay stretched out on a generous bed in opulent surroundings, courtesy of Brezhnev – another strong man, the 'Kremlin Casanova', the General Secretary of the Community Party of the Soviet Union. Fidel wasn't alone, nor, like Coventry and Jose, was he fully dressed atop bed covers for a badly needed rest before a badly needed shower. With help, Fidel had already wiped the grime of the flight from his body. He was naked and had company. Brezhnev had seen to that. He had provided a willing woman for Fidel. She was a tart who also worked for the KGB and Castro was giving her a mouthful of Cuban hospitality that was proudly erect – a white Havana of sorts. It wasn't Cuba or its people that were being serviced at this moment. It was Fidel. Lying on his back, his beard wet with sweat, his eyes were open and floating in his head.

In another wing of the palace, Brezhnev was also with a female, but it wasn't Elena, his wife. His Mrs. was tucked away in Kutuzovsky Prospekt, the Brezhnev's official dacha in the city of Moscow. He was with Maria, one of his many lovers, all of which were KGB operatives, and all of which he had hammered with his sickle throughout his married life. He and Maria were performing unmentionable sexual acts. They were bolder and more erotic than anything Coventry could dream about, and neither Mother Russia nor the Bolshevik Revolution was on Brezhnev's mind as he slavishly laboured for his milky reward.

Leonid was happy. His teeth had been fixed. No Russian dentist could manage it, but thanks to his pal, the British Prime

Minister, his teeth were at last mended and his pain was gone. Using a US go-between, the British PM had secretly flown two top British dentists to Moscow, contrary to the wishes of the KGB. They were livid and paranoid over the matter. At best they felt the British or Americans would bug Leonid's teeth, at worst they thought he would be poisoned. Neither had taken place, so Leonid, who was now on his knees with his head in the furry crevice of Maria, was a happy, humbled comrade. The rain against the windows did nothing to divert the pair, nor was the Kremlin Casanova thinking about the black box beneath his bed containing the nuclear button. Only the burly Russian general outside Brezhnev's door, who had medals on his chest and who wore a big round hat, had the box and what it held on his mind.

At the American Embassy, Big Ben was dealing with another matter. Four people had beaten a path to his door minutes earlier – Tina, Tanya, and the two CIA men. The latter's surnames were Mulkins and Warden. In dealing with them Big Ben had a fine line to walk. He knew Tina and Tanya. Working together he and the two women had been the go-betweens who had helped spirit the dentists into Russia with false Canadian passports. That's how Big Ben had become privy to Prime Minister Jones' closeness with Brezhnev and many other Russians inside and out of the Soviet Union. Mulkins and Warden were not aware of all this. Their interest was Coventry and whether or not she could possibly be the assassin. This too was Tina and Tanya's concern.

The spoke in this wheel was Big Ben, the person at the Embassy American newcomers to the city would come in contact with. He knew what Coventry's real mission to Moscow was, and knew that she was no killer, but he had to go through the motions to keep this complex equation of deception balanced. The object of the meeting was to pool opinions as to whether Coventry was the assassin. No clue had surfaced when her luggage was tampered with on arrival in Moscow. All this was taking place in Big Ben's office as the rain fell and Coventry lay in bed thinking with her eyes closed.

In London it was three hours earlier. Prime Minister Jones was in Downing Street chairing a cabinet meeting. It was raining hard. He

106

and his government had a monkey on their backs that refused to jump off. The monkey on his back wasn't about his dealings with Russia and Brezhnev. The suspicions about him that had taken Coventry to Moscow were not on the cabinet's agenda.

That was an unspoken subject. It was only a matter that was whispered about in the corridors of power. The cabinet's agenda centred on three issues – The Aberfan village mining tragedy of 1966, the results of the Tribunal of Inquiry dealing with the tragedy, and the thirty-year rule that allowed the government to hide embarrassing facts uncovered by the tribunal. The country was up in arms over Aberfan. The heat was on the government of Jeremy Jones.

The facts growing from the inquiry crucified the government and their aim was to hide as many of these facts under the thirty-year rule. These were the facts. On the morning of 21st October 1966, a tip holding a thousand tons of coal waste atop a hill overlooking the Welsh mining village of Aberfan, had thundered down and killed a hundred and forty-four people, a hundred and sixteen of them children in a schoolhouse. The tip was the responsibility of the Government's National Coal Board. There was not the slightest doubt that the disaster was caused by the Coal Board's negligence. After three years, no one from the government had been found to be at fault. The Labour minister in charge of the environment had run for cover in the wake of the tragedy and acted like a coward. He had also disclaimed any responsibility for the accident.

The Tribunal had found the government to be insensitive to the tragedy on a scale that made a mockery of their claims to be a political party of the common man, which the people of Aberfan were. They were found to have treated the parents and kin of the dead as troublemakers. They had retained money from a disaster fund and given the parents of the dead children only five hundred pounds, and then forced them to prove a close connection with their kids, before the government considered parting with more. The fund had raised eighteen million pounds – more than forty million dollars. Three years after the tragedy, the insurance companies and Coal Board were still at odds over responsibility, while the gutted village of Aberfan remained in ruins. As Coventry lay stretched out, the Prime Minister and his cabinet were deciding how many of these facts could be kept from the nation under the thirty-year rule.

Tiplady was in his office at the *London Evening View*. His elbows were on his desk. His fingers were laced and he was cracking his knuckles. He was thinking. Minutes earlier, Big Ben had called him on an embassy secure line. He had brought Tiplady up-to-date in a coded manner the two had worked out before. Northwest of London, two hundred and fifty miles away, on the Isle of Man, the island was shrouded in fog, but Juanito and his passengers were safe. It was 1.10pm, the same as in London. Juanito, his crew and all his passengers were scattered around the northwest corner of the island in small hotels and in the homes of hospitable islanders. The next day, weather permitting, Manx Airways would fly them to London where they would board a Spanish plane that would take them to Madrid. Juanito was in a small hotel stretched out on his bed with his eyes closed. He had spoken on the phone with his bosses in Spain and he was happy to have saved his passengers and crew. He was also doing something very rude to himself while looking at a photo of a male.

In upstate New York at Attica State Prison, Willie Sutton was at breakfast with scores of angry fellow convicts. But he wasn't angry, just weary. He knew he was getting out soon, but he had not yet told his fellow inmates. They could be vengeful and envious when someone was getting out and they weren't, some for the rest of their lives. They were a mixed bag of very bad apples; murderers – rapists, crooks of every hue, more than half of them black and every one of them pissed off over the harsh Attica regime and Governor Rockerfeller's 'do nothing' attitude to their plight. Riots were coming and Willie knew it. He also knew he was too old to be in the midst of such turmoil.

Willie was sitting at the end of a long wooden table along with other inmates. Their language was appalling. Soon he would be away from the daily mental hiding he was getting from constantly hearing words like fuck, bastard, ass-hole, scum bag, shit and so on. At this moment, Willie was switched off to these words. His mind was on his future, just as Coventry was thinking and wondering where on earth she was.

As he lifted coffee to his lips, Willie's mind was in overdrive. He was too old, sick and tired to be a crook again. Once he was free, no longer would his daily needs be provided by the state of New York. He needed money once he was out in order to live a reasonably comfortable existence in his remaining years. His health was bad, so he needed money. He also needed an operation on his legs.

Social Security would give him a pension of six hundred and ten dollars every month and he would get a check of perhaps six thousand dollars for his work in prison over seventeen years. Helen, his sister in Florida, with whom he would live, was secretly holding twenty-three thousand dollars of his money from past crimes he had committed. The cash was in a safe deposit box in a Florida bank. The box was in the name of a third person that was no longer living. Willie was reasonably secure, at least for a while, but he needed more money and his mind was fixed on a chance that had arisen to earn money legally.

A writer who knew his lawyer had approached him and proposed that they collaborate on a book called 'The Life And Times of Willie Sutton'. Willie was considering the proposal because a ten thousand dollar advance on royalties was on offer. A New York firm had jumped at the chance of publishing the book when the writer approached them.

So as Coventry lay in her Moscow bed, wheels were turning in Moscow, Britain and Attica State Prison. As Willie thought the proposal over, rain began pelting the prison windows and the convicts began banging the tables and chanting: Rain, rain, fuckin' rain. Then the guards blew their whistles and their keys began to rattle.

SEVENTEEN

The rain punching her window had a soothing, yet odd effect – it triggered a bazaar little dream. When Coventry awoke she was perplexed. Strange as it may seem, her dream was about the boxer Muhammad Ali. He kept calling out: 'I shook the world, I shook the world'.

She lit a cigarette and thought: Why should I dream about him? Why him? Maybe it was because he was always in the news. Soon after becoming champion he had converted to Islam, changed his name and refused induction into the US army. He was against the Vietnam War and because of his refusal to do his two-year military service he had been stripped of his title. Yet he had not been jailed. He had evaded prison because the government knew that locking him up would cause militant blacks to riot in cities all across America. Liberals and others who were also against the war were on his side, so the government was stymied. Had Ali been white, he would surely have been locked up and few would have protested. Now Ali was lecturing all across America at mostly black colleges, talking his usual talk as if royalty in exile. Maybe that's why Ali crept into Coventry's dream.

After showering, Coventry spent two hours waiting to be served in the Ukraine's almost empty dining room. It was a frustrating experience. A large staff of waiters and waitresses in blue jackets idled and stared into space as the few waiting customers became more and more agitated. It was only when German tourists with irate red faces began thumping tables with their fists that service began, with no reaction from the dining room staff. They had seen this all before and could not have cared less.

Since all expenses linked with travel to Russia had to be paid in advance before visitors could gain visas, the staff at Moscow hotels didn't give a hoot about service. You got what you got, when you got it. If you didn't like it, tough! Nor was the food much to shout about once it finally arrived. Coventry returned to the third floor, picked up her key from Olga and slipped into bed. She was tired and somewhat disoriented. Tomorrow would be another big day. She was to see George Bolchekov, report to the American Embassy, and contact from Big Ben was soon sure to come.

The rain continued and in the distance there was the rumble of thunder, then a crack of lightning. Coventry looked at the radio with no dials and wished she could play it. A bit of music would have been nice. Her eyelids were heavy and soon she was in a deep sleep, and soon after that, a multi-headed dream came like a dragon. It was set in an odd place where she had no history or interest. The dream was vivid. Her eyes began to dart behind closed lids, her hands became fists and her body was primed for the battle.

She's in New York's Madison Square Garden and part of the main attraction. The arena is filled to overflowing with spectators. She's fighting Muhammad Ali for the World Heavyweight Championship. The spectators are noisy and excited. Coventry is wearing her contact lenses. She forgot to take them out in the pre-fight excitement. Most of the central people in her life are in the audience. Her mother and Sutton are not among them. They're in her corner, just outside the ropes ready to help her between rounds. Her mother will bring in and remove the stool. Willie will treat any cuts and bruises. Ali's ringside helpers are John and Robert Kennedy. Ali is clowning around as usual, while waiting for the bell to ring that will start the fight. He's playing to the crowd, acting the fool, oozing with confidence. He's a showman and the ring is his stage. Blacks love him, some whites hate him, but no one can ignore him. His persona cries out:

"I am black!

I am pretty!

I am the greatest!"

Ding! The fight begins. "Allah is great, let's rumble," yells Ali as he springs to his feet from his stool. "Gonna give this honkey a whippin," he yells to the crowd. Many in the crowd respond with "Ali, Ali, and Ali." Sister Margaret-Mary, who is dressed like a vamp yells out: "kick him where it hurts, Coventry."

"Gonna come out dancing," Ali says while bouncing up and down in his corner. A black woman in the crowd yells: "Bull shit, kick his ass, Coventry."

Ali's in white trunks, his opponent's are red, white and blue. Coventry is topless, her breasts are primed for the occasion, the eye of one nipple is blue, the other brown, both are fixed on Ali, notably his crotch. His trunks are snug. He looks to be well-hung. Both fighters are now in the middle of the ring, moving clockwise, sizing each other up. "Kick him in the nuts," yells the holy nun.

This is an old-fashion bout, turn of the century style; bare knuckle, no mouth-piece – a fight to the finish, no referee, anything goes, each round three minutes long. Ali and Coventry can talk freely to one another as they bout. Ali towers over Coventry, but her eyes dominate the ring. With her lenses in place, they cast lasers that lock on Ali. Allah, a new arrival, is fearful, perplexed. Coventry can't see Allah in her dream, but she feels his spirit, feels him drawing near. Her Eyes of God are not his will. Jesus the Jew may be meddling, thinks Allah. Coventry's not clowning. She's very serious; she means business. She's ready, threatening in demeanour. Her fists spell danger. This woman has a mean-on, thinks Muhammad. "Dammmmed right!" yells the black woman in the crowd.

Ali and Coventry are dancing round the ring. A punch has yet to be thrown. "Nice titties," says Ali as he shoots out a left, but misses. Coventry answers with a left to Ali's head, then a right, then a left, and then a right cross blow that lands on Mohammed's jaw. The crowd's shocked!

Ali's legs wobble; he staggers back.

"How do you like that, Cassius?" says Coventry.

"I don't, and don't call me Cassius, that was my slave name."

"I'm no longer a slave – my name is Mohammed Ali!"

"Bull shit," says Coventry, "Clay's your name – a white man's name."

Ali is furious, he pulls himself together and yells to the crowd, "I'm pretty, I'm pretty, I shook the world when I beat Sonny Liston, I beat him twice. He's too ugly to be champion!" Ali connects with a lightning uppercut to Coventry's jaw. Her head whips back. Her hair is in her eyes. She can't see, she moans in her sleep, then she turns in bed, then her fists tighten further. Goodfellow is in the crowd. He calls out, "take out your lenses, take out your lenses!"

Coventry says, "Jesus Christ, I forgot all about them."

McAvoy, her Godfather, yells out, "Shame, shame, you took the name of the Lord in vain." Coventry's mother also yells shame.

Willie Sutton is appalled. That's the language he hears and hates in Attica. Coventry swipes the hair from her eyes then rids herself of lenses. She opens her mouth and out they tumble then up they rise like smoke and vanish. "Holy Shit," yells Ali. "This bitch is weird, she's a witch doctor."

"Correct," responds Juanito to Ali. The Spaniard's been sitting in a cheap seat way back in the arena. "Correct," he repeats, "she's a witch, finish her off, and then meet me in the alley. I know you're a queen, so are I."

Tiplady pipes up. He's also way back in the arena. "Don't forget me, I'm queer too, let's have a threesome."

"It's a date," Ali responds. "I'll take you both on once I whip this witch."

Big Ben, whose wearing a mask that covers his face yells, "Get on with it Coventry, finish him off, we have business. The Prime Minister's shit runs deep."

Everyone's excited and yelling. Fists from the audience are punching the air. So too are Coventry's as she sleeps. In Ali's corner, outside the ropes, the Kennedy brothers are hollering, urging Ali on. "Whip the witch", they chant. The contest is now frenzied. Ali and Coventry are in a punching mood. He digs her in the belly with a left, then a right, and then another left. She retreats for a moment. She then responds with a hail of blows: a left uppercut to the chin, a right to the temple, a left to the belly, then she kicks Ali in the crotch.

Sister Margaret-Mary is beside herself. She's jumping up and down, "That it," she yells. "That's it."

Ali is doubled over, he's breathless, humiliated. He drops to his knees. His head is hanging. He's vulnerable, a sitting target, open to attack.

"Go for the kill," yells Sutton. "A knee to the head should do it!" The crowds falls silent, they're on their feet, can't believe what they're seeing. Tina, Tanya and Olga are opened mouthed. Calvert is a force to be reckoned with – they know it now. RFK and JFK had better do something.

They jump in the ring and come to Ali's aid. They push Coventry away, then attack her. The crowd goes berserk. Many jump into the ring. It's a free for all. Black and whites are battling but not always with each other. It's a mixed bag of conflicts, with blacks on whites, whites on whites, and blacks on blacks. You name it, it's happening. Mayhem!

Little Willie Sutton is in the middle of it all, trying to bring order. He's the only one with a level head. The bell to end the round is overdue. More than three minutes have passed since the round began. What's going on?

Cannon shots go off. Bang! Then we hear, Da da da da da da da da da da – Bang! Da da da da da da da da da da – Bang! Coventry's eyes open. She sits up in bed. It's morning. Her radio is playing Tchaikovsky's 1812 Overture. The music is near the end, at the crest of its crescendo. Moscow's church bells are chiming victory over the French and Napoleon. As Coventry slips out of bed, she thinks about the thrilling overture; she loves the ending because the French turned tail and ran. Coventry's first real day in Moscow is about to begin and it starts with a dream that makes her think.

EIGHTEEN

While she was sleeping, the temperature had dropped like a rock and Moscow was now in the eye of a snowstorm, whose iris was huge. The snow was belting down and winds from Siberia were digging into the city's belly. The wild flakes were thicker and more active in flight than any Coventry had ever known. The storm had struck west Russia in the early morning, just like the one that hit New York the night Willie Sutton escaped from jail. It didn't take her long to link the two in her mind and go back to that day, her tenth birthday. That snowstorm was great, but this one was the mother of them all.

She could see it swirling from her third floor window. Below, there was a growing blanket of white where yesterday there were streets, rooftops, cars, people and trolley-cars. Sights that yesterday were new to Coventry had vanished, just as familiar sights had vanished in New York the day back in December 1951, when Slick Willie had vanished after escaping from jail.

Déjà vu. As a girl Coventry had known this snowy scenario before. Now she was a woman – an American woman working for a British newspaper – and she was here, in Moscow, about to play a dangerous game behind the Iron Curtain with people she didn't know – people who were often ruthless.

At the conclusion of the 1812 Overture what Coventry thought to be news began coming from her radio, but since the language was Russian she was well and truly in the dark. She was preparing to pull herself together to face the day when the unexpected happened. There was a tap on her door. It was Olga, who stood framed in the door, big as a bear, wearing a grumpy face but with hands laden with things that defied her bearing. In her left hand, she deftly balanced a breakfast tray, and in her right she clasped a fur hat, boots and a pair of heavy woollen gloves.

Coventry was taken aback and moved by what Olga had brought because they spoke of forethought and consideration. Coventry appreciated Olga's gesture because she was hungry; she did not look forward to a restaurant wait, and was unprepared for such weather in October, even in Moscow.

"Please, come in," said Coventry, while adjusting the belt on her bathrobe. Olga entered the room with measured steps, her eyes on her balanced tray. Coventry moved her head from side to side and said, "What snow!"

"Will get worse," said Olga, who put the tray on the table, boots on the floor and hat on a chair.

"Thank you so much."

"It is my job," said Olga with a wry smile, "or I go to Siberia."

"Really?"

"Yes, we want you to write good about Russia." Not expecting such candour, Coventry was again taken aback. Since entering the room, Olga couldn't stop looking at Coventry's eyes. Finally, turning to the boots she said, "Try, and see if boots fit." Coventry slipped them on. The boots fit fine. So did the gloves.

"Perfect!" was Coventry's verdict. A smile ran across Olga's big round face.

On and on came the chatter from the radio. Glancing at the radio, Coventry asked, "Is it news?"

Olga's head moved up and down in the affirmative.

"What's being said?"

"Snow, more coming," said Olga "and Spanish plane with three hundred people that..."

Olga's words stopped when the phone rang. It was Tina to say that she and Tanya would be there at nine and that Coventry should dress warmly and wear something on her head. "Yes, I'm prepared, thanks to Olga," replied Coventry into the phone. When she hung up she conveyed the gist of the call to Olga. Coventry then began her breakfast and Olga withdrew, leaving her to prepare for the day.

Maybe it was the dream, maybe it was the 1812 Overture, maybe it was what lay ahead, or perhaps the anticipation of meeting Bolchecov, but when Coventry awoke that morning, she was in a state of arousal.

After breakfast she stripped, stepped into the bathtub, turned on the shower and forcefully ran the water over her body. It felt good. She felt buoyant and her loins were purring. Coventry was thinking, and it wasn't about the Prime Minister of Britain, Big Ben, Willie Sutton or anything dealing with Moscow. She was hot! Her mind was on what her body was craving – a release – like the ones during and after her dream about Juanito.

Had she been aware of Juanito's plight the day before, she may have started the day in a different frame of mind, but she didn't know. She might not have had last night's dream had she known, but she did, and now she was in the shower with a personal agenda that was contrary to her convent teachings. She was careful not to wet her hair. That would never do. Going out with wet hair on a frigid day was not a good idea. Coventry, for sure, was not a frigid lady.

With head tilted back, Coventry let the water splash over her face. Whatever boundaries of inhabitations she may formally have had, were not on tap this day. She soaped her forehead, face, her shoulders and her arms. Next in line was the inside of her arms up to the hollow of their pits, where she lingered in one, then the other. This action felt erotic, as if her shaven pits were wired to her loins. Next for a visit were her breasts. Both were now at attention, boasting a lively lift. Down to them she went with soap. Down, over, round and under until with soap in one hand, both were cradled, snug in the hands of their master. Gathered as her breasts were, Coventry's loins reacted

118

with a force eager for release. Down, down streamed the water from the showerhead.

Her whole body was primed, geared to a single goal, and as a matter of course her most intimate orifice was next for cleansing. In the mood she was in, the zone was sensitive to the touch. It reacted with excitement when the touch came. As the water showered down and vanished down the drain, the feelings within her were strange. They were sinful, erotic and in league with Satan. Had Sister Margaret-Mary seen Coventry's encounter with herself, she would not have understood. She would have prayed for Coventry's salvation, but the last thing on Coventry's mind was Sister Margaret-Mary. Only her agenda was in her mind. Her body was wet, yet on fire, her nipples hard, fiery bullets. Now, from the front, Coventry's hand reached down and found the slot whose condition was mint but hot; the nest whose first eruption was triggered by a dream and then by a self-induced hand me down. Into the nest went the soap. Further still was Coventry's inclination. The more she soaped the spot, the more her pulse raced and the more she recalled the pilot that inspired the thunderbolt which she yearned to repeat, in the shower on this frigid morning, with the snow falling hard and the wind blowing into the belly of Mother Russia.

Coventry didn't know it but she was aping Juanito on the Isle of Man the day before. He thought of her and stroked, she thought of him and probed, he thought of her and stroked, she thought of him and probed, and finally, like the thrilling end of the 1812 Overture, her probing hit home and at the stroke of eight on her radio, her rigid trembling and breathless moans began.

Coventry was seated in the hotel lobby waiting for Tina and Tanya. The snow was falling, the wind was icy and she was properly dressed for the day. She looked stunning in her fur hat. She was poised, relaxed, and ready for whatever the day would bring. She was ready to meet Bolchecov and act out her charade.

NINETEEN

Coventry was seated in the lobby, facing the hotel entrance doors. She was looking out at the street. She could see scores of bundled-up men and women outside shovelling snow. Every now and then a bus or trolley-car would pass the Ukraine with lots of snow on its roof. It was not a day for Muscovites to be out, but the wrapped-up citizens of the city had to labour. Not working because of a snowstorm was not an option, so they had to wait in the open, shivering in the arctic blast until their trolleys or buses came along. This yearly struggle with winter was a form of brutality Russians were use to and accepted because they had no choice and knew nothing else. Suffering was a way of life in the Soviet Union and the country's history was testimony. These thoughts ran through Coventry's mind as she looked out at the street from her comfortable seat in the Ukraine's lobby.

Half a dozen business-type men were waiting in the lobby for a taxi to appear at the kerbside. No matter the weather, the taxis always came. For taxi drivers too, the weather was no excuse. They had to crank-up their frozen little Ladas, pray that it would start, and venture out for a living and the kopecks that they brought.

The Ukraine Hotel was one of Stalin's giant monolith constructions of the early 1950s and as Coventry waited for Tina and Tanya, she noticed the frescoes on the vaulted ceiling. They had escaped her notice the day before because so much was happening at the time, like handing in her passport and registering when she arrived. Surrendering her passport was a bit threatening and looking at the ceiling was not on her mind when this was taking place. Now, after her showery escapade, she was at ease, and above her were the frescoes looking down.

A man with an Irish-looking face was also looking, but not at the frescoes. He was taking Coventry in and his mouth was watering. He was seated to her left with his short legs crossed. He was most unnoticeable, which suited him fine until he chose to draw attention to himself.

His name was Enda McShane, an arms dealer from Ireland who was also on a secret mission. He was in Moscow willing and able to buy weapons for the Provos – the breakaway wing of the IRA. His master and paymaster in Ireland was Sean McStefion, the chief of the breakaway wing. McShane's hobby was bedding women and Coventry looked like one hell of a good potential lay. Her eyes leapt out at him and her striking face looked at home, nestled beneath the halo of her smart fur hat. Coventry's plan that morning was to wear her lenses but the weather had vetoed it. Goodfellow had warned against their use in windy conditions and today was such a day.

Like Coventry, McShane's true mission to Moscow was cloaked in bogus cultural matters. He too had a date that day at the Soviet Press Agency Novasti. He too would later meet with the catalyst in his mission, someone like Big Ben, and McShane was waiting for his driver to arrive to ferry him to Pushkin Square. If his mission gelled, the arms he would buy would be shipped to Libya. From Libya, where Colonel Gadaffy was now in power, the arms would be shipped to Dundalk, a town on the east coast of southern Ireland near the Northern Ireland border. Not knowing just who Coventry was, McShane decided to defer his assault on her nest until he knew more about her. He didn't want to mess with a woman from the KGB. On the other hand, there was a polish about her that looked anything but Russian. He would wait and keep his eyes opened for her tonight in the hotel lobby.

The Ukraine was located on Kutuzovsky Prospeckt near the banks of the Moscow River. It was easily within walking distance of Novinsky Boulevard fifteen, the address of the US Embassy. It was no more than a mile from Red Square and two miles from Pushkin

Square. Travelling by car on a normal day, the drive from the Ukraine to Pushkin Square would take fifteen minutes, but today it would take much longer. This was on the mind of Tina and Tanya as they slowly drove along the slippery, snowy streets of Moscow to pick up Coventry.

When they finally arrived at the Ukraine, the two women were full of apologies. The KGB did not tolerate lateness. The chain on a wheel of Tina's Lada had broken so extra care was needed and this had delayed them.

"Quite alright," said Coventry. "I was enjoying drinking in the sights."

"We go," said Tanya anxiously. "Must be at Novasti soon. Bolchekov will not be happy if we are late – busy man."

Looking like Eskimos, and with vapour streaming from their mouths, the three women were quickly out of the hotel, down the slippery steps and into Tina's Lada. As they did so, the severity of the weather hit Coventry. It was beyond her experience – bitterly cold. The arctic wind cut like a knife and the snow was falling like daggers. She was ever grateful for the gear Olga had lent her, but even though her raincoat was lined inside, it was not nearly suitable for the weather. She was freezing, and once inside the car, Coventry felt every bit as cold. The car heater was useless. Communism could do with the uplift of a capitalist car, she thought. For an instant, Coventry's mind zipped back to Willie Sutton and how he had laboured through the snow and wind and how he must have suffered after he escaped the Pennsylvania jail.

From 'Kutuzovsky Prospekt', Tina drove a short distance until she reached 'Uitsa Nova Arbat'. Then, with her windscreen wipers squeaking, she swung north on 'Novinsky Boulevard' until the road became one jaw-breaking name after another. Then, after a mile, Tina turned right on 'Tverskaya' and continued until she reached Pushkin Square. In the centre of the Square, oblivious to the falling snow, stood the statue of Alexandr Pushkin, the liberal, nineteenth-century poet, novelist and dramatist of Russian and African blood, who died in a duel at thirty-eight defending his wife's honour.

The Press Agency Novasti was a spooky-looking ten-storey building. It was filled with Russian bureaucrats following the party line and when Coventry and company climbed its steps and entered its doors it was ten o'clock exactly. As Coventry's driver, the meeting had little to do with Tina, so she waited in the lobby by a heater, brushing the snow off her clothes and warming her frozen body.

George Bolcheckov's domain was on the seventh floor and the building's elevator was an ancient machine with a sliding gate similar to the one in the film Grand Hotel. When Tanya slid its gate closed and pressed the number seven button, the old elevator lurched. It made a grunting sound then lumbered its way up, and all the time since entering the building, the eyes of a uniformed attendant were on Coventry.

The seventh floor held a long, clean corridor with door after door issuing no sound, but this was not so at the door bearing the name G. Bolchekov. It was open and revealed a room with typing secretaries and the sounds of tapping messages arriving on teletypes that were ancient. At the desk of one secretary stood a tall, handsome man with greying hair at the temples. He was dark, looked like a Spaniard and was reading something a male secretary had just handed him.

When Coventry and Tanya entered the room his eyes rose from what he was reading, he smiled. As he approached the two women, he looked Coventry over in an approving manner and his smile grew. He was good looking. Tanya was right, thought Coventry. Only one thing spoiled her image of the man. Tanya had failed to mention that he dragged his left leg when he walked.

Without saying a word he oozed charm. Coventry could see how women would be drawn to him. He had a warm and welcoming style but was no fool. He knew what buttons to press. He was a cultured man.

By way of Tanya, he welcomed Coventry to Moscow and paid her a compliment that would have charmed the most cynical of women. With his rich, brown eyes fixed on her, he said he thought she was beautiful, and that even today, as cold as it was, should she fall into the river, she would make the water boil. It was the type of compliment a woman might hear from a Spaniard, Greek or Italian, not a Russian.

Having so charmingly welcomed her, Bolchekov asked Coventry and Tanya to follow him to his office, which was at the far end of the room. When the formalities were over, he gave Coventry a list of five places he had arranged for her to visit and which he hoped she would write about in her newspaper. They included the Bolshoi Theatre, the Cathedral of the Assumption, the Pushkin Museum, the Tretiakov Galley and the Moscow Circus. She would attend the ballet at the Bolshoi that night accompanied by Tanya. Tina would drive them to and from the theatre.

Bolcheckov and culture were as one and even though he spoke through Tanya, Coventry could see the passion he held for cultural expression and the degree to which he felt Russian culture was reflected in Moscow. The city was the home of Russian theatre. Of that there was no doubt. The famous Bolshoi of opera and ballet was one of many theatres open to the public most of the year. The range of music, cinema and circus available dwarfed that of any city in Europe. As well as exhibitions, the city's many museums had a wide range of special displays. Few cities in the world were more culturally rich than Moscow. Through Coventry, Bolchekov was eager to remind readers of her paper of these facts. Unspoken by Bolchekov but obvious to Coventry was the fact that Russia needed hard, foreign currency to compete in the arms race. Increased tourism was one way of getting it.

The meeting went very well. When finished, Bolchekov offered his guests coffee but Coventry declined politely as it was clear he was a busy man. His secretary had popped her head in his office to say that Mr. McShane had arrived. Since she was free for the rest of the day, Coventry decided to report to the American Embassy, as was her duty. It was a golden opportunity to link up with Big Ben under cover of a well-known requirement placed on newly arrived Americans to the city of Moscow.

At this minute plans were being made for the dinner Leonid Brezhnev was giving in honour of Fidel Castro, the dinner at which Cuban cigars would be passed. Knowing that Coventry's visit to Novasti would be brief, and that she would report to the American Embassy thereafter, the CIA agents were there waiting. Only they had no idea what her real mission to Moscow was, and that Big Ben was the key to her mission. While the agents waited, Big Ben was alert to the unfolding events, and while all this was taking place, the clock by Willie Sutton's bunk in his prison cell was ticking. All the cell lights were out. It was 3.30am but Willie was awake. He was thinking of being freed. In London the Prime Minister was at the Antheniam Club having an early breakfast with a trusted advisor. They were discussing the Aberfan tragedy, and by now, Juanito and his passengers had been flown to London and were boarding a flight at Heathrow for Madrid. Trevor Tiplady was already in his London office, pacing up and down – he was cracking his knuckles and wondering if sending Coventry to Moscow would blow up in his face.

TWENTY

Getting to the US embassy was a nightmare, which began when Tina was pulling away from Pushkin Square. Her Lada skidded, hit another car, which in turn hit a Cadillac belonging to a government official, who literally hit the roof. The accident was unavoidable, but it delayed the official who was rushing to catch a train to Leningrad. He gave Tina a tongue-lashing and took her name for disciplinary action, but Tina was not concerned. Intimidation was a way of life in Russia. She and others had a plan for the future that would sever their tether from the belly of Mother Russia.

More slipping and sliding and other delays were in store on the way to the embassy. The snow was falling and whirling as hard as ever, but Tina eventually made it. She pulled up and parked in a shovelled pathway in front of the embassy building. The icy wind was blowing and the American flag outside the embassy was flapping loudly. Coventry drank in the sight and sounds of the flag as she entered the building's front doors.

She thought that on a day like today the flag would be indoors, but this was not the case. It was out there, battling the elements, chin out, symbolic of the home of the free and the brave, and even of the crooks in New York jails like Willie Sutton. It symbolised a mixture of many things to many people. It symbolised the most successful nation ever conceived; a nation without a monarchy – a nation whose only royalty was money, Duke Ellington and Count Basie. A nation that was armed to the teeth, and despite Vietnam, race riots and other stresses, was at ease enough with itself for its people to eat hotdogs and drink beer at sports venues across America, and the next day be

126

free enough to bitch openly about Vietnam and the US government – an inconceivable freedom in Mother Russia.

Two, young, tall US Marine sergeants in blue uniforms stood smartly inside the embassy entrance doors. From head to toe their uniforms were immaculate and they wore white gloves. When Coventry and company entered the building and brushed the snow from their clothes, the marines snapped even further to attention. Chests out like barrels, buttons and buckles glistening and shoes like mirrors, they towered over Coventry, Tina and Tanya, but hard as the Marines tried, they could not take their eyes off Coventry. One of them – a lad of Irish extraction – swallowed hard. Never in his life had he seen anyone with eyes like hers. Inwardly they threw him off balance, but he remained at attention. "I'm American, here to register my arrival in Moscow," Coventry said.

"Yes mam," said the other Marine, who pointed with precision to a door that said US Citizen Registration. "They'll help you there, mam," he said. Glancing at Tina and Tanya

Coventry asked, "May my Russian friends wait for me?"

"Yes mam," said the other Marine, "please follow me ladies," which Tina and Tanya did until they and the Marine disappeared into a room at the far end of a corridor.

Tina and Tanya were playing it cool with Coventry. They had visited the embassy before. Their most recent visit had been yesterday, when they met with Yearwood and the men from the CIA. The two marines had recognised them from the day before, but said nothing.

"Come in," said a voice in reply to her knock. When Coventry entered the office she saw a young woman sitting at her desk that momentarily took her breath away. "Hi," said the young woman. "I'm Kathy Honey. Welcome to Moscow." She bore an uncanny resemblance to Coventry's mother in her youth when she too worked for a US Embassy.

"Thanks, I'm Coventry Calvert."

"Oh yes, you're staying at the Ukraine."

"That's right."

"Please, Miss Calvert, take those wet clothes off."

Happy to comply, Coventry did so after pushing her gloves in her raincoat pocket.

Wheels within wheels were at play, involving two embassies privy to the same information. The result was that Honey already had Coventry's registration form completed and ready for her signature. On it were her Visa and passport numbers, her arrival and departure dates, where she was staying, her place and date of birth and the purpose of her visit to Moscow.

"Your form is ready for signature. Will you please look it over and sign," said Honey. Coventry read it and signed. "That's it," said Honey, "all done. Oh, just one more thing. Two gentlemen would like to speak with you, will you please follow me?" It didn't take long for Coventry to guess who the men were.

Honey led Coventry to a conference room, one flight up. She knocked on the door. A man's voice said enter and the two women did. The conference room was large and neat and on one of its walls there was a photograph of President Nixon flanked by two upright American flags. A long conference table, lots of leather chairs and scores of books on shelves dominated the room. The tall agents were on their feet at the far end of a long table and Honey introduced Coventry to them.

"We know each other," said Coventry in an icy tone.

"Yes," replied Mulkins and Warner in a gentlemanly manner. They were being careful. No ordinary American was she and their suspicions might be wrong. They had not forgotten how, with eyes blazing, she had turned to confront them at Heathrow Airport. They knew she had balls.

Turning to Honey, Coventry said, "These men were stalking me at Heathrow. And they were in the Ukraine's lobby when I arrived yesterday." The agents looked at one another. Their expressions said it all. They were not happy. Sensing fireworks, Honey excused herself and quietly withdrew.

After she had gone Mulkins said, "I take exception to the word stalking."

"Well what would you call it?" Coventry retorted.

"You were being observed."

"What's the difference? You were threatening. To me that's stalking."

"Do you know who you're speaking to?"

"Tell me."

"The CIA."

"Should I swoon, or faint. What do you want of me?"

"Some answers."

"You ask, I'll answer," said Coventry her eyes burning through Mulkins.

Mulkins was getting irritated – hot under the collar. He and Warden needed answers. They were getting heat from Washington. A tip had come from Interpol that an attempt would soon be made to assassinate someone of importance in Moscow and that dire global consequences could result if the killing took place.

"We'll need your fingerprints," said Warden.

"Why?"

"Not at liberty to say."

"I see," said Coventry with a lift of an eyebrow. "Well I'm not at liberty to give you my fingerprints, unless I see your ID."

This gal really does have balls, thought Warden. He and his partner looked at one another. Neither said a word. They reached in their pockets, pulled out ID and handed them to Coventry.

She looked them over and handed them back. "Fine, you can take my fingerprints."

"Good," said Mulkins, "but first we need some answers."

"You ask, I'll answer," Coventry repeated. The agents asked basic questions, such as date and place of birth, where she grew up, where she was educated. Her answers seemed to satisfy them.

Then they asked. "When were you last in Texas?"

"I have never been to Texas."

"When were you last in Northern Ireland?"

"I have never been to Northern Ireland?"

"Have you any links with Northern Ireland?"

"My grandparents were from there."

"When were you last in Memphis, Tennessee?"

"I have never been there."

"What was your mother's maiden name?"

"McComb, Paula McComb."

"What was your father's name?"

"I wish I knew."

Mulkins came back like a shot. Her answer should have been Charles Calvert. "You don't know?"

"Yes, I don't know."

"Is not his name Charles Calvert?"

"That was my stepfather – he's dead – you asked the name of my father. That I don't know."

Warden went no further; the quiz was over. He and Mulkins led Coventry to another room, where her fingerprints were taken. That done the agents thanked Coventry and said she was free to go. Mulkins suddenly remembered something. "Mr. Yearwood, the cultural attaché here went to school with your boss. He would like to meet you and say hello."

"How nice."

"I'll take you to his office."

Yearwood's office was two flights up and within minutes, Coventry and Mulkins were at his door. Mulkins knocked and Miss Tripp, Yearwood's secretary replied with a cheerful, "Come in." When they entered, Mulkins introduced Coventry to Tripp.

"Oh yes," said Tripp, "Mr. Yearwood has been hoping to meet you. Welcome to Moscow. I'll let him know you're here." Tripp crossed the room, knocked twice on Yearwood's door and stuck her head in. "Miss Calvert is here," she said.

"Outstanding," replied a deep voice. Seconds later, the tall, well-dressed Yearwood appeared at his door. He was smiling. He shook Coventry's hand, thanked Mulkins for showing her to his office and invited her in.

"How's old Tiplady?" he asked laughingly.

"Fine, fine," Coventry said.

"We go way back," said the black man. "Way back."

He also went way back with Willie Sutton. Just as it was snowing a blizzard the day he helped Willie, it was snowing like crazy in Moscow today.

TWENTY-ONE

Bugs, bugs and more bugs! At the time of the Cold War, electronic eavesdropping between some nations was a way of life. The Russians were notorious buggers of American embassies and the US was bugging theirs too. Each was eager to know what the other was up to and therein lays the tale of Cold War espionage. It was all about electronic eavesdropping. One country would neutralise the other's bug until another, more sophisticated bug came along and all concerned had a jolly time living in their world of intrigue. Far be it for the British to be excluded. In London they were bugging any European country they could get their bugs into. They were paranoid about Brits going over to the other side as Philby, Burgess and McLean had done.

All these buggers had amazing ways of bugging and no nation was safe from being bugged. While Coventry was being quizzed in the conference room of the US embassy, the British were listening. They had a nifty little bug in the room. A Russian bug had been found and disabled by the Yanks, but not the British bug because the Americans weren't looking for it. Had they been looking and found it was British, they would have wondered how their sneaky cousins had managed to install it. They really should have looked for it because they had bugs in every British Embassy around the world. In Moscow alone, one of their bugs was in the British flag in the office of the ambassador. Since Coventry wrote for the *London Evening View*, it wasn't hard for the British to identify who she was, so having listened in on her quiz, they now had to keep a close eye on her.

The only room in the US embassy that wasn't bugged was Big Ben's office. He knew all about bugs. He knew where to look for them and how to render them mute. He, especially, had to be on guard.

While the British were listening to Coventry, so too was Big Ben. Not only were the Americans and Russians bugging each other, they were also bugging themselves. They didn't always know what their own folk were up to – bugging themselves was a way to find out. Not only had Philby, Burgess and McLean defected to the Russians, but three Americans had defected to them too. By listening in on the Coventry quiz, Yearwood could judge how much he could reveal to her. It was a dangerous game he was playing and no one must ever know that the dirt on the PM had come from him – and he had plenty.

In 1961, Jeremy Jones was Shadow Foreign Secretary. By various means, Yearwood had come by copies of letters written to him by a Kremlin official in January of that year. The letters were as bold as brass. One of them spoke of plans to send missiles to Cuba and asked: 'How did Jones think JFK would react when he found out?' This letter was dynamite. The FBI under J. Edgar Hoover knew about Russia's plan, but he hated JFK and the CIA so he kept them in the dark. Yearwood was performing a dangerous, high-wire act. Few could be trusted, so he had to be sure of Coventry's discretion. He would see if she mentioned her quiz by the CIA and the events leading up to it.

Big Ben was forty-nine years old, and rose above his colour to the extent that after anyone met him, his skin became irrelevant and of no concern to anyone other than people who disliked blacks. He neither lived in a black man's skin, nor did he crave another. He was the best man he could be, who happened to be black – or in his case, dark brown. His parents had been domestics from the Leewood Islands who identified with the British Monarchy during the reign of King George V and Queen Mary. They had emigrated to New York at the end of World War One and Vincent – or Ben as they would call him, who was a change of life baby – was born there in 1920. Both his parents had died before he was ten. He had no siblings.

In 1941, three years after he graduated from high school, Japan attacked Pearl Harbour, America joined the war and Ben joined the Marine Corp immediately after. He fought the Japs in Battan, Guadalcanal, Iwo Jima, Wake Island, and when released from service at the end of the war, he emerged a First Sergeant with a chest full of medals – one of them being the Purple Heart. He had shed lots of blood for America and of this he was proud.

After military service, he took advantage of government help and under the GI Bill of Rights he studied accountancy and journalism at City College in New York. In 1950, after five years of classes by day and working by night, he gained his degree in accountancy. After graduation he took a wild shot in the dark. He applied to the FBI and was accepted. His degree in accountancy and his shining military record helped him to become one of only twelve black FBI agents in America. In order for a black man to be accepted by the FBI in the America of the 1950s, he had to have something special.

Starting as a field agent, one upward step led to another and he eventually entered the Foreign Service. By his hard work and skills, he rose to the position of cultural attaché in American embassies in Trinidad, Panama and finally Moscow. The latter posting was a huge step up for him. He had forged a friendship with Trevor Tiplady when both attended a summer course at South-Eastern University in the state of Florida. Now, having welcomed Coventry and invited her into his office, he would try and determine how much information about Prime Minister Jones he could reveal to her.

He was easygoing and did not stand on formalities. He could put people at their ease and knew all about Coventry's eyes, didn't stare or make a fuss. Nor did he sit behind his desk like a figure of authority with his knees knocking like his friend, Trevor Tiplady. He and Coventry sat in soft, leather chairs in a cosy conference area of his office. A pot of freshly brewed coffee and a tray with sandwiches was already on its way, thanks to the efficient Miss Tripp. They were chatting about Tiplady.

"Does he still wear sharp clothes?" asked Yearwood. Coventry still had no inkling that Yearwood was Big Ben.

"Yes, very sharp."

"Have you even seen such snow?" he asked.

"Yes, well, sort of, in New York, but not like this – in 1951 – the day Willie Sutton broke out of jail." Yearwood, who was sitting with his legs crossed, reacted by re-crossing them.

"Yes," he said. "I was there too. I was truck driving for a living and studying too."

"I remember it well, it was my tenth birthday," said Coventry.

Yearwood made no reference to Sutton.

"I understand you're here to write pieces on cultural matters."

"Yes, I've just come from Pushkin Square. I met George Bachekcov of the Press Agency. He's arranged things for me. Tonight I see the Bolshoi ballet."

"Great, you'll like it. If I can be of help, let me know."

The coffee and sandwiches arrived and the pair tucked in. Being out in the cold had given Coventry a fierce appetite. As they munched away, Yearwood casually asked if she had a nice chat with Mulkins.

"Oh yes," she replied between sips of coffee. She did not expand on the matter.

"Do you know what he's all about?"

"I don't know what you mean," Coventry replied with a look of innocence.

"He and Mr Warden, the fellow who's always with him are CIA."

"Really," Coventry said. She was giving nothing away and this Yearwood liked. He thought of the Jewish couple that had brought him up after his parents had died and he said to himself, This goy (a gentile) is Kosher. It was time for him to be open with her.

"Do you know who I am?" he asked.

"Yes, you're Mr. Yearwood, a friend of my boss, also cultural attaché to the US Embassy in Moscow – and a sharp dresser too."

Yearwood smiled. Yes, he thought, she's Kosher, also cunning.

He told her who he was and for an instant Coventry's jaw dropped. Then he said, "You've read the file haven't you?"

"Yes."

"What think you?"

"On the surface, it's very incriminating."

"Well," said Yearwood, as he slipped out of his chair, "welcome to the sub-surface." He walked across the room, took down a picture of Nixon, opened the safe behind it and pulled out a file twice the size of the one Coventry had read. The information it contained about the Prime Minister and his links with the Soviet Union was devastating. Two hours later, after Coventry had pored over the file, Yearwood said, "If the source of this file is revealed, I'm dead!"

In the meantime Tina and Tanya were down in the waiting room, not wondering what was keeping Coventry.

TWENTY-TWO

Despite the damning evidence, the question that concentrated the mind was whether or not Prime Minister Jones was truly a communist. The matter was complex. If the file's documents were incorrect, and acted upon, goodness knows what the consequence would be. Yearwood and Coventry hoped they were not tampering with a hornet's nest that would wrongly engulf Jones, as well as themselves. Caution was required.

But if the evidence reflected the truth, Jones had to be exposed. But did it reflect the truth? Or was it too tilted to be true? That was the question. Yet too much was at stake for undue caution. British and US secrets were slipping away with steady regularity and the moles that were giving them away were mostly British. Philby, Burgess and McLean were a constant reminder of British turncoats in the pockets of the Russians. The whole situation was unreal – the thought that the Prime Minister, America's closest ally, was a communist in league with Russia. Neither Yearwood nor Coventry wanted to believe it.

There were American turncoats too, but they were not civil servants like Philby, Burgess and McLean. They were not part of the US government. They were mostly scientists with misguided thinking who were passing secrets to the Russians to – in their minds – equalise the balance of power between the east and west. They felt America was too strong and that this was dangerous. There were other Americans who were ideologically in tune with communist thinking, but they were less significant than the scientists. They were idealists, liberals, dreamers who believed that the state should run people's lives from the cradle to the grave.

Senator McCarthy – the hunter of communists – thought that the Hollywood film crowd was full of communist sympathisers. A few were, but they were small fish. Some had been wrongly accused and their careers wrecked. Britain however was different. The fish now under scrutiny was no ordinary kipper, no show business liberal. He was the Prime Minister, and the rumours about him and the Russians were rife.

What was hard to fathom was how a Russian in high places could so boldly put in writing Russia's intentions. This was perplexing. No attempt to mask his letter's meaning had been made by its writer – a former Russian army general. The writing was careless, stupid, or deliberate. The latter seemed more likely, but why? Was the PM being set up? Was he being used? Was the writing of the letter intended to tip off the Americans? Was the writer working both sides of the street? The questions were endless.

Of all the documents in the Jones file, this letter was the most incriminating. It had arrived at 'Dover House', Parkgate, and Jones' constituency office in Cheshire. It had been hand delivered. Someone in his constituency office – perhaps Jones himself – had written the date of its arrival on the letter. Big Ben had come by a copy from someone in the FBI. It was a Xeroxed copy of a Xeroxed copy. On the upper right hand side of the letter appeared the initials JEH, which meant that J. Edgar Hoover himself had read it. There was little doubt that knowledge of Russian intentions were known in Britain and America three months before the soviet missiles arrived in Cuba.

Did Jones, a rising politician in the Labour Party with the job of Shadow Foreign Secretary, inform the Tory government, or his party leader, or Washington? If not him, did anyone from his office sound the alarm? This was unknown. It seemed unlikely that the contents of the letter ever travelled up the political chain of command, either in Britain or America, or the missiles would never have reached Cuba. Instead, the world was to come within a hair's breath of World War Three. Fortunately, the first to blink were the Russians, who withdrew their missiles from Cuba after a tense standoff between Premier Khrushchev and President Kennedy. The American promise to withdraw their missiles from Turkey had helped to defuse the threat of a nuclear war. One would not have thought that a cultural attaché and a newspaper reporter would be privy to such lethal information. Unlikely, yes, yet it certainly was the case. Unlike the Jesuit Order, Coventry and Yearwood were, not by design, but by fate, in a strong position to influence the influential. It was not one they relished.

Yearwood's file on Jones was second to none. It was more comprehensive than the FBI's file, MI5's, MI6's, or even the file of the CIA. Somehow, in league with God knows whom, Yearwood had managed to raid everyone of their files, so that his file included all they knew about Jones, but for reasons they were keeping to themselves. His file contained the names, dates and places leading to the dental work Brezhnev had done, and the part Jones played in arranging to have the work carried out. Yearwood was the American middleman in this project. The folder in his file giving details of this project was called 'Project Canal'. The project was so secret that not even the FBI knew about it. But the KGB knew. The British dentists had arrived in Moscow as tourists on false Canadian passports and had been quietly taken to a secret location where dental work was carried out. They were in and out of Moscow in fourteen hours. Accompanied by Tanya, Tina had chauffeured the dentists during their brief stay in Moscow. All these details were in the 'Project Canal' folder.

Yearwood and Coventry agreed that careful thought should be given before they took any action. They would mull it over and make a decision in eight days time, before she left Moscow. She would come to the embassy that day on the pretext of collecting a gift Yearwood was sending to Tiplady. She would casually mention this to Tina and Tanya ahead of time, so as not to arouse their suspicions. She would explain her extended stay with Yearwood by saying that as fellow New Yorkers, they had much in common and that time ran away. Yearwood had mentioned his friendship with Tiplady to the KGB women the day before when he met with the CIA agents.

If Yearwood and Coventry decided to proceed, and if her newspapers lawyers agreed, Coventry's piece would need documentation, like the letter about the missiles. Sending anything in the file to London by diplomatic pouch was not possible. Too many variables were involved. The pouch was out of the question. Spiriting the file out of Moscow was the only method that would not involve others. Coventry would have to take the file out of the country herself. It was tricky and dangerous, but it did not involve others.

Yearwood had thought ahead. In order to ensure against mishaps, and as a form of insurance, he had microfilmed the file twice – a skill he had acquired with the FBI. He had reduced the file to film no larger than a thimble. If he and Coventry decided to go ahead, he would give her selected filmstrips of the file and she would take them out of the country hidden on her person. They would each mull this over and decide where on her person would be the best place to conceal it. They had to be careful. This was not a game. Cold War Russia was a tightly controlled outpost. Foreigners entering and leaving Russia were carefully checked. Everything was searched. If anyone fell under suspicion, all sorts of nasty things could befall them. So that was that – the plan was hatched. Yearwood and Coventry would meet again in eight days.

Before leaving his office, Yearwood whispered something chilling to Coventry. They were just inside his office door. He leaned forward and brought his lips close to her ear. "Listen," he said quietly. "When you come next week, I will greet you in one of two ways, 'Hello Coventry', or 'Hello Miss Calvert'. If I say the latter, we must abort everything and you should leave Moscow quickly."

The snow continued falling. When Coventry stuck her head in the waiting room door she found Tina and Tanya none the worse for wear. In fact they were mellow. The embassy staff had seen to that. Again thinking ahead, Yearwood had arranged for their hospitality – soup, sandwiches, coffee and several stiff, double shots of Johnny Walker Red Whiskey. The KGB girls were slightly tipsy and when Coventry entered the room, neither Tina nor Tanya asked what had delayed her.

That night Coventry attended the Ballet at the Bolshoi. Thanks to George Bolchekov she and Tanya sat in the best seats, but because of the weather the theatre was only half full, a pity, because the performance was brilliant. Fidel Castro, the Cuban trade delegation and Leonid Brezenev were in the audience.

The show was a thrilling experience. The ballet was Swan Lake and Tatiana Bolchekov – the Prima Ballerina – who was George's sister, was out of this world. Her body was fine tuned, her movements seamless magic. She was as one with the music and the company with who she danced. The experience was uplifting in more than music and dance. The intermission too was an unusual treat. Coventry would write good things about her night at the Bolshoi, and they would all be well deserved.

TWENTY-THREE

Olga was waiting. She was dying to hear what Coventry thought of the Bolshoi ballet, but Coventry was frozen. The snow had stopped but the icy winds from Siberia had been leaving her with a nasty, lingering chill in her bones.

Off came her coat, hat, gloves and boots. What a relief! She flopped on the edge of the bed with a sigh. There were times she thought she would not survive the day's cold. She rubbed her feet, wiggled her toes and sank within herself. Her room was a welcomed haven and growing in charm. It was warm and cozy and Olga wasn't a bad sort – she just gave that impression. She was sweet in a rough kind of way. After opening the door and handing her the key, Olga slipped away to make tea. "I think you need some," she said as she lumbered away down the third floor corridor.

After Tina and Tanya had dropped her off and plans were made for the following day, the three women had gone their separate ways. Tina had gone home to her sex-starved husband and Tanya rushed to the bed of her lesbian lover, who, as it happened, was the Prima Ballerina, Tatiana Bolchekov. Yearwood had tipped Coventry off about their affair.

Coventry's plans for the following day were to visit Gum department store in Red Square. She needed to purchase a few things. On her list was a fur hat – like the one Olga had lent her – a pair of gloves, a heavy coat, and boots with fur lining were a must. She had heard about Gum and was toying with the notion of scribing a piece about the store from the viewpoint of an American who had shopped in stores like Harrods and Macys. Nothing critical, just how they compared and differed, with perhaps a few comments from Gum shoppers. These were pleasant thoughts that distracted Coventry from her growing concerns about the decision she and Yearwood had soon to make. Then there was the matter of slipping the microfilm out of Moscow.

When Olga reappeared, the tray she carried was laden with a steaming teapot, a large cup, buttered brown bread and a small dish of caviar. Coventry's eyes lit up.

"Will you join me?" she said. Olga declined with a backward step.

"It is not permitted." Coventry was weary and Olga could see it so she didn't ask if she liked the ballet. The question could wait. "You tired," she said. "You eat, you sleep." She then left quietly shutting the room door behind her.

By the time Coventry had finished her treat and tumbled into bed, she was spent. She had intended to shower but put it off until morning. It had been a punishing day but by-and-large the day had gone well, which was not always the case for others.

In Madrid, Juanito was being hailed a hero and the accolades were embarrassing him. Women with rampant hormones were fluttering around him like butterflies. Newspapers around the world had carried the story of his coolness under pressure and that included Pravda, the Russian Daily. Coventry was unaware of this.

In Moscow, Enda McShane, the sex-obsessed Irishmen who had weapons to buy, had also met with Bolchekov on bogus cultural matters. With the snow falling and the wind howling, he had walked to nearby Tverskavs Station and taken a train to Kitai Gorod, where he sat on a platform bench pretending to read a guidebook of the Moscow underground system. None of this was new to him. He had done it all before, but the man he was to meet who would sell him weapons was new to him. They had never met before. McShane was sitting in the seat arranged, so the man would know him. The Irishman had purchased weapons for the IRA before thanks to a fellow countryman who had set the whole thing up – a former Fina Fail minister in the Irish Government.

McShane waited and waited. Trains came and went, and when the man finally arrived, the two of them sat together, looking at the guidebook as if one was giving the other directions. In the course of all this, a deal was struck. A numbered account in a Swiss Bank would be the method of payment for the weapons. The seller of weapons was Polish, he spoke adequate English and the weapons were Polish made. They would be shipped from Poland to Libya when half of the payment had reached the numbered account. The other half would be sent to the account when the arms reached Libya, at which point the IRA would take possession of the weapons. The money for the weapons had been raised in America from Irish Americans who hated Britain and longed for an Ireland United.

In New York, night had arrived and in Attica Prison all the inmates were now in their cells. The barred doors of the cell were open as it wasn't late and some of the prisoners were visiting fellow inmates in adjoining cells. The sounds of radios, voices and harmonicas were echoing throughout the double-decked compound and a rare element of calm was in the air. As usual the back and forth banter of the inmates was laced with bad language, but tonight Willie Sutton wasn't bothered. Governor Rockefeller had made a decision. Willie would be released from Attica before Christmas. Over the years, Willie had been in and out of jail and had spent half his life behind bars. What did he have to show for it? "What a waste of my life!"

In London, Jeremy Jones, the Right Honourable Prime Minister was in his Downing Street office with one of his ministers who had been careless and would soon be exposed. No senior civil servant was present to take minutes. Jones and his minister were at it, back and forth, and their language was no better than in Attica State Prison. All the press knew about the minister's indiscretion. Labour Party Headquarters had issued no denial and the government was in hiding from the media. Jones was apoplectic; newspapers, TV, and radio, were primed. Soon they would strike and Jones was in a twirl. He could see the headlines.

MINISTER'S SHAME:

'Indecent Act at Café de Paris'.

The minister had been seen with a Filipino pickup in the stairwell where Coventry was conceived. The pickup had been caught on his knees in the act of paying the minister homage and the Filipino – a nurse who worked in a London hospital – was a man. A similar embarrassment had engulfed the previous Tory government and had led to their loss of power to the Labour government. In the case of the Conservatives, the minister's passion was a lady – a lady that was no lady – a lady who was a prostitute, whose hangout was the Café de Paris.

In London, an editorial meeting was under way at *The London Evening View*. The next day's news was on the agenda. Of seven people seated round a table, Tiplady's knees were knocking. The decision had been taken to hold off on the story of the Labour minister. Unbeknown to his staff, Tiplady had bigger fish to fry with Labour and Coventry's findings in Moscow might well do the cooking.

Next on the meeting's agenda was a huge protest soon to take place in Washington DC, demanding an end to the Vietnam War. It would be one of the newspapers features for tomorrow. Also, a few days earlier, Concorde had made its maiden flight and had broken the sound barrier. This would also be featured in depth. The supersonic Anglo/French aircraft had done it – broken the sound barrier! The tone of the piece would be that, the British and French have at last done it – conquered the sound barrier. Only the piece would fail to mention that the sound barrier had been broken years earlier by Gus Yeager, an American Air Force Pilot in a slim, bullet-shaped jet, which Yeager had named 'Glamorous Glenys'. So went the meeting at *The London Evening View*.

Back in Moscow, Jose Del Valle de La Rosa was alone in his room at the Metropole Hotel. He was playing solitaire but his mind was not on cards. It was on the dinner Brezhnev was giving for Castro in two days time, during which he would give Castro a box of cigars. In the palace on the outskirts, Fidel was again undercover, but with a different woman this time. This one was as black as coal, courtesy of Brezhnev, who was down the hall with Maria, his lay for the day, who was as white as snow.

Two hours before, Castro and Brezhnev had not been in Moscow. Early that morning and despite the weather, a helicopter had flown them to a secret location fifty miles from Moscow at the edge of a forest. There they had met the leader of an African country with rich oil reserves who was waiting with a group of Russian minders. The year before, he had ousted his country's king, kicked the American and British oil companies out of his nation and now his country was suffering an economic embargo. He needed foreign currency. His joke of a nation was grinding to a halt. Trade with America and Britain was gone, leaving him with thousands of barrels of unsold oil. Castro and Brezhnev were keen to get their hands on the oil at a knockdown price. And they had.

When Coventry fell into bed and closed her eyes, the concerns she had earlier pushed aside with thoughts of shopping came flooding back. Even as she slept, they remained.

TWENTY-FOUR

What if? What if? What if? Coventry pondered the questions. What if Yearwood is bogus? What if Jones is only pretending to be a Red? What if Yearwood and I proceed and I'm caught with the microfilm? What if I get it through airport customs and write the piece and everything crashes down on our heads? What if the CIA keeps after me? What if they know about the file? What if all this is just a crazy dream? What if? What if? What if?

The questions hung heavy on her mind, but finally, after tossing and turning and pacing the room, Coventry fell into a deep sleep – and into a troubled dream that ebbed and flowed like pieces from a jigsaw that failed to fit this crazy puzzle of a dream.

She's in a deep, deep sleep. Her eyes are darting wildly beneath their lids as she watches the dream unfold. The setting is familiar – the Café de Paris. She's down in the main dance floor. The Café is crowded with patrons. The balcony is filled to overflowing with people who are out on the town for the night. Coventry is scanning the patrons, neither thinking nor looking for Juanito but thinking and looking for Richard Nixon. He's not in view but a large banner bearing his face is hanging down from the edge of the balcony. Nixon is here somewhere in the Café but not in view.

The Café's patrons are immaculately dressed and snow is falling from the ceiling. Also falling and bouncing up and down are red, white and blue balloons. The snowflakes aren't streaking down with anger, like those that fell on Moscow. These float through the air with the greatest of ease, like slow-motion butterflies. It's not cold and when the flakes reach the floor they vanish like magic and the floor remains dry.

This time Coventry is not dressed like a floozy. Nor is a cigarette dangling from her lips like a tramp-like lady of the night. Nor is she down to bra and panties. This time Coventry looks smart. Her contacts lenses are in her eyes, so her eyes are brown. A black sleeveless dress with high collar, white pearls and black shoes adorn her. The dress is snug and nothing of her figure is left to onlooker's imaginations. Her auburn hair has a glow. Everything about her is inviting yet unattainable. She's looking for Nixon; she needs to have a word with him. She needs to know what the CIA wants of her.

The band is not playing 'The Windmills of Your Mind' or any other romantic music. It's playing the 1812 Overture. At last Coventry catches sight of Nixon. He's dressed for the occasion and just spotted Tanya dancing with the Prima Ballerina. The two are snug in each other's arms. Nixon licks his lips with a view to cutting in. The Prima Ballerina looks tasty to him. Nixon's attempt to cut in fails. Tanya thumps him away with a straight-arm blow to the chest. Nixon staggers back and in a flash Mulkins and Warden appear. They come to Nixon's aid and hustle him away by his arms. Coventry follows them. She soon catches up and taps Nixon on the shoulder. He turns, fixes her with his gaze and the CIA men hover to protect him. "It's alright, boys," says Nixon, "back off." The agents move back four steps.

"I'd like a word," says Coventry.

"By all means," says the president.

"What do your boys want of me?" Nixon turns to the Mulkins and Warden and asks.

"What do you want from this lady?"

"We're not at liberty to say, Mr. President."

The snow and balloons continue to fall and a red balloon is bouncing around the feet of dancers, whose steps attempt to match the Overture music. They are unaware of the bouncing balloon and a lady with high-heels bursts one by mistake. 'Bang' goes the balloon and this is mistaken for a gunshot and the president's men rush him away up the back staircase where Coventry was conceived.

When the balloon bursts, out from its belly pops Willie Sutton. He calls out to Coventry, "I'll ask him. I'll ask him, I'll ask Nixon what they want from you."

"Good, you ask him," Coventry replies.

Willie, then hot in pursuit, scampers up the staircase two steps at a time. He's not far behind Nixon and his boys; the three have just reached the top of the staircase. They've just pushed open the fire doors and are now outside the Café on Coventry Street.

It's snowing indoors but outside it's pouring. In her dreamful state of mind, Coventry reacts to the change and turns in her bed. Her eyes are missing nothing. She sees a black bullet-proof limo with its windows down, screeching around a corner and stopping at the kerbside, where Nixon and his boys are waiting in the rain. The driver is Tina, next to her sits Olga. Coventry sees the CIA bundle Nixon into the limo and all its windows elevate. Just as the windows rise she sees Willie Sutton tapping hard on the limo's rear door window. He's motioning to Nixon for the window to lower. "What do you want from her?" he asks Nixon.

"I'm not at liberty to say," Nixon replies. The windows slide up and the limo speeds away through back streets of Piccadilly, heading towards Victoria Station. Coventry sees this all and lives it. She tosses again in her bed.

The scene shifts back inside the Café de Paris. Coventry is sitting in a chair near the main dance floor. Her head is in her hands. She's sobbing. It's snowing indoors harder than before and the flakes are angry. Her tears are not liquid, but snowflakes and her head is not hers but a red balloon, a hammer and sickle are where her mouth should be. Yearwood appears. He kneels before her and asks, "What's the matter?" She says she's worried about the CIA. He says, "I don't know what you mean." Then she asks if he's really Big Ben. "I'm not at liberty to say." Then she asks what would happen if the file is wrong and they act upon it. Yearwood says, "I'm not at liberty to say."

"And what if I get caught with the film?" she asks, "What then?" Yearwood replies that he's not at liberty to say. Then he vanishes.

Then, weaving towards her through the dancing couples, Bolchekcov appears and he's not dragging his leg. Coventry sees he has no legs, that he's only a torso in a wheelchair. He rolls up before her and in perfect English he asks how she liked the ballet. She responds by saying she's not at liberty to say. Then Bolchekcov too vanishes. Then a short plumpish man with grey hair appears. He's smoking a pipe. He's Jeremy Jones, The Right Honourable Prime Minister of Great Britain and Northern Ireland.

The snow keeps drifting from Coventry's eyes, that are vacant holes in the red balloon. "What's wrong young lady?" asks Jones.

"Are you a Red?" asks Coventry. Jones says that he's not at liberty to say. Then she asks if he knows who she is.

"About you," says Jones. "I am at liberty to say." And with this comment Coventry suddenly wakes up and springs out of bed with her hands on the sides of her head. Then she reaches for a cigarette and lights it. Then she thinks What if?

TWENTY-FIVE

Since travelling to Moscow, her thoughts had not been about her father. Other thoughts were on her mind. At best he was a curiosity and no doubt killed in the war. This was not the case. Her father was alive in London. He was a member of the Athenaeum Club and when Coventry and her minders were driving through the snow from Pushkin Square to the embassy, her father was in his room speaking on the phone with a friend. An hour after that, he was standing at the kerbside in front of Harrods waiting for the traffic light to change. He was waiting to cross the street to see someone Coventry knew. Wheels within wheels were turning and their impulse had much to do with eyes.

When Coventry was poring over the PM's file in Big Ben's office, her father, a tall, handsome man, was strolling into the premises of Hawkins-Goodfellow. He looked thirty-five but he was nearly fifty. Smartly dressed, the aura he projected was strength and confidence. Nothing about him was pedestrian. A year earlier he had acquired contact lenses and they were now bothering him. He was dissatisfied with the lenses and a friend had suggested that he should consult Goodfellow.

So who was this man who rose from the past to see someone Coventry knew? He was John Travelyan, a wealthy, Tory member of the House of Lords, a hereditary Peer from Cornwall whose title was 'Lord Crantock of Travose' – 'The Earl of Crantock'. He was a soft-spoken, educated Englishman much in appearance like the actor Walter Pigeon, except that his hair, though greying at the temples, was blond.

Crantock – a Cornish village – was in the north coastal region of Travose and Trevelyan's domain was an old country mansion on the outskirts near the Bristol Channel. His family had acquired their title for services to the crown in the 1700s and their wealth was old money derived from tin mining. A graduate of Oxford with a flair for mathematics, John – the eldest of four brothers was – by the age of twenty-two, a war hero of the highest order. He was 'One of the Few'.

He was not a spoilt Peer with a sense of self-importance. He was enterprising and his outlook was far-reaching. Above all, he was keenly aware of his accident of birth. Unlike some Peers – be they life Peers or hereditary – he wore his title well. There was no pretence about him. What you saw was what you got. He disliked being made a fuss of and took his duties in the Lords as a Tory speaker on 'health issues' very seriously. Unlike some Peers, he did not attend the Lords for an afternoon nap and the daily pay for attending.

He was nineteen when his father died and as the eldest son he inherited his father's title. This was a good thing because his three married brothers, Peter, Oscar and Philip, were less than they could be. They were too inclined to having good times, to bandy their lesser titles, and to live off their inheritance; there was little grit and enterprise in their makeup. In the war years, few of John's RAF comrades knew much about his family background or title. He sought no special treatment because he was an Earl. Neither did the fact that he was rich turn his head. In this and other ways, Coventry was very much like him. Unlike his siblings, John Trevelyan was the best John Trevelyan he could be. So what happened that night in 1941 when he and Paula left the Café de Paris? Why did Paula not hear from him again?

German bombing of British cities would start after the sun had set. At night, cities were blacked-out and woe betide the person that showed lights when blackouts were in force. Flashlights had to be of low voltage with shields to pitch light down. Streets were stripped of names, road signs and traffic lights were done away with, cars were hitting people and many vehicles hit another. There were traffic accidents galore, and if you needed a taxi, you were usually out of luck. Being out at night in wartime Britain was fraught with dangers. If a bomb didn't crush you, a vehicle just might. Senses needed to be primed. Even though people planned their outings around full moons, they still had to be alert because the Luftwaffe planned raids around them too.

When the all clear had sounded and the anti aircraft guns had stopped, John pushed open the fire doors at the top of the Café's staircase. He and Paula slipped out onto Coventry Street, and with his hand holding hers, they made their way through the darkness and mist to Victoria Station. In all the excitement caused by the bombing, John and Paula had left their gas masks in the Café de Paris, but John had his flashlight to help mark the way.

The bombs had hit Tower Hamlets east of Piccadilly Circus. The smell of incendiary fumes hung in the air and the glow of fires in the distance could be seen from the vicinity of the Café de Paris. The darting beams from flashlights cutting through the darkness and mist was everywhere. The warning sounds from ambulances and fire trucks filled the air, as well as the voices of police, home guard units and the fire marshals that oversaw Britain's life in darkness and were always vigilant for looters.

Now that the all clear had sounded, the bomb shelters near the Café de Paris were emptying and flashlight-bearing people were scurrying home, or to shelters as another raid might soon come. On their way to Victoria, Paula and John gingerly picked their way around rubble and the shattered glass caused by the nightly bombings. In and round the gutted shells of buildings and shops the remains of fires continued to smoulder.

Paula's flat was on Old Pye Street near Victoria Station and John saw her home. Before leaving her, he gathered her in his arms, kissed her good night, and said he would call soon. Then he vanished through the mist on his way to Victoria Station. There he took the train to the south coast of England and his Bexhill aerodrome posting.

Later that night, while on his way from Bexhill Station to his airfield, the Luftwaffe returned over the south of coast of England. As their bombs fell, coastal searchlights ran across the sky and anti aircraft guns pumped shells upwards to smash the foe. Scrambling to take cover, John was injured by a blast and spent sixteen months in hospital. At one point it was thought he might lose a leg, and it was not until 1943 that he was fit enough to be released from hospital. Although his injuries had put an end to his flying days, there was nothing wrong with his mind. When freed from hospital, his skill with mathematics came into play.

Still attached to the RAF, he was seconded to the hush-hush Bletchley Park decoding unit in Bedfordshire. Its job was to intercept and decipher wireless messages and John was one of a team that broke the German's Enigma Code. All this was secret at the time and even after the war, John never mentioned his Bletchley work to anyone.

When the war ended, John was twenty-six and became a publisher of books dealing with military history. In 1950 he had married Blanca Consuelo Ruiz, a Spanish beauty distantly related to King Juan Carlos and they soon had twin girls. In 1965, Blanca died tragically in an accident while skiing in the Austrian Alps. This was John's life as he strolled into the premises of Coventry's optician, Mr. Leslie Rupert Hawkins-Goodfellow.

In 1943, following his release from hospital, John had tried reaching Paula. By then she was back in New York and the US Embassy would give no details. The war moved on, then ended, time passed, and the memory of the American he had deflowered faded from his mind. Now, at the age of nearly fifty, and with sixteen-year-old twins, Lord Crantock of Travose strolled into the optician's shop to enquire about new contact lenses. He wanted to equalise the colour of his eyes because just like Coventry, his right eye was blue and his left brown. He wanted both to be brown and the two brown lenses he was using were causing him bother. He also wanted to discuss the possibility of lenses for his twins because like him, they too had the same eye discrepancies. It was a family legacy passed on by his father which – except for John – only one of his brothers had inherited. John's father's eyes were normal –both blue.

Around the time all this was taking place, other wheels linked with Travelyan were turning. Father Powell in Rome had telephoned Father Stewart – his fellow Jesuit priest who taught at Stoneyhurst College. Stewart in turn had called Adam, his brother, at the Ministry of Defence. On behalf of Coventry and at Powell's request, the Stewarts were looking for clues as to who Coventry's father was and if he had been killed in the war. Adam was searching the Ministry's records but was finding it a difficult task. He had so little to go by – just the first name of a pilot called John who flew in the Battle of Britain aged twenty-two. The job was near impossible, because of the near two thousand four hundred Britons who flew in the Battle, more than two hundred had been killed in action; some three hundred others had been killed on missions after the Battle of Britain, and scores of these flyers were then twenty-two with the first name of John. Also, of those still thought to be living, further scores had the same first name and no addresses for these men were known. The best Adam could do was to track down the list of British flyers involved in the Battle of Britain who where killed and see if a clue could be gleaned from the list. When he tracked the list down he found that those killed numbered eight hundred, and many were called John. The task was clearly impossible. If Coventry and her father were ever to meet, it would only be through the will of God, whose wheels within wheels he kept turning.

TWENTY-SIX

His face looked familiar the minute he walked through the door. Goodfellow was sure they had met, but he was damned if he could remember where or when. It was one of those awkward moments in his life when he recognised a face, but could not pin a name to it. He searched his mind for clues but none came. The last thing he considered was meeting the man in the war. The smartly dressed chap looked too young to have taken part.

Trevelyan smiled. "Mr. Hawkins-Goodfellow?" he asked. Still wondering where they had met, the optician responded with a smile of his own.

"Yes, that's me."

"A friend recommended you."

"Very nice to hear. May I ask who?"

"Roy Russell."

"Oh yes. We go back a way – we met at RAF Duxford."

"Good Lord," said Trevelyan. "I met Roy there too – you were at Duxford?"

"Indeed," replied Goodfellow. "Late '40 to '43 on Lancasters. And you?"

"Late '40 to early '41 on fighter escort."

"Well, well, well, who would have thought it? The years have been kind to you." Trevelyan was pleased with the compliment but could not reciprocate. "I thought your face looked familiar. Maybe we met there."

"Very likely," said Trevelyan, "but I can't recall, much was happening then."

"Indeed," agreed Goodfellow. Trevelyan introduced himself and the men shook hands in the warm, friendly manner of old comrades, who knew what was needed to be tough, when their country needed tough men.

After chatting about the old days in Duxford and discovering that both were recent widowers, Trevelyan broached the reason for his visit. He failed to mention that his eyes were different colours, and that matching them was the purpose of the contacts he was wearing. While the Peer was explaining the trouble the lenses were causing, the optician noticed that the brown in the iris of Trevelyan's left eye was richer in tone than the other. He assumed that the contacts were prescribed. He asked if he could see the prescription. "They're not prescription lenses," said Trevelyan. "They're tinted brown. My sight is perfect. My right eye is blue, my left is brown." Déjà vu? The flyer Goodfellow had met in the war and had mentioned to Coventry had the same type eyes. Could this be the same man? When Trevelyan removed his lenses and Goodfellow looked into his eyes, the answer was 'yes', and the meeting between them came flooding back – it was after the Battle of Britain at RAF Duxford in late 1940.

It was at a time when Bomber Command was striking Germany's cities with daylight bombing raids, a time when fighter planes like Spitfires and Tornadoes were escorting bombers that flew from bases in the east of England. The two of them had spoken a few words prior to a mission. They were sitting side-by-side at a mission briefing, taking notes. Most of the flyers were smoking, Trevelyan's pipe had gone out. He had run out of matches. He asked for a match and Goodfellow had obliged and it was then, when Trevelyan struck the match and lit his pipe that Goodfellow had noticed his eyes. They had jumped out at him. When he recalled the moment, Travelyan could not remember the occasion, but said that it must have been him. "It had to be me."

"Well, well, well," said Goodfellow.

"Well, well, well indeed," said the Peer.

Aside from his daughters and one brother, Trevelyan knew of no other person with eyes like his. Even his father, who had passed on the trait, didn't have them and he had only heard about the trait in his family. Except for two sons, John's father had never seen anyone with that eye-colour mismatch.

By 1969, the quality of contact lenses were improving. They were changing from hard to softer plastic and Trevelyan's lenses were state of the art. Goodfellow checked them and could not find a flaw. When he tried fitting them over the irises of Trevelyan eyes, he found the cause of the problem. The lenses were a shade too big. Instead of only covering the iris, they were ever so slightly touching the whites of the eye. This was causing the irritation. New lenses were in order, and after examining Trevelyan's eyes and finding them to be fine, Goodfellow said that Trevelyan should see David Corcoran at Moorefields Eye Hospital. "He's top in his field," said Goodfellow. "I recently sent him someone for tinted lenses with eyes like yours." Trevelyan was intrigued.

"You don't say."

"Yes, a lassie from New York. Her father was RAF, killed in the war. Her mother was a Yank."

"You don't say," said the Peer pensively. He had met flyers in the war that were married to Americans.

Travelyan was eager to see Corcoran, but in two days time he had business in Crantock, so he had to leave London soon. "Will I have to wait for an appointment?" he asked.

"Let's see." Goodfellow picked up his phone, rang Moorefields and got straight through to Corcoran. He explained what his customer needed; he had to return to Cornwall in days and could Corcoran possibly see him soon.

"He's an RAF friend from the war," said Goodfellow to Corcoran. Corcoran was free for the next sixty minutes and if Treveylan could get to him fast he would see him right away. Goodfellow smartly put down the phone and said, "The balloon is up, if you get to Moorefields sharpish, David will see you now."

Travelyan flagged down a taxi and twenty minutes later he was there.

Corcoran examined his eyes, took measurements, and said that the new lenses would be ready in ten days. That was fine, by then Trevelyan would be back in London. The doctor wasn't thrilled with the quality of the tint in the Peer's old lenses. Their tone was too rich and they made one eye look browner than the other. The tints in the new lenses would compliment each eye and give them a more natural look.

Corcoran was amazed how similar the Peer's eyes were to those of the American girl who came to him for tinted lenses. "Your eyes and hers could be clones," said the doctor. "Brown and blue eyes in one head are rare. It's a genetic hand-me-down, as you know." The similarity prompted a question from Trevelyan.

"Do you know much about her?" he asked. Corcoran thought for a moment. There was a pile of folders on his desk. He fished one out, opened it and began to read from notes he had made.

"Miss Coventry Victoria Calvert. She's twenty-eight, single, eye health good, writes for a newspaper, and lives in London. Her mother died of cancer recently." Corcoran looked up. "As far as I recall," he said. "Her mother was in London when the war started. She worked in the American Embassy and married an RAF flyer that was killed in action. Miss Calvert was born in New York after he died. Since the eye mismatch never occurred on the mother's side, the trait almost had to have come from the father. His eyes may have been identical to hers."

When Corcoran mentioned the American embassy, Trevelyan began to think. On the train on the way back to Cornwall, he continued to think. The names Coventry and Victoria also made him think. What was the name of that girl who worked in the American Embassy? He couldn't remember, but he still had his diary from the war. Her name must be in it. He would look it up. He knew the date – could never forget it; March 7th, 1941, the day he was injured by the bomb. With that thought, as his train sped through Devon, the memories came flooding back about the girl, the bombs and the Café de Paris. In Moscow Coventry continued to think, What if? What If? What if?

TWENTY- SEVEN

It was her third day in Moscow. What with her dream and the questions running through her mind a decent night's sleep was impossible. Her mind was disturbed. What should she do? That was the question that perplexed Coventry. Whether it was nobler to give the Prime Minister the benefit of the doubt, or by mistake oppose him. She had a week to decide. Then she would see Yearwood and be alert for his 'Hello Coventry' signal that it was safe to proceed. She would then need to say if she was in or out. She hoped his greeting would be 'Hello Miss Calvert' – it would signal danger and mean 'abort'.

Her instructions from Tiplady were for three pieces to be written on cultural events or places she had attended. She would write them in London. Although cultural matters were the excuse to get her into Moscow, whatever she wrote had to have substance. The Soviet Press Agency was not to be taken to be fools. Whatever about the real reason for the trip, Russian culture was second to none and *The London Evening View* was obliged to treat it with respect. That afternoon Coventry would attend the Moscow Circus with Tina and Tanya, but in the morning she would visit Gum Department Store on her own and get there by taxi.

The decision she was wrestling with had preyed on her mind all night. She would doze, and then wake, then doze, then wake. At one point she got up, had a cigarette, wandered around the room and looked out the window at the snowy streets, empty of life. The city was asleep but Coventry was wide awake, thinking.

She distracted herself with thoughts of Juanito. She hadn't thought of him since the morning before, when she loved herself in the shower. Had she known of the danger he had faced, and what he was up to, a shock would have followed. Juanito had a weakness that he fully acknowledged – a weakness that for years he had failed to conquer. It was the demon that appeared when least expected and drew him into acts that led to self-loathing. Only his Jesuit-priest brother knew of his weakness and tried to help, though he had the same weakness, but felt no need to conquer it. For Juanito's brother the weakness wasn't a problem. The inclinations of the siblings were seemingly unknown to their parents.

Juanito was not with his parents at this moment, or in his flat on the outskirts of Madrid. He was in the lavish Hotel Cuzco in the heart of Madrid. Chased and celebrated by the media all day, he had made the rounds of the TV studios where one interview had followed another; he was a hero, he had saved three hundred lives. He was a shining example of a noble Spaniard; his background was steeped in Jesuit teachings by a brilliant religious Order of Priest and Brothers, whose founder was another Spaniard, Ignatius Loyola.

Bi-sexuality was Juanito's demon and master. As Coventry wandered round her room, Juanito was in his hotel room in someone's arms – a man, a bald, youngish-looking fellow who was rough on looks. The man was a reporter for a French newspaper who had interviewed Juanito and was now the Satan in his bed. Both of them were naked, and rigid. Juanito slung the sheets aside. He then changed positions. The pair then went down for a slurpy encounter.

The new day finally arrived. Coventry's radio began its customary music early in the morning. It was then followed by the news. When Olga appeared, Coventry asked what the news was all about. Olga said that the announcer was asking: "Did he jump, was he pushed, or was it an accident?" According to the announcer, the chairman of a Cuban Trade Delegation had fallen from the platform of the Borovitskave Metro Station; he had instantly been killed by an incoming train. His legs and arms had been severed and had flown in all directions. Coventry cringed, hearing Olga's grizzly translation.

Coventry didn't know it, but the background to the bloody incident had some connections with her.

The day before, after being quizzed by the CIA, the agents had received word that cleared Coventry of all suspicions. The information had come from the FBI, who had received it from Sinn Fein. By way of a priest in Cuba, Sinn Fein had discovered whom the real political killer was, and that he worked alone. The killer was not a woman, but a man posing as a woman, who for reasons of his own, used names containing the initials C.V.C.

His name, of course, was Jose del valle de la Rosa, the man whose sliced body still lay on the tracks of the Moscow underground station. A handful of people knew the truth behind his death. He did not jump, nor was his death an accident – he had been pushed! The question was, who did the pushing? Was it a lunatic – or was it a made-to-order killing? Was the KGB involved, or the CIA, a Cuban operative – or maybe all three? Only those involved knew. The world of political intrigue in the Cold War was a nasty one, and God help the person whose death happened to be convenient. It was certain that Fidel Castro had to have known of de la Rosa's plans to kill him, because Castro and the Cuban priest that fingered de la Rosa were friends of old. The CIA was now off Coventry's back, but she didn't know it.

As usual, Sinn Fein was playing it cleverly, building credits with the powerful, while at the same time furthering their cause of ousting Britain from Ulster. They had revealed the real assassin, while at the same time their man McShane was in Moscow cutting a deal for weapons to be used against Britain. Could it be that McShane pushed de la Rosa? It was more than a possibility.

The snow in Moscow had stopped, the sun was out in London, the weather was filthy in Cornwall, and in Attica Prison, Willie Sutton was one day closer to freedom. The State's governor was dragging his feet over the date of his release and Willie was still mute with fellow convicts about his coming freedom. The day of his release couldn't come fast enough because the Attica inmates were in an ugly mood. A riot was poised to erupt and Sutton didn't want to be in jail when it did. He was too old for that shit; he didn't want to be involved, and it could put a damper on his release.

While London was enjoying a bright, autumn day, in Cornwall it pelted down with rain. Like Coventry in Moscow, Trevelyan had slept very little the night before. He had not found his diary and this had upset him. On his trip from London, he had thought about the night in 1941 when he was injured, and of his fling with the American girl. He remembered that he met her in the Café de Paris but could not recall her name – and this was bugging him.

Except for Phil and Eileen – the couple who tended to Trevelyan's stately home – the house was empty when he arrived from London. Schools were on a break, so his twins were away. The rain was hissing down and Trevelyan could not get to his study fast enough.

"Bring the tea and sandwiches to me there please," he said to Eileen. The Earl scoured the study for the diary. "Where the hell could I have put it?" he mumbled to himself. He looked high and low, but no diary. He knew it was there, but where? "What on earth was her name?"

TWENTY-EIGHT

The weather had changed for the better. It was a beautiful, crisp day and Moscow was basking in sunshine. The streets were nearly clear of snow, the temperature was up and what little snow remained was melting. Time had moved on; the last six days had flown by and tomorrow Coventry would return to London. Today in the afternoon she would visit the US Embassy to collect the gift Yearwood was sending to her boss. That was the reason for her visit, but then there was the visit's sub-plot – the signal! She would be alert for Yearwood's sign that it was safe to proceed. If the signal was 'go', she would then need to say if she was 'in or out'. She still hadn't made up her mind what to do, but she was hoping for a negative signal from Yearwood. All week she had been nagged by those 'what if' questions. The matter of the microfilm was a worry on top of other worries, so she was hoping for a 'thumbs down' signal from Yearwood.

In addition to attending the ballet and circus, during her nine days in Moscow she had visited St. Basil's Cathedral, The Pushkin Museum, The Tretiakov Gallery, and The Cathedral of the Assumption – all the places Bolchekov had suggested. She had also been to Gum in Red Square, but for obvious reasons she had avoided the Moscow Metro. Although all she had seen was worthy of literary comment, she would only write pieces about the three places that were most cultural – The Boshoi Ballet, the Pushkin Museum and the Moscow State Circus. Her idea to write about Gum had to be abandoned. Except for her visit to Gum, Tina and Tanya had accompanied Coventry everywhere. By this stage in her visit, they were sanguine with Coventry, so they had given her slack on the day she went to Gum. They knew that she was no killer, but as KGB, they still had a job to do, which was to keep an eye on her. She was a foreigner, so she had to be observed. Watching people was a way of life in Cold War Russia and those doing the watching were often watched themselves – more wheels within wheels.

Gum, a Russian acronym for 'State General Store', was a popular trading hall for merchants dating back to the Tsarist period. In 1969, as in 1900, it boasted an ornate turn-of-the century interior, comprising three parallel arcades, the upper two of which were linked by bridges. There were hundreds of shops in the arcades and light streamed into the building through its glass roof. The centrepiece of Gum's lower floor was a fountain overlooked by the galleries.

On her visit to the store and to thank them for their help, Coventry sought gifts for Olga, Tina and Tanya. They had treated her well and this called for recognition. In 1969, at the height of the Soviet reign, there was a great contrast between the ornate design of Gum and its lack of consumer goods. After searching in shop after shop, Coventry finally found something that she knew the women would appreciate. A supply of colourful materials had just arrived from Kenya that was suitable for making summer dresses, and Coventry bought generous lengths for all three women. Her plans to buy things for herself were dashed because none were on offer. Most of Gum's cupboards were bare.

Since the weather had been fine for several days and the forecast for tomorrow was good, Coventry had suggested that it was pointless for Tina and Tanya to take her to the embassy. It wasn't far from her hotel; she knew the way, and she would walk there and back. The venture on foot would offer a pedestrian's feel of the city. She would also stroll down to the river, have a look around and if the weather turned bad she would take a taxi. Tina and Tanya were amenable to the idea and made arrangements to take Coventry to the airport the day of her departure. Her flight was at 3pm and the carrier was Aeroflot. Her flight number was a more acceptable 211.

Olga was sad at the thought of Coventry leaving. The lumbering Russian with the big heart had bonded with the svelte Yank with the fetching eyes. As she had planned, Coventry headed first for the bank of the river for a look at the waterway she had read so much about – a river once awash with the bobbing bodies of Stalin's purged victims. A low stone wall ran along the edge of the riverbank. Leaning on the wall and thinking about the purges of the 1930s, Coventry looked out at the river and thought about how the devil had flourished in Russia when Stalin was in power.

From where she was standing – a spot with a gap in the wall – five stone steps ran down to the river's edge, on the lowest of its steps, two boys sat talking. They were a few feet from the water. When they noticed Coventry above them, they immediately knew she was American. They called up, "USA?"

"Yes," Coventry called down. The boys jumped to their feet excitedly.

They smiled. "You know Elvis Presley?" Coventry returned their smile.

"No. I don't know him." The boys sagged a little. Then, in English they began singing, 'You ain't nothin' but a hound dog,' and one of them simulated playing a guitar.

It was time to bite the bullet, so Coventry headed for the embassy. She had still to make up her mind what to do if Yearwood's signal was positive. When she arrived at the embassy, the US flag in the front of the building wasn't buffeting wildly, like on that snowy, windy day the week before. This time it was waving gently in a slight breeze. At the entrance of the embassy the same two marines with their shoulders back were on duty, as precise and efficient as they had been before. The younger of the two was just as fascinated with Coventry's eyes, and just as before, they smartly directed Coventry to Miss Honey's office. Once inside, Miss Honey continued to bare a remarkable resemblance to Coventry's mother, the young woman whose name the Earl of Crantock could not remember, nor found his diary that held her name. This time Coventry didn't have forms to fill or CIA men to see. This time she was here to pick up a gift Big Ben was sending to his friend in London.

Miss Honey led her up the stairs to Yearwood's office. She knocked and Miss Tripp said come in. Honey then slipped away down the stairs. Tripp was as friendly as before and just as before she stuck her head in Yearwood's office to let him know Miss Calvert was here. "Oh great," his big heavy voice thundered out. In a flash he appeared at his office door and said "Hello Coventry." That was it – the signal was to proceed. There and then Coventry decided to go ahead with the plan.

"Please come in," said Yearwood.

They were together for an hour. We don't know exactly what was said, but we do know three things: it was safe to go ahead; Coventry was 'in, not out'; and the gift for Tiplady was a bottle of Vodka.

The next afternoon, Coventry returned to London. Before leaving Moscow she gave Olga, Tina and Tanya their gifts and all three were moved. It was a pleasant trip back to London and the weather on route was fine. Yearwood was sending the microfilm to Tiplady through a circuitous route, so Coventry was relaxed. This was not the case with the Earl of Crantock. He had yet to find his diary, he had yet to remember the name of the girl from the past. Nor was this the case with Willie Sutton; the date of his release had yet to come through. Nor was it the case with Prime Minister Jones. He was up to his eyes in problems. Nor was it the case with Juanito; he was still at odds with his sexuality; he was still being pulled by a body of men. Nor was Coventry totally relaxed. She was entering dangerous ground. She had chosen, therefore something had to be renounced. There was always a price to pay.

TWENTY-NINE

It had taken courage for Paula to confess her indiscretion as she lay dying, but there was something about Coventry's father that she never mentioned. She never said a word about his eyes, so Coventry never knew. In any event, her eyes were not something about which Coventry thought deeply – they only came to mind when someone brought them to her attention. It was only when Corcoran focused on the anomaly that the thought crossed her mind that maybe her father's eyes were like hers. If this was the case, the question was why did her mother not mention it? Did she think it a quirk greater than her indiscretion? Still, it was an odd matter never to have been broached since it dealt with a trait Coventry so obviously reflected.

While flying back to London, Coventry thought about the possibility that her father's eyes were like hers. Why she should think about it then was odd. Maybe it had something to do with Father Power pulling strings from Rome in his attempt to learn details about her father. It popped into her head when her thoughts should have been elsewhere, like how she should approach her pieces on the ballet, museum and circus, and more importantly, what the next step would be regarding the Prime Minister. Her thoughts should have been on how Tiplady would view the information on the microfilm and whether the newspaper's lawyers felt it safe to go public with the story, but they were not. They were on the nagging question of whether her father's eyes were like hers. Perhaps it was mental telepathy that made her think of it then, or the fact that at the same time, her father was thinking about her mother.

He was still looking for the diary. The more Trevelyan thought back, the more he recalled. He could see the girl's face, but he was damned if he could remember her name. He recalled the two of them swaying in each other's arms on the small dance floor when the sirens began to sound. He recalled how soft she felt in his arms. He remembered the heat he felt in his loins. He remembered how, with no sense of alarm, the Café's patrons quickly left the dance floors they occupied when the sirens signalled danger. After all, because of its depth below street level, the Café de Paris was supposed to be the safest dancehall in London. He remembered taking the girl by the hand and making for a nearby stairwell, thinking that the stairs led down, but instead they led up.

He remembered that the stairwell was empty except for them, and that it was damp. He recalled the impact of the bombs that were landing and how they fixed his mind of the danger marching their way. He recalled the sounds of explosions getting closer and closer, and of the fear they provoked. He remembered his impulse to follow the stairs up, and how he and the girl climbed to the very top of the staircase, and that they led nowhere. He recalled the scent of the girl's anxious, sweating body, the shape of her heaving breasts, and how, at the top of the stairs, fearful, she fell breathless and trembling into his arms. How his body reached to hers – so close to his own – and how rigid he became. At that moment, the bombs no longer mattered to either one of them. Only the act of union mattered. He recalled how they joined, she standing with her back to the wall, her legs astride, while he thrusted with her arms round his torso, she urging him on – urging him in. He recalled the jolting spasm of life from his scrotum that triggered his legs to tremble. He remembered all this, except the girl's name. Whatever the reason, while Coventry was flying back to London, her mother's confession and her own visit to the Café de Paris came flooding back, along with thoughts of her father's eyes.

Maybe it was because her father was remembering, that these thoughts returned to Coventry. He was thinking too. Could the American girl with eyes like his be his daughter? All the pieces seemed to fit. Her mother worked in London at the US embassy during the war. He was frequently in and out of London at the time, frequently in and out of many a woman, but only one of the women was American and worked at their embassy. Eyes of different colours were rare. They ran in his dad's side of the family. This girl, the daughter of an American woman, had the same eyes. Dr. Corcoran said they could have been clones of his own. Her Christian names, Coventry and Victoria rang a bell.

"Where could that diary be?" What was that girl's name? What should he do? Should he leave the matter an open question, never to know, or pursue further? No! He had to know!

If the girl was his daughter, he had to know.

Dr. Corcoran said the girl's mother was dead, that she had been married to a British pilot who was killed in the war. Trevelyan thought and thought. This may only have been a tale on the part of the mother. Having children out of wedlock was shameful at the time. He had to know, had to find the link; the girl's name had to be in his diary. If he could find it, he would have something to go by. He didn't want to stir a hornet's nest only on a hunch. With a name he could go back to Corcoran and see what more he could learn. He would need to be open with Corcoran, tell him everything. He would soon see Corcoran and collect his lenses and take up the matter with him then, but first he had to find that blasted diary. To square this crazy circle of wheels within wheels, on no occasion during her stay in Moscow had Coventry worn her contact lenses. They were only inserted in her dreams.

THIRTY

It was hard to get a taxi at Heathrow. Many flights had arrived around the same time as hers and scores of people were eager for rides into London. Finally, when her turn came in the queue, Coventry jumped into the Black Cab and took off, headed for Belgravia. Among the things she carried was a bottle of Vodka for her boss.

It was late afternoon. The weather in London was typically autumnal, crisp and windy. Clocks had gone back an hour, so it was rapidly getting dark. Leaves were falling and winter, with its long black nights, was drawing in. The traffic into London was heavy. Still, it was a pleasant enough ride and Coventry's mind was at ease. She had accomplished what she set out to do and tomorrow would speak for itself. She would report to Tiplady, bring him up to date and he would choose what course their work would take. Until her next role was ready to be played, the ball was now in his court.

Her immediate aim was to get home and sleep. She was tired and had not slept well in Moscow. One thing, however, was especially on her mind. She was intrigued to know how Big Ben would get the microfilm to London. It was a relief for her not to have carried the microfilm. What she didn't know was that Yearwood and her boss had worked out the film's way of transport in advance, and that she had carried it from Moscow.

The taxi driver wasn't chatty like the one that drove her to Heathrow ten days earlier. Neither was it raining or misty, or was a Jaguar tailing her taxi. Neither was she thinking about Holmes and Watson, or Willie Sutton, or the fiendish professor Moriarity. She was relaxing with a cigarette and taking in the sights of the speeding traffic heading for London on the motorway. She was feeling fragile, looking forward to entering her flat, shutting the door behind her, kicking off her shoes, having a bath and falling into bed. Her tiny bed in Moscow had been an interesting experience, but she was glad about her big, waiting bed in Belgravia.

She wasn't hungry. The food on the Aeroflot jet had been good and the woman that attended her had made her comfortable. Her name was Anna – a tall, powerfully built woman with huge arms whose English was better than average. Coventry's eyes had transfixed her, just as they had done Olga. In some ways, Anna was like Olga except that though powerfully built, Anna's body was fine-tuned, like a hammer-slinging Olympian. She was in her thirties and the deep lines on her face spoke of struggles, and from the chatty questions she asked, it was clear that Anna's mind was fixed on defection to the west.

At last, after an hour of fighting traffic and red lights, Coventry's taxi pulled up in front of 23 Wilton Crescent. Coventry breathed a sigh of relief. Thank God, home at last. By now it was dark. The driver placed her luggage by the entrance door building. She tipped him handsomely and he drove away through the winding streets of Belgravia, in search of another fare at nearby Hyde Park Corner.

When Coventry opened her flat door there was mail on the floor mat. One letter was from Willie Sutton. The rest were bills of one kind or another in brown envelopes. She would read them all in the morning; she was too tired for that right now. Within minutes she was soaking in the bath. Her eyes were closed and the nipples of her breasts were bobbing on the surface of the soapy water.

The TV in the living room was on and she was listening to the news in the background, trying to catch up on local and world events. Trevor McDonald, a young black newscaster was reading the news on ITN. He was reporting on Concorde, which that day in France had made its maiden flight. He was also reporting on the daily sectarian killings in Northern Ireland, on the war in Vietnam, and on the growing hints that president Nixon was planning a trip to Red China.

After her ablutions, Coventry had tea and tumbled into bed with a sigh. Soon after, she was fast asleep and no dream would visit that night. The next thing she knew it was seven in the morning. She had slept ten hours – she felt better for the sleep but was still a bit tired. She perused her mail and Willie Sutton's letter was first for her attention. He still didn't know the date of his release but was hopeful it would be before Christmas.

It was Friday and by ten o'clock Coventry was in Tiplady's office. Smartly dressed she was sitting opposite her boss with her long legs crossed and the Vodka, Yearwood had sent was standing at attention on his desk. Tiplady's eyes were on the neck of the bottle and not on her legs, as was usually the case, but his knees, as usual, were knocking. He turned his gaze to Coventry. "Good to have you back," he said.

"Good to be back."

"Did you enjoy meeting Yearwood?"

"Yes. I can see why he's called Big Ben. He hopes you enjoy the Vodka."

"I will," said Tiplady, but his mind and eyes were back on the neck of the bottle.

Coventry reported on her trip and when she had finished, Tiplady's eyes returned to the neck of the bottle, then back to her.

"Did you find the file's convincing?" he asked.

"Very," replied Coventry. Then she asked. "How will he get the microfilm to you?"

Tiplady flashed a naughty smile. "It's here," he said.

"Already, how did Yearwood do it?"

"You brought it with you." Coventry's eyes widened. She uncrossed her legs.

"Me?"

"Yes."

174

"How?"

"In the Vodka bottle."

Coventry's jaw dropped. She fumbled in her handbag for a cigarette. "Where?" she said as she lit up.

"It's in the hollow of the screw on top."

"Well I'll be damned," said Coventry between drags on her cigarette.

"We thought it better you didn't know."

"I'm glad I didn't know," said Coventry casting her eyes upward.

"I'll show you," said Tiplady.

He unscrewed the top of the bottle and in its hollow behind a circular metal disk was a roll of microfilm, no larger than a thimble. It contained the entire file. Coventry cupped her chin in one hand, closed her eyes and moved her head slowly to the left, then to the right. Her boss threw his head back and laughed, but Coventry was straight-faced.

Tiplady pulled himself together. He said that the ploy was a simple way of getting small objects through Russian customs, that one bottle of Vodka was much like the other; so they never drew attention. He also said that Yearwood's FBI training came in handy. This was news to Coventry; she had no idea of his FBI past. After the newspaper's lawyers had studied the information on the microfilm and come to a decision, Tiplady would get back to her. Right now, her boss said that she should head home, rest, and on Monday start writing the first articles. He wanted to publish the first one in the 'special features' page the following Friday. This too was news to her.

The following evening, Coventry visited the Café de Paris. The Spaniard had come again in a sexy dream so she had taken a chance, hoping he would be there. She stayed for a while and had a few dances, but Juanito wasn't around. By now, the publicity about his landing on the Isle of Man had died down and he was back flying the

Lima, Peru route. While she was dancing with a stranger that night, Juanito was milling around the lobby of his Lima Hotel, looking for a young man to bed for the night. In the meantime, Trevelyan had yet to find his diary.

THIRTY-ONE

By Monday, she was totally recovered from her trip; being back on familiar ground was a relief. October in London, with its trees shedding leaves was a lovely time of year. There was something different and special about autumn in London. Coventry couldn't put her finger on it, but there was something unique about the rhythm of autumn in Old London Town.

Not meeting up with Juanito again at the Café had been disappointing, but not a tragedy. Her on again, off again carnal pulses were on hold and not a hint of a sexual dream had come her way of late. It was time to get back to business and write her piece on the Boshoi Ballet. She had mulled the job over in her mind, was eager to get it into words and then into her column in *The London Evening View*.

By nine o'clock she was in her cubicle at work, ready to begin. The notes she had made in Moscow were at her side by her typewriter. She had a good idea how to slant the piece. She had given it thought and had already written the piece in her head. Getting it down on paper was next. No trace of politics could enter into her writing – that was a no-no. She wanted her account to be more than a piece on the Bolshoi and Swan Lake. She wanted it to be about a cultural event, performed in a beautiful theatre for an audience of hundreds who had braved the weather. She wanted it to be about the perfection of an art, the Prima Ballerina who suspended belief, and of the company of dancers who supported her leaps, pirouettes and plies and were also swan-like to the eye. It would be about a brutally snowy day with rapier-like winds that cut one's body, and about Swan Lake, which fed one's soul.

Coventry lit a cigarette, slipped paper into her machine and clicked it into position. She was ready to start and focused. She was about to type when her phone rang. It was Father Power calling from the Vatican to say that she should ring Adam Stewart at the Ministry of Defence. Adam had called his brother at Stoneyhurst College, who in turn had called Power.

Since he had little to go by, Adam had failed to unearth anything about who Coventry's father was or what had become of him. There was no solid trail for him to follow, but he wanted Coventry to know that he had tried. He did, however, have a list of RAF men who flew in the Battle of Britain, that showed which had been killed in the war. The list contained over two thousand names. Adam had gone through the list carefully and although it gave no clue as to which man was her father, he wanted Coventry to know that she was welcome to a copy. Coventry was grateful for Power's call. She took down Adam's number and rang him immediately.

Adam sounded a friendly, obliging man and she thanked him for his efforts. His offer to send Coventry a copy of the list was accepted with gratitude. She gave him her address and Adam said he would mail it later in the day.

As she was hanging up, John Trevelyan was calling Mr. Green, his dentist in nearby Newquay. His twin daughters – whose birthday it had recently been – had received many gifts, one of them being a large box of Belgium chocolates. He had helped himself to one, thinking that it was soft but it was hard and he had broken a tooth. The molar needed quick attention. It had been a year since he had last seen Mr. Green. His dentist said that he should come straight away, that he would somehow fit him in. Within the hour, the Peer was in Green's chair having his tooth repaired.

As Green was probing in Trevelyan's mouth, something suddenly popped into his mind – a brown, bulky envelope Trevelyan had left behind during his last visit. The envelope contained his wartime diary. Green had put it away, intending to mail it but had forgotten. It was on a day that his receptionist was off with the flu so his place of business was not running smoothly. Trevelyan had the diary with him, after collecting it from a local bookbinder that had repaired the diary's spine. Just like Green, the entire episode had slipped through the cracks of Trevelyan's memory.

The diary covered a five-year period from January 1940, through December 1944. Trevelyan immediately turned to the page for Thursday, March 7th, 1940, the day he was injured by the bomb. It was blank from that date forward for the next month. His first entry after that was Thursday, April 11th 1940. By then he had been in hospital for nearly five weeks. His entry read:

'Royal Exeter Hospital. Last five weeks a blur. Injured by bomb March 7th while returning to Bexhill from London. Nearly lost right leg. Many torso wounds. Will be here ages. Flying days are over. In London went to Café De Paris. Met sweet Yank girl there – we were naughty during air raid. Paula McComb, US Embassy, London, Mayfair 2334 Ext. 11. Also, flat 14C, Peabody Buildings, Old Pye St. London W1. Bombing raids every day along S/E coast. Chamberlain weak. Churchill tough!

Britain under siege!

God help us!

All the pieces of the puzzle, but one, was now in place. The one missing piece was the key – the link – that would confirm that he was the father of the American girl with eyes like his. Was the name of her maiden mother Paula McComb? That was the question – the key. Perhaps Dr. Corcoran could provide the answer. He would see him soon to pick up his lenses. Wheels within wheels were laying the path for the Earl and his daughter to meet. It remained to be seen if they would.

For the rest of Monday, Coventry worked on the Bolshoi piece. One draft followed the other, and by late afternoon the piece had reached the standards that Coventry always aimed for in her work.

Tiplady had asked to see it before anyone else, so on her way home she dropped it off at his office.

Coventry was growing less enchanted with her lenses. She had worn them to the Café de Paris the previous Saturday night, but with a measure of discomfort, so she had to remove them.

She had excused herself from her dancing partner for that purpose and when she returned and he looked into her eyes, the poor fellow grew wobbly in the knees. At the first opportunity, he excused himself and vanished. A pity, thought Coventry, he was a good dancer but thanks to her eyes, Lady Luck was with her that night. The poor fellow was a thief who had pilfered a safe at the Mayfair Hotel and had ducked into the dancehall for safety. Unbeknown to the patrons, the cops had grabbed him just as he was leaving the dancehall. In his right-hand trouser pocket was a 32.calibre pistol, which, Coventry had mistaken for a measure of affection.

THIRTY-TWO

The word-code dealt with the Jones affair – it was the first time Yearwood had used it while speaking on the telephone with Tiplady. He had to be careful; there was always the threat of someone eavesdropping. He and Tiplady had set up the code if the Jones affair suddenly needed to be dropped. In the course of their talk, Yearwood would say: "By the way, have you seen Casablanca on TV lately?"

When Coventry entered Tiplady's office to hand in her Bolshoi piece, her boss was speaking on the telephone. From the other end of the phone came, "Have you seen Casablanca on TV lately?" The message was clear – the Jones matter had to be dropped. Yearwood could say no more. Something was brewing in Moscow and it wasn't good.

Yearwood's message was God-sent for Tiplady because a problem had also arisen at his end. It involved Lord Baxter, the owner and chairman of *The London Evening View*. The rich Peer had not been privy to what his editor had been up to, regarding Jones. Like so many in high places, Baxter had heard the rumours about Jones, but had no idea that his newspaper was trying to expose him. Tiplady had informed him over the weekend. Baxter had given Tiplady total freedom in the running of the newspaper, but this was a venture too far. Not only had he been kept in the dark, but so had others of importance at the newspaper. The only one who knew and was deeply involved was Coventry, a reporter who was new to the newspaper, and a Yank to boot.

Before taking up the matter of the Jones file with his lawyers, Tiplady had met with Baxter at the 'Oliver Plunkett Club', where Baxter was a member. The London club boasted a membership of Britain's Catholic cream. They had met in the club lounge and when Baxter heard what Tiplady was planning and who was involved at the newspaper, he doused his cigar in his drink and hit the roof. It was an outburst that startled other club members in the lounge. Baxter then stormed out, leaving the shaken Tiplady with a very pink face.

A week had past since Coventry had met with Tiplady and not a word had been said about the microfilm. Neither had he mentioned the Bolshoi piece she had written, that had yet to appear in the newspaper. It was clear he was avoiding her. She had nonetheless completed all her other pieces related to her Moscow trip on cultural matters. Each one employed a creative slant and she looked forward to seeing everything she had written in print. Finally, nine days after returning from Moscow, Tiplady told her that the Jones matter was on hold. The excuse he gave was that the lawyers were still studying the microfilm. His words were few and their meeting brief. She had no reason to doubt him, but there was something about his manner that cast doubts in her mind. The knocking of his knees was most pronounced and the worried look on his face was not one she had seen before.

Tiplady didn't know what lay behind Yearwood's coded message, but the black man did and was in position to tell. It had to do with a secret, Yearwood had recently learned that not even J. Edgar Hoover knew about it. The rumours that the British Prime Minister was a communist and which Yearwood's file suggested were a myth based on suspicions that went back in time. That was not the secret that prompted Yearwood's word-coded telephone message. He had heard about the secret by accident from Clark Thompson, the hard-drinking senator from Utah who was in Moscow on US government business. Other than Nixon, Eisenhower and Harold Macmillan, only Thompson knew the real truth about Jeremy Jones.

The genesis of all this went back to 1959, at the end of Eisenhower's term in office as president. Nixon was then vice-president and in Britain the Conservatives were in power, under Harold Macmillan. At the time, Jones, an unabashed socialist from a working-class background was only a member of parliament. Jones and Eisenhower – a Conservative – were at opposite ends of the political spectrum. During this period, America and Russia were armed to the teeth, the Berlin Wall did not exist, Phiby, Burgess and MacLean had defected to Russia and other turncoats were lurking in the British civil service. In the middle of that year, the Labour Party had sent Jones and other MPs to America to observe state primary elections that would determine who the Democratic Party would choose to oppose Nixon in the 1960 election. Politically, the British Labour Party and the American Democrats had much in common. One of the contenders from the Democratic Party for the job of president was the junior senator from Massachusetts, John F. Kennedy.

In the course of their visit, the British MPs were invited to a Washington dinner, whose host was President Eisenhower – a pragmatic realist and hard as nails. The dinner was the brainchild of the president. He had a job in mind for Jones, but first he had to vet him, so steps were taken for Jones to be seated next to Eisenhower.

Prime Minister Macmillan had suggested Jones for the job to Eisenhower. Though Macmillan and Jones came from different political parties, and were polls apart in ideology, over the years Macmillan had come to know, like and respect him. He knew Jones to be a man of convictions who would never betray Britain. He knew the rumours about him were false. He knew that Jones had never been a member of the communist party, that he had no links with Philby, Burgess, MacLean, or any of the Cambridge University clique from which they came. He and others were also keenly aware that Jones could waltz in and out of Russia at will and that he was always welcomed by the highest Russian officialdom. To them he was a long-standing, pipe-smoking socialist from Britain, who could disagree without being disagreeable. In other words he had the ear of the Russians.

The suspicions about Jones grew from the fact that in the late 1940s, and as President of the British Board of Trade, he had made many trips to Russia. He often visited Russia, was friends with a Russian who lived in his home constituency, the friend was known to have links with the KGB; and the convenient coincidence that Jones had gained the leadership of the Labour Party when his predecessor died suddenly from an odd illness after a trip to Russia. These facts formed the core of the suspicions. They were there, in the corridors of power, and wouldn't go away.

In 1959, America and Britain were not on speaking terms with Russia, nor were the Russians speaking to them on any official level. Relations were cold between east and west. Distrust and espionage were the order of the day and the military establishment of these countries were paranoid about what the other was doing. In addition to this, there was the continued testing of nuclear weapons by all sides. It was a standoff that was escalating at an alarming rate.

What Eisenhower needed was a trusted middleman through which issues of importance between America and Russia could be addressed. This was why Jones had been seated next to Eisenhower and why, in 1969, no further fuel could be added to the suspicions already linked with his name. He had enough problems at home, not least the ongoing aftermath of the Aberfan mining disaster.

Jones passed the test of Eisenhower's scrutiny and after considering the president's plan he took up the challenge. If he could help to secure a more orderly, safe future for the world, he would, and with the passage of time, Jones had never flinched from this task. Quietly, his contributions to global equilibrium were showing results. In 1959, his talks with the Russians had led to the Nuclear Test Band Treaty of 1963, the first of its kind involving Britain, Russia and America. His input paved the way for the erection of the Berlin Wall – an Eisenhower idea of great foresight, which few knew about then, or even now.

There were concerns on all sides over the number of people escaping to the west from Iron Curtain countries. It was felt that what was then a trickle of people escaping, might result in a flood. Something had to be done. It was causing added frictions between east and west and the exodus could eventually destabilise the social and economic fabric of Western Europe. People had to be kept behind the Iron Curtin and Jones helped sell the idea of the Berlin Wall to the Russians. The soviets welcomed the idea. They were livid and worried over the growing number of people who preferred freedom in the west, rather than the tyranny of communism.

Now, in 1969, Jones – acting on behalf of President Nixon – was in the process of trying to assure Leonid Brezhnev that Nixon's attempts to dialogue with Red China was not a US ploy aimed at America and China ganging up on Russia. This is what Yearwood had learned from Thompson and why exposing Jones to further falsehoods could not continue. How did Yearwood come to learn all this?

At a dinner in the US Embassy, Senator Thompson drank too much and Yearwood helped him to his room. While Yearwood was putting him to bed, Thompson started talking about Jones and didn't stop until he had passed out. In the morning the senator could remember nothing of all the beans he had spilled. As for the file on Jones, virtually everything in it was a fabrication that came from the FBI. Under J. Edgar Hoover, the FBI was a law onto itself.

As Coventry was slipping into bed that night, a multitude of thoughts were running through her head. Way off in Cornwall, her father was thinking too, and across the Atlantic, in Attica, Willie Sutton was sitting on his bunk. His legs were bothering him. He was giving them a rub. He was thinking: when the hell will my release date come through? This jail is ready to explode with a riot!

THIRTY-THREE

The list of Battle of Britain flyers had arrived. It was waiting on the doormat in a big, brown envelope. Coventry began looking it over, even before taking off her coat. Her eyes danced over the pages. The list was lengthy with over three thousand names. She had no idea that so few from Britain and other countries had beaten back the strength of the mighty German Luftwaffe. The first sheet of the list gave the number of Britons involved, just as Adam Stewart had said. The rest were nationals of other nations. She could see how impossible it was to identify her father. No Christian names preceded surnames, only initials. It was a hopeless task – a dead end. Oh well, it was just a shot in the dark, she thought.

Titled 'Battle of Britain Roll of Honour', the list covered sixty-two pages that triggered a very strange feeling. An eerie sensation that somehow brought her in touch with men who triumphed against huge odds in one of the defining air military battles of the twentieth-century – the battle that kept Hitler at bay and that gave Britain time to breathe and fight another day.

Page after page told a story. In addition to the Britons that took part, nearly six hundred flyers from the British Commonwealth and other nations had also helped Britain in her hour of need. They were the tough guys in life who take up the challenge when tough guys are needed. Among them were New Zealanders, South Africans, Czechs, Australians, Canadians, and Irish. They were not the only ones from other nations to pitch in – to make the enemy bleed, and in some cases bleed and die themselves. A sprinkling of tough guys from Belgium,

Palestine, South Rhodesia and America had also put their shoulders to the wheel in Britain's defence.

No, the list could not help identify her father. What it did was connect Coventry with his comrades, and the reality that more than four hundred had been killed during the four-month battle. The list cried out with the fact that their sacrifice was far from over – it told the sad tale. Of those not killed in the Battle, nearly eight hundred more had later been killed in subsequent actions. The result was that almost half of those who flew in the Battle of Britain were dead by the war's end. The odds were that her father was among them. So that was that – the end of a trail, but though the trail had reached its end for Coventry, this was not the case for John Trevelyan in the hunt for the answer he sought. Was the mother of the American girl with eyes like his named Paula McComb? If the answer was yes, then he was her father.

The immediate question for Trevelyan was which of two paths should he follow in pursuit of the answer he sought? The oblique one through Goodfellow, or the more direct route, through Dr. Corcoran? There were pros and cons for each approach. Not a person to waste time, Trevelyan chose the direct route. Tomorrow he would ring Corcoran, make arrangements to pick up his lenses, and try to seek his help.

The Earl was back in London at the Travellers Club, a mile from Wilton Crescent where Coventry was perusing the list. Whatever hope she had of discovering who her father was, and what had happened to him, was gone.

At work, Coventry had been in a state of flux, treading water and slightly disappointed since learning that the Jones story – even with the worries that it brought – was suspended. She had been given a silly assignment and had completed it with ease. She had been shunted into a cul-de-sac and she knew it. The fact that Tiplady was staying at arms length had equally disappointed her. Something was amiss. She could sense it.

In the war, Trevelyan had faced dangers head-on. Time after time, he had gone up to battle the Luftwaffe, and each time he had returned while some comrades had not. The bomb in Bexhill should have killed him, or at least he should have lost a leg. Neither had happened. On all but one occasion, he had escaped unscratched, and when he was hurt he had come through in tact. Like many surviving airmen, he had pondered his luck and asked – Why me? Why have I been so lucky, not just in the war, but throughout life. Why was I born into privilege? His answer was that it had to be for a reason, perhaps so that his sights would forever be pitched honourably high. It followed that if this girl was his child, he had to know. Then he had to let her know. But in letting her know, he would not bring conflict into her life, so he would approach with caution and sensitivity.

When the next day came, he phoned Corcoran.

"Yes," said the doctor, "come by at 2pm."

Trevelyan was prompt. The lenses were in a small box identical to the one Coventry had been given several weeks earlier. The Earl hoped that the lenses would be less troublesome than his last pair and his wish was granted. They felt fine and Corcoran was pleased. Trevelyan knew the procedure of putting them over the irises, how to clean them, and what to avoid – like not wearing them on windy days or in dusty places. None of this was new to him, and having tried them on, he liked how natural the irises looked with the new brown tint in the lenses. Now came the hard part – the broaching of a sensitive subject. The Peer had to be careful with his words for fear of encroaching on Corcoran's medical ethics.

Corcoran was a busy man, so Trevelyan was brief. He started by saying that he had a sensitive, personal matter to discuss and would the doctor be prepared to listen.

"Yes, by all means," said Corcoran. The Earl held nothing back; he revealed everything and ended by saying that he thought the American girl might be his daughter, and that if her mother's first name was Paula, that name would confirm it.

188

Corcoran was slightly thrown back. He stood, wandered around his office, looked out the window and thought. The clock on the wall ticked loudly. The doctor thought back to Trevelyan's first visit and as he thought, the clock ticked on. Although medical ethics prevented divulging patient's details, he recalled that during that visit he had told Trevelyan something about the girl, but only because of their uncanny eye similarities. He never dreamt that there might be a family link between them. That information however, was as far as Corcoran could go. Corcoran turned from the window. He continued to think and the clock ticked on.

He took off his spectacles, cleaned them and slipped them back on. Then he said, "I can tell you this, the girl is a reporter who works for *The London Evening View*. Her name, as you know, is Coventry Victoria Calvert. That's all I can tell you."

Corcoran had already gone beyond what he was permitted to reveal, but he recognised the Peer's sincere intentions. He was aware also that Trevelyan was an RAF comrade of his friend Hawkins-Goodfellow. He wished Trevelyan well, and the Peer thanked Corcoran.

What to do next? That was the question Trevelyan thought about for days. He eventually chose a course of action. He would write to Coventry at *The London Evening View*. All things considered, it was in his view the best way to approach her.

THIRTY-FOUR

Lord Baxter of Battle lived in an old country mansion similar to John Trevelyan's home in Cornwall. Situated in Sussex on the south coast of England, the town of Battle had derived its name from the days of the Norman Conquest and the 1066 Battle of Hastings.

The Baxter wealth, like that of the Trevelyan's, was old money, the calibre of wealth whose lineage looks down on the new. The lord and kin were upper crust – English to the core with the emphasis on English. They were, in their view, English, not British. They considered themselves the country's core-people in origin, not 'blow-ins' tacked onto the fringes of England with the passage of time. A man in his late fifties, Baxter, like Trevelyan, was also 'One of the few'. Unlike Trevelyan however, his bark and bite could be severe.

On this particular day, Baxter was in an ugly mood. He had summoned his editor to his home for a dressing down and that's just what Tiplady had to endure. On the receiving end of a savage assault, he left Battle in no doubt as to his master's wishes. Baxter's edict was clear; on no account was a story about the Prime Minister's links with Russia to appear in *The London Evening View*. The entire matter should be dropped, forgotten and never referred to again.

The shaken Tiplady gave Baxter his assurance that he would obey his wishes.

"And what about this Yank, will she keep her mouth shut?" thundered Baxter. Tiplady again gave his assurance. "God help you both if I ever hear of this matter again. Good day to you, sir," snapped the angry Lord.

Tiplady left Battle with his tail between his legs, lucky to still have his job. He drove off with ribbons of sweat running down his face and in no doubt that he was on probation.

John Trevelyan was having a battle of his own, trying to compose a letter to Coventry – a letter whose tone he had to get right. Assembling his words was difficult; in a way it was an ordeal almost equal to the Luftwaffe-dogfights he had flown and survived over England. In some ways those battles were easy compared to writing this letter. He had ripped sheet after sheet of paper from his typewriter after a few sentences. The words weren't right, their tempo was erratic and the tone of his words were banal. His efforts were getting him nowhere.

Better leave it for a while – I had better show my face at the debate, he thought.

He was in the House of Lords. The debate was on agriculture and when he entered the chamber, the Labour leader in the Lords was on his feet, speaking on earthy matters of little interest to most present. The chamber was largely empty, and the Peers present were mostly dozing, recovering on the chamber's long-rowed and comfortable red leather seats, after one of their hardy lunches with glasses of wine. The scene was one of democracy at work, in a state of cosy relaxation and Trevelyan's mind was not on the speaker's words. It was on which words to use in his letter to best convey a delicate, personal message. He had a hurdle to leap with his letter. How does he tell a girl that he had deflowered her mother in a staircase in the middle of a bombing raid? What was the best way of saying that he thought he was her father? That was the hurdle for Trevelyan to leap.

There was little about the Lord's debate that gripped Trevelyan. The subject, as important as it was held little interest, so he slipped away from the chamber back to his typewriter. Finally, after several hours, his battle with words was over, his letter written and mailed. It concluded by saying:

'If it should be that I am your father, be assured that I take no pride in the manner of your conception, but that I remember your mother with warmth. I am happy that you exist, and should you wish to meet me, be further assured that the wish is also mine'.

The letter was totally honest as to how he came to know of Coventry and where she worked. He also said that he regretted the death of her mother at such an early age.

Trevelyan's battle with words was over, but this was not the case with Juanito and his men. Coventry was still unaware of his exploits on the Isle of Man and since seeing him last, neither did she suspect that the manly Spaniard was a strong homosexual at heart. Juanito was back in Madrid visiting his parents and the three of them were having dinner. His homosexual leanings were no longer impulses he could deny or hide. He knew he could no longer live a lie; he had to tell his parents and hope for the best. Now the time had come, for the confession of his life.

The dinner was over. Unable to look them in the eye, Juanito spoke down to a plate of food he had not been able to finish. Like John Trevelyan, he was struggling to find the words, battling inwardly to give voice to his feelings. The words fell clumsily from his lips as his eyes welled with tears; the feeling of shame, guilt and sin gripping his total being.

When he had finished there was silence at the table. His head was still down. When it came up and faced his parents there was nothing but calm on their faces – no traces of despair, looks of surprise, or reactions to sins revealed. His parents were not surprised or shocked as Coventry had been when her mother confessed her sin on the staircase of Café de Paris. Juanito's parents had known of his nature for years. The devout Spanish couple had long since come to terms with the wayward course of their son's sexuality. They did not condemn, just as Father McAvoy had not condemned Coventry's mother on that stormy ocean voyage years before. All his parents could do was pray that God would look with compassion on their son. They stood, embraced him and said they understood.

Willie Sutton's battle with the silence of New York's governor was over at last and the famous old thief was greatly relieved. He would be out of prison before Christmas. Only one obstacle remained. Thanks to the persistence of his lawyer, all but one of his old criminal cases that had added over a hundred years to his sentence had been overturned, on one technicality or the other. The last case – for which he owed ten more years – would be considered in the Brooklyn district court early in December and was sure to be overturned. Prison would soon be behind him and hopefully the Attica riots that were bound to come would not erupt before then. Most of the weight of uncertainty on Willie's little shoulders had at last been lifted.

Now Willie had four letters to write. One was to his lawyer, another to his sister, a third to Coventry and the last one to a friend who worked abroad. Unlike John Trevelyan, he would not need to battle to find the words. The letter to Coventry would not be coded; there was nothing secret now about his coming release – everyone knew, including the press. What they didn't know was the date – and neither did Willie.

Willie Sutton had done it again, broken out of jail – this time legally. Once he was out, he would take up the offer of the writer who approached him to collaborate on a book about his life.

THIRTY-FIVE

Coventry was preparing to retire for the night. She had to catch an early morning train to Diss in Norfolk to interview 'One of the few'. It was a thrilling and timely assignment. It was Monday the 27th of October; the 31st of the month would mark twenty-nine years since the end of the Battle of Britain and the article she would write would mark the occasion and one of its heroes. Since Lord Baxter was also 'One of the few', Tiplady had to be careful who he gave this assignment to. He was in enough trouble with Baxter as it was. His lordship would be on him like stink on shit if the article was not first-rate.

Before choosing a reporter, Tiplady had discussed it with some of his veteran scribes who were not working on assignments with deadlines. He hadn't seriously considered Coventry, but since there had been silence between them, and she was still in limbo, he thought he would at least talk to her about the job; his gesture would help break the ice between them. He was glad that he did.

He found her to be eager for the job and amazingly *au fait* with facts dealing with the Battle of Britain that even he didn't know about. This was not always the case with the other reporters he had spoken with. She was astonishingly up on dates; the numbers of flyers that had taken part, the nationality of those from other countries that had participated, and even the fact that one hailed from Ireland, whose surname was Hemmingway. This amazed him because he had met Hemmingway several years earlier at the home of Baxter. That did it. The assignment was hers. The man from Norfolk she was to interview was former Wing Commander V.T. Galbraith, the chair of the Battle of Britain Veterans Association.

Coventry slipped into bed, set her clock for 7am and clicked off her bed light. Along with other tools of her trade she would take to the interview, she would also bring the Battle of Britain Honour Roll list. The list was certain to come in handy and impress Galbraith. Everything she was taking was at hand, ready for tomorrow. Coventry was soon asleep.

It had been days since she had dreamt, but tonight one would come in the form of a premonition, a dream with two people who were one – Juanito and her father. As she fell deeper into sleep, the dream became more vivid, and real.

It was a wild, windy autumn day in 1940. Crisp leaves were whipping past her, some of them slapping at her face. She is sweeping them away with her hands. She's standing at the far end of an aerodrome runway somewhere in southern England. At the other end of the runway, Spitfires and Hurricanes are revving their engines, ready to take off because German bombers are coming to drop bombs. Sirens are howling, signalling the bomber's eminent arrival – the aerodrome would soon be attacked.

Coventry's hair is blowing wildly. She's smartly dressed, just as she was when she flew to Moscow on that miserable rainy morning. A voice coming from a megaphone in the elevated aerodrome radio tower calls out.

"You, lady in the raincoat, leave the runway at once."

Coventry cups her hands over her mouth and calls back. "Mind your business. I'll stand where I want."

A man dressed as a pilot with a parachute bobbing on his back runs across the runway in her direction. When he reaches Coventry, she sees it is Juanito. He sweeps her in his arms, bends her over and kisses her madly, taking her breath away. His tongue is deep down her throat.

Then he says, "I'm your father. You haven't been born yet, just letting you know in case I get killed today. If I survive, I'll see you when you're twenty-eight."

"You can't be my daddy," says Coventry. "You're Juanito, I met you at the Café de Paris, remember? You called me Eyes of God – remember?"

"No," says her daddy. "You've got it wrong, and it was your mother I met at the Café De Paris, and what I called her was Face of an Angel. But you can call me Juanito if you like. Got to go, dear, got to take off and fight the Hun."

"Take me with you, take me with you," says Coventry.

"Can't do, only room for one in a Spitfire."

"I'll sit on your lap, on your lap."

"Can't do it – too dangerous."

"Take me with you, please."

"Very well, little girl, very well." Coventry and Juanito race down the runway towards his Spitfire. As they run towards the plane, Spitfires and Hurricanes whiz past them, ready to lift into the air. Zoom! Zoom! They thunder past, missing Coventry and Juanito by feet.

The day is a beautiful one. Clusters of lovely clouds are overhead and Hitler's bombers are coming. In the distance the familiar unsynchronised 'hurrang' sound of bombers engines can be heard. Bombs whistling down and explosions can be heard coming from nearby aerodromes. Coventry and Juanito finally reach their Spitfire. All the other planes have gone; they are now above in the sky, locked in battle with the enemy. Machine gun fire can be head. A Spitfire is hit. It bursts into flame and spirals downward.

"I'll get in first, you sit on my lap," says Juanito. Done! The plane's propeller is spinning. The Spitfire is rolling forward, moving faster and faster. Juanito is strapped in. Coventry's on his lap; his arms are cradling her close. He's aroused, and she can feel it.

"Nice," she says. Juanito can't see in front of him, Coventry will need to pilot the plane and fire its guns.

"Follow my instructions," says Juanito.

"OK," she replies.

"See the speed gauge?"

"Yes," says, Coventry.

"See the control-stick in front of you?"

"Yes."

"When the needle reaches a hundred on the gauge, pull the stick back slowly towards you."

"OK, this is fun." Coventry follows instructions, pulls the stick back and little by little the Spitfire is airborne. Her touch on the controls is beautiful. She's a born pilot and Juanito says so. She smiles proudly. Her hair is blowing all around as the cockpit dome is open.

In bed in the throws of her dream, Coventry moves about as she lives every moment. Her right hand is gripping the Spitfire's controls. She banks the plane to the left, then to the right. She goes in and out of clouds. She and Juanito can see dogfights all around them. Spitfires and Hurricanes are laying into bombers and the bombers are responding with bursts of fire. At the same time, the bombers are dropping explosives. They hurtle down, hitting the ground one after the other like footsteps of volcanic eruptions.

"When can we attack," asks Coventry. "Where are the guns, and how do I shoot them?"

"Attack at will," Juanito replies, "the guns are in the wings; the button atop the stick you're holding is the trigger. Shoot at will."

Coventry swings her craft behind a bomber. She throttles back to slow down her plane, lines up her shot and fires her guns. She misses. She can see the face of the tail-gunner in the bomber she's attacking. He can see hers. He's lining up a shot to attack her. He shoots and hits the left wing of Coventry's plane, disabling it. The nose of her Spitfire is a ball of fire.

"Got to jump clear, got to jump clear," yells her father. "Hang on to me, little girl," he says, "we only have one parachute."

The Spitfire is out of control. It begins to spiral. Coventry tosses and turns in her sleep. Somehow she and Juanito manage to jump clear of the falling plane. She's holding onto her father for dear life. Her legs are flopping in every direction, as down they fall. Her father pulls the ripcord on his chute and silk streams out like a ribbon of life.

The chute fills with air and pops open. In so doing, it jolts the two up as the chute finds its wings. Now down, down they go as the weight of two bodies is asking too much of the chute, which is only meant for one. Down they go with the ground getting closer and closer. The sweat is pouring from Coventry's face. Her eyes pop open like a parachute and instead of seeing the opened chute above her, the ceiling over her bed is what she sees. It was all a dream and Coventry is happy, because Juanito was her father and her father was Juanito and the whole damned dream was a load of stupid shit.

THIRTY-SIX

As Coventry's taxi was leaving Wilton Crescent for Euston Station, a postman near Piccadilly Circus was delivering mail to *The London Evening View*. Amongst the mail the paper was receiving that morning was the letter from her father, sent two days earlier. Since she would be away from London that day, she would not see the letter until tomorrow.

Coventry was looking forward to meeting her interviewee, Mr. Galbraith – he was special; not only was he a hero of the Battle of Britain, but was only one of eleven airmen in World War Two that had escaped from Colditz Prison. Many had tried but few had escaped.

On meeting Galbraith, she immediately could sense he had no vanity. Tiplady had failed to mention that Galbraith was a knight – Sir Vincent Thomas Galbraith. The Queen had dubbed him a knight when he was only thirty-four.

When her train pulled into Diss at 9.43am, Galbraith was at the station waiting, and gentleman that he was, his charming ways were swiftly winning. A tall, well-built man with greying brown hair, Galbraith was the type of Englishman portrayed in Hollywood films by the likes of Walter Pigeon; he was cultured to the bone and understated. For the next eight hours, he, his wife and the setting they called home, captivated Coventry.

Sir Vincent's domain was a fifty-acre estate in Harling and Anne, his wife, was a delight. Only eighteen when the Battle of Britain took place, Gathbraith defied his fifty-three years and the war experiences that should have undermined his future looks. His

199

youthful appearance gave no hint of the ninety-four missions he had flown, the three years he had spent in Colditz and the five escape attempts he had made, before succeeding with the sixth. Just like 'The Shadow' the mythical American radio character of the '30s and '40s, Galbraith had fogged the minds of the Colditz guard at the gate and brazenly walked past them on a snowy night, dressed as a German officer. He had returned their salute smartly, said nothing and disappeared into the night just as Willie Sutton had done. With the help of his fellow prisoners, the Colditz guards didn't know that he was gone until morning, and, as in the case of Willie Sutton's escape, by morning the only thing left of Galbraith were his footprints in the snow. Nearly thirty years on, Galbraith didn't look a day over thirty-five. Just like Coventry's father.

In arranging the interview, Tiplady had described Coventry, so Galbraith knew what to look for when her train arrived in Diss Station.

"He'll know you when he sees you," Tiplady said to Coventry. Needless to say her eyes were top of the agenda when Tiplady described what she looked like, and the fact that she was a Yank, who was always easy to pick out in a crowd. What Galbraith looked for at the station is just what he got – a tall, handsome, well-dressed woman with an air of confidence, whose breeding spoke for itself.

For a very good reason, foreknowledge of Coventry's eyes gave Galbraith a sense of anticipation. He had mentioned her eyes to his wife before Coventry arrived. He had good reason for this. He had only met someone with eyes like hers once, and it was someone he knew well – The Earl of Crantock, a Battle of Britain veteran, and member of the Association. He had recently seen him at the Athenaeum Club in London.

Coventry and the Galbraiths hit it off from the start, in a seamless blending of people from different backgrounds brought together by chance. The knight responded to her questions in direct, detailed ways that gave Coventry insights and anecdotes to draw on about the Battle of Britain, from the viewpoint of someone who was there and survived. The honour roll list Coventry had brought impressed Sir Vincent – not that he hadn't seen the list before. What impressed him was that she had done her homework and taken more than a surface interest in the subject at hand. In discussing the battle and those who had taken part, she proved a depth of knowledge about the battle. She did not mention that her father had taken part. Maybe later, she thought – if they ever met again.

The morning was spent reliving the Battle of Britain. The afternoon would be devoted to Colditz and his escape. After a lovely lunch, prepared and presented by Anne, Coventry's hostess slipped into her riding gear, mounted 'Banjo', her horse, and clip-clopped away for her afternoon ride along a narrow lane that was covered by leaves.

Galbraith's story was extraordinary and his soft-spoken ways gave no hint of the steel in his character. Along this line of thought, Coventry asked: "Did the war mellow you, make you the easy-going man you are today, or was the spirit of a lion always in you?"

A bit embarrassed, Galbraith thought for a while. "Tyrants like Hitler are always the same, they want to cage free men – they bring out the beast in free men. I jolly well don't think myself a lion," replied Galbraith. Enough said. Coventry got the message. When Galbraith was certain the interview was over, he broached the subject of her eyes, but not wanting to embarrass her, he asked if he was free to do so.

"Of course, Sir Vincent."

The honour roll list was on a table near Coventry. Galbraith asked if he might see it again. He turned to page fifty-five, which is where the surname of flyers starting with the letter T began. When he found the name he wanted, he showed it to Coventry. "See this name?" said Galbraith. Coventry had a look.

She read the name aloud. "Flying Officer John Trevelyan."

"Well," said Galbraith. "He's the only person I ever met with eyes like yours. He's a good friend of mine. I saw him in London a few days ago."

That night, while on the train back to London, Coventry was reviewing the notes she had put to paper. She was especially interested in the notes she had made after the interview was over, about the man who had eyes like hers. She thought about her dream of the night before, and of Juanito, who appeared as a pilot and said he was her father, and what her father had said in the dream: 'I'll see you when you're twenty-eight'.

Her mind leapt. Then she shook her head and thought, this is stupid, this is weird, and this cannot be possible.

THIRTY-SEVEN

The following morning, two things were about to shock her at *The London Evening View* when she arrived for work. News of the first was tapping into one of the newsroom's Teletype machines from the Amalgamated Press at 9.59am local time.

Amalgamated Press, Paris, France

FOR IMMEDIATE RELEASE

28 October 1969

AMERICAN EMBASSY MAN FOUND DEAD

CIRCUMSTANCES MYSTERIOUS

Vincent E. B. Yearwood, 49, a US Embassy cultural attaché in Moscow, USSR, was today found dead in the River Moscow. His remains were recovered at 6.31am local time. Neither his embassy nor the US State Department could give further details about his death.

Mr. Yearwood was cultural attaché in three US Embassies prior to his Moscow posting. Randolph Coin, the US presses attaché at the American embassy in Moscow said, "Mr. Yearwood's death is a mystery. We are investigating his death."

–End-

There was a buzz running through the newsroom when Coventry arrived at work. Three reporters were in their cubicles working the phones, calling contacts in East Berlin, anxious to know further details about Yearwood's death. Questions remained unanswered. Was it murder? Was it politically linked? Was it suicide? Was it an accident? His death bore all the hallmarks of Cold War intrigue.

The London Evening View's first edition had to go to press by 11.30am. Who, When, Where, How and Why? These were the questions that needed answers if the paper was to cover the story in its first edition professionally. Tiplady could say nothing about his link with the dead man and no one at the paper knew anything other than what had come from the Amalgamated Press. They knew who Yearwood was, what his job was at the embassy, where his body had been found, and the fact that he was dead. They knew nothing about HOW and WHY he had met his death. On these questions, Tiplady too was in the dark. The newspaper's front page for the first edition had already been composed. What remained to be written was as much about the story as was known. The front page read:

US EMBASSY MAN FOUND

DEAD IN MOSCOW RIVER

Tiplady was in the newsroom hovering over one of the Teletype machines. He was reading a dispatch from the Reynolds News Agency that contained no further details about Yearwood's death other than those given by Amalgamated Press. The hour was nearing the 11am deadline. Two reporters who were working on the story were at their typewriters waiting for more information.

Tiplady was jumpy. When he spotted Coventry, he discreetly signalled for her to slip into his office. His hand gesture said it all. Everyone in the newsroom around him was busy so nobody noticed. If he was jumpy it was not only due to the deadline he had to meet if the story was to be covered in the first edition. It was because Yearwood was a friend with whom he and Coventry had been in league over a matter getting out of hand. He knew that Yearwood could not possibly have committed suicide, and he knew something else: if Yearwood had been murdered, it probably had something to do with what he knew about the Prime Minister. If this was the case, he and Coventry could well be next – because they knew about Jones too – so if Tiplady was jumpy, it was for good reason.

Everyone at the paper knew that Coventry had been to Moscow on a cultural assignment. That's all they knew. Tiplady had to be sure that Coventry kept quiet; he had to alert her of the possible dangers. He had already informed Lord Baxter of Yearwood's death and had received another blast, so Tiplady was under the hammer of unfolding events.

Coventry had yet to speak with anyone from the newspaper, but from the atmosphere she knew something of importance was happening. With a coffee in one hand and a cigarette in the other, she waited in Tiplady's office for him to arrive. He was colourless when he finally appeared. He quietly shut the door behind him and fell into his chair. His knees were knocking more furiously than Coventry had ever seen. He reached for a cup on his desk – whose coffee had chilled – and gulped down a swallow. It was obvious he was finding it hard to say something unpleasant. By now, Coventry's eyes were like saucers, wide open and on guard for what was coming. Tiplady leaned forward and spoke in a whisper.

"I have bad news," he said.

"What's happened?"

"Yearwood's dead."

"He's what?"

He's dead," replied Tiplady, his head moving up and down in the affirmative.

"When? How?"

"This morning. His body was found in the river near the embassy. " Coventry was shocked. She reached in her handbag for another cigarette. "The news started coming over the wire services at ten this morning. AP had it first."

"What happened?"

"Don't know yet. We're trying to find out." Tiplady had to be quick; he had to stay on top of this story if some of it was to be covered in the early edition. "I must be brief, Coventry. Have you told anyone that you met with Yearwood in Moscow?"

"Not a soul."

"Good, keep it that way. His death may be linked with the PM's file. We may both be in danger. I don't want to scare you, but it's best you know."

"I understand." Coventry's heart raced.

"Carry on with what you were working on and keep your head down."

For the rest of the morning, Coventry did just that and spoke to no one; she carried on with the Galbraith piece. The envelope containing the letter from her father was sitting on her desk. So much was going on around her that she failed to notice it till noon. There was no return address on the envelope to say whom the letter was from. All she could tell was that it was mailed from Parliament Square two days earlier. I'll open it when I return from lunch, she thought. People who had read her column would often write and this is whom she took the letter to be from – a reader of *The London Evening View*. She slipped the envelope into the top drawer of her desk.

She didn't go to her usual place on Shaftsbury Avenue for lunch. She did what she never did; she went to a local pub. She needed a drink to calm her nerves. A woman alone in a London pub was a bit rare at the time, and when she entered the 'Dog and Bone', the all male clientele looked her over. To hell with them, thought Coventry and she ordered a gin and tonic.

An hour later, she was back at her desk. The last thing on her mind was the envelope she had slipped in her top desk drawer without opening. It was this drawer into which she always put her handbag, but she failed to this after lunch. She kept it on her desk because in it was her address book, and she had to call Galbraith to check on something she wanted to include in her piece. When she had made her call, she opened the drawer to slip in her handbag and there was the envelope. I'll open it later she thought, I must push on with the Galbraith piece.

When she was leaving for the day, she opened the envelope and read the letter. Her jaw dropped, and a chill ran through her body. One shock had followed another.

THIRTY-EIGHT

Her mind was in turmoil that night. If she drifted into sleep, it did not last long; thirty minutes later, she was pacing the floor. Two shocks had come within hours of each other; her mental equilibrium was off balance. Added to this, something else was keeping her awake, an angry wind buffeting her windows and whistling through her building.

Earlier that evening, a lady from Norfolk had called BBC TV to say that a weatherman in Holland had predicted that a hurricane was headed for Britain that night. With a wry smile of superiority, the TV weatherman reported the lady's call to the nation, and assured the viewers that no such hurricane was on its way.

The Dutchman was right! A hurricane was heading for Britain and by morning it would leave a trail of destruction across all of Great Britain. But the force of its power had yet to arrive. As Coventry tried to sleep, as her mind leapt from one concern to the other, the hurricane's vanguard was paving the way for its wicked, angry body and its lashing tail.

Coming to terms with the day's shocks was difficult. Yearwood was dead in mysterious circumstances and this had thrown up dangers for her and Trevor Tiplady. Although twenty hours had passed since Yearwood's body had been found, nothing further was known about the circumstances of his death. A wall of silence was up and Coventry had a good idea what lay behind the silence. That was one thing. Then there was the letter from her father. The faint hope she had of discovering who he was, whether he had survived the war, and if so, of finding him, had been granted. She was mindful of the saying: 'Be careful what you wish for – you just might get it'. Now she was wondering if what she wished for was worth the ambition. She didn't know what way to feel about it now. Then there was the matter of her recent odd dream, the one that foretold her father's appearance. The whole dammed thing was spooky as hell, as if driven by an eerie force. What should she do? Respond to her father's letter, or let the matter die? She had to think the matter through, and while she was thinking the wind kept rattling her windows. It kept hurling trash bins all over the street of Belgravia, whistling through her building, and the longest she was able to sleep in one stretch was an hour.

When morning came, the hurricane's damage had been done and Britain was a scene of destruction. The hurricane had hit full-force in the night as predicated. Even after it had struck it remained nameless – not given a name by the Brits, not given the respect it deserved. Despite their high tech computers, the British weathermen had got it wrong. The PhD's of the British Meteorological Office and the BBC didn't know where to put their faces. The country had not been warned and the tail of the hurricane was now whipping the nation. British to the core, the excuses from the weathermen abounded but the damage had been done. Millions of trees had been uprooted and some had killed people when they fell. Rooftops and chimneys had been blown away. The country was in a mess. At Hyde Park Corner, where Coventry and others waited for their bus, there were trees across the road, causing hazards and delays.

Trying to get a taxi was a waste of time. Like many people on their way to work, Coventry was left with no option but to walk. She couldn't take the day off; her piece on the Galbraith story had to be finished within hours. Yesterday's shocks had thrown her off stride and delayed its completion. She would decide what, if anything, she would do about her father's letter as she walked to work. Not responding to mail was not her style, but her father's letter was no ordinary missive.

The walk to Piccadilly Circus was not a long one. With her hair blowing wildly, Coventry covered the distance briskly with the help of wind on her back. At Piccadilly Circus, she slipped into a coffee shop for a visit to 'the ladies' to see what on earth she looked like. While she fixed her hair, she thought about her father's letter, and as she drained the last of her coffee, she decided what to do. She would call him.

He had written and his letter was respectful so she decided to call him that night. Although his letter was written on House of Lords stationary, there was no mention in the letter of his Peerage. His letter had given her two numbers to call. One was the number of the Athenaeum Club; the other was in Cornwall in case he had left London. She would ring the London number first, but before she called, she would do some research – she would check the British 'Who's Who' and the 'Book of Peers'.

The silence thrown up by Yearwood's death had continued and what appeared in the papers that morning was sketchy. *The London Evening View* had covered the story in the previous day's late edition and it too was thin on facts.

Those who knew the facts weren't talking, and this wall of silence would remain until interest in the story was lost – which was what the people who weren't talking had in mind. In the end, none but they would ever know the real story behind the death of Yearwood. If his death was foul play, and was linked to the PM's file, then Coventry and Tiplady had no cause to worry. No one but Yearwood knew they were privy to the file – or about the microfilm they had – or what they aimed to do with it. Yearwood had taken the secret of their involvement to his grave. No one knew except Lord Baxter. And he was above reproach. Or was he? The problem was that neither Coventry nor Tiplady knew that they were in the clear, and probably never would.

That afternoon, Coventry looked up Trevelyan in 'Who's Who' and the 'Book of Peers'. Bingo, there he was – The Earl of Crantock, a man of distinction, a man from an ancient Anglo Saxon family, 'One of the few', a member of the House of Lords, a publisher of military history books, a widower with twin daughters – Celia and Charlotte – the list went on. In addition to all this, Coventry discovered that she had half-sisters named Celia and Charlotte. The revelations left her breathless. Not only was her blood partly English upper-class, but also her father was a Lord to boot. She had to compose herself, calm down. That evening, Coventry picked up the phone and called the Athenaeum Club.

A man at reception answered. "Athenaeum Club, good evening."

"Good evening," said Coventry. "May I please speak with Mr. John Trevelyan?"

"Oh yes," said the man. "Lord Trevelyan. I think he's in the lounge, who may I say is calling?"

"Miss Calvert, Coventry Calvert."

"One moment please."

Coventry's heart was thumping.

Three minutes passed and Trevelyan came to the phone. Before he spoke, Coventry could hear a sigh of relief coming from the other end of the phone. Then a refined voice said: "Miss Calvert?"

"Yes."

"Good evening my dear... I'm glad you survived the windstorm." His voice bore a velvet tone and Coventry could not help drawing closer to this stranger.

THIRTY-NINE

Trevelyan wore cavalry twill trousers, a navy blue blazer, a cream colour shirt and a neat red tie. Tan suede shoes rounded off his outfit. He was wearing his contact lenses. As in the case of Vincent Galbraith, one would never guess that he was in his early fifties. Coventry was soberly dressed in a light blue blouse and navy blue skirt of modest length. Her hair was swept back but she was not wearing her lenses. Except for her eyes, she was a picture of perfection. When she and Trevelyan met, shook hands and he fixed on her eyes, the Peer could see that her eyes were a mirror image of his own. This was his kid, of that there was no doubt.

Coventry and her father reflected class, just like the exclusive-member club they were in. They met, they talked, they drank each other in and little by little, each conquered the other. That was the way the lunch unfolded. Since she had not worn her lenses, but he had worn his, Trevelyan discreetly jettisoned his own and once this was done each of them drank the other one in fully. They reflected each other in many ways and each could see the likeness beyond just eyes – the shape of the chin, the firmness of bodily tone, the shoulders straight back and the propensity for height. In their case never was the saying so true than the phrase: 'An apple doesn't fall far from a tree'.

They each knew the manner of her conception so the subject was not broached – that could wait. What happened to him after was more important, so Trevelyan explained. What her mother was like then was also more important, and this too he spoke of.

They were lunching at the Athenaeum a few days after Coventry had called Trevelyan. The Club's staff treated the Peer with deference and by the company she kept, Coventry was treated with equal respect. The members and guests of the club in nearby tables would warmly signal hello across the room to them. In their minds, she was probably a romantic interest of the Peer. A widower he may have been, but Trevelyan was far in appearance from his sell-by date. Not in the most fertile of minds would anyone have thought that the stunner with him was his daughter – a tryst, maybe, but not his daughter.

As in the case of Vincent Galbraith, there was nothing boastful about Trevelyan. He was the acceptable face of a superior person, one in whose company a miner from the deepest coal pit in Wales could feel at ease. He spoke about his time in hospital after his injury and how – once he had been released – he tried reaching Paula, only to be told that she had left England. Without trying to make excuses, he spoke about those days and how people lived for the moment. He talked about how time had moved on and how his life had unfolded. He spoke of how his wife had been killed, about his kids and the rest of his family. He made no mention of being a Peer and a member of the House of Lords – that spoke for itself. He didn't talk of being wealthy or being special or being 'One of the few' those facts too were apparent. Nor did he speak of being her father, which, was self-evident. He spoke about coincidence and the hand of fate that so often joins parts of a whole even though time, space and events have disjoined them. He said that, "this, for him, with her, was a gratifying moment, that he hoped could be built upon." He spoke almost poetically in deep, meaningful terms, all of which struck home with Coventry.

Now it was her turn to fill in the past, to speak of her mother's sad ending and deathbed confession; to say that she knew how life was lived by people in wartime Britain; to say that she was happy he had found her, and that she also hoped that this meeting could be built upon. All this and more she would say.

It was obvious to Trevelyan that his daughter had a brain. He was happy that her schooling had been superior, that her mother had married well, that Coventry's work was challenging, and that she was financially secure. He was an Anglican and she a Catholic, but that mattered little to Trevelyan. What mattered to him was her outlook – this, from what he saw, he liked. His daughter was a worker, not a malingerer or good time girl, not a typical young product of the sixties. He knew her views on liberalism and with them he was greatly in accord. He knew she was unmarried but didn't know about her virgin state, but had he known he would have been glad. He didn't know she had visited the Café de Paris and had seen the spot where her mother had surrendered to him. This would have shamed him, so Coventry hadn't spoken of it. He didn't know about Juanito and her ambitions of surrender to him. He didn't know about her dreams so often laced with sex, nor of her penchant for self-love.

He was amused and amazed at her interest in Willie Sutton and the fact that she knew him. He was amazed for good reason. In all of Britain, he was one of very few people that had heard of Willie, or knew anything about him.

He first heard of Sutton in 1941 while recovering from his injuries in hospital. The chap in the bed next to him, who had been badly burned, was Flying Officer Joe Masefield, a Canadian who knew all about Sutton's exploits in New York and Pennsylvania. Masefield was a Sutton fan and would often talk about Willie's captures, and of his slick escapes from jail.

While browsing in a Cornwall bookshop after the war, Trevelyan had come upon the book: 'Great Crooks of the 20th Century'. At the time, the name of Willie Sutton hadn't crossed his mind for years. When he opened the book and looked at chapter one, he found that the chapter was all about Sutton. So when Coventry said she liked and knew Sutton, Trevelyan was amazed. When he learned that Willie was still living, that he was in Attica State Prison in New York, and was soon to be released, he became was fascinated. He thought Sutton was dead.

"Willie will be released just before Christmas," said Coventry.

"What will he do then?" Trevelyan asked.

"He'll live with his sister in Florida. He may co-author a book on his life."

"Will you see him at any point?"

"Oh yes, his first stop after his release will be Manhattan. I plan to be there."

"May I join you?" Coventry was taken aback, but with delight.

"Of course," she replied.

"May your sisters come too? They've never been to New York."

"Absolutely. You'll all be my guests at the Plaza."

"Jolly good," said Trevelyan. "Jolly good,"

I like her style, thought Trevelyan. She reminds me of me.

FORTY

The day after meeting her father, Coventry made four important phone calls. One to Father Powell, one to Adam Stewart, a third to Hawkins-Goodfellow and the last to Dr. Corcoran. They deserved to know that her father had actually found her. She especially wished to thank Goodfellow and Corcoran because the link between them was the trigger of it all. The four men were delighted with the news and when Powell heard what happened, there was an intake of breath from his end of the phone. "Good Heavens," he said.

The year 1969 had been an eventful, revealing year for Coventry and it was now drawing to a close. The date was the 10th of December; soon it would be Christmas. Much had taken place in the weeks gone by and now Coventry, her father and her sisters were poised for their trip to New York and possible snow at Christmas. Soon they would be gazing on Central Park from their expensive suites in the Plaza Hotel. Soon Willie Sutton would be free from his prison cell, whose floor tapped at night from the sounds of darting mice.

Coventry had written to Willie, passing on her news and giving her arrival date, where she would be staying and how long her visit to New York would be for. Her letter suggested that upon his release, he should call her at the Plaza and give his name as Mr. Warren. Willie had replied and would do as she suggested, but said that when they met they should do so discreetly. He said that the press might be on his trail and he didn't want her or her father linked with an old crook like him. 'They would have a field day', he said in his letter. Coventry agreed. She could see the headlines in the New York Daily News:

SLICK WILLIE FREED

MEETS BRITISH 'PEER'

'GOOD LORD!'

Relations between Coventry and her father had developed nicely. In the weeks since their meeting, the reality of 'he who begat her indecently' was not an issue and more and more they had become friends as well as father and daughter. He called her Coventry and she called him John. The Peer had visited her flat and she spent several weekends at his home in Cornwall. Trevelyan had been open with his family and friends as to who Coventry was – they all accepted the fact in the same spirit as the news was conveyed to them.

Coventry found the thirteen-year-old Celia and Charlotte to be delightful girls. Just like their father, there were no airs or graces about them. Their behaviour was typical of girls of that age, but without an edge. They were thrilled with their American sister whose eyes matched theirs and whenever Coventry spoke about New York, their eyes would grow big and their jaws would drop. When their father said that they should wear lenses like his, the twins would hear none of it and their veto to the notion was clear. They liked looking different. Their friends thought their eyes were 'cool' and the girls urged their father to throw his 'wretched' lenses away.

"And they're jolly hard on the eyes too," Celia and Charlotte said in perfect unison.

At work everything was back to normal, and much to the envy of other scribes, Coventry's name was becoming well-known in journalistic circles and throughout Britain. Tiplady was his old self, but as usual his knees continued to knock, even though Lord Baxter was no longer on his back. Yearwood was dead and mostly forgotten but there was life in him yet. In New York, and from the most unlikely of sources, Coventry learnt astonishing facts, about him and Willie Sutton.

Her pieces on Russian cultural matters had been well received. Bolcheckov was very pleased with the articles but something else was bringing him grief. Coventry's piece on Vincent Galbraith's role in the Battle of Britain and his escape from Colditz was described by one critic as, 'A gem, a story laced with pathos about a true knight'.

On the social side of her life, now and then she visited the Café de Paris with the hope that Juanito would be there. No luck. No Juanito. On each occasion she had simply said: "C'est la vie." Little by little, something else was developing for her – a romantic interest, at least on the part of someone else. He was a dinner guest she had met at her father's home on one of her weekend visits. He was a nice, tall, well-spoken man who was easy on the eyes, but Coventry felt he was not for her. She wasn't crazy about his HRH initials, they smacked too much of royalty, too much like His or Her Royal Highness. They actually stood for Harry Robert Halfpenny.

"What do you think?" her father said, on the phone to Coventry once she had returned to London from Cornwall. "What do you think?"

"Not for me, John," she said. "He's a nice fellow, but he's not for me."

"Fair enough," her dad replied.

She was so engrossed with her work and new kin, that Coventry's virgin state of being rarely entered her mind. If the urge for release came along, she knew how to handle it. Though nearly thirty, her views had not altered. She felt that marriage and all that went with it were a waste of time. Sex was another matter. When the time and place and right person came along – hopefully Juanito – then she would hoist her flag of surrender. If romance followed, that would be another matter. A long-term commitment was serious business that had to be carefully broached with full knowledge of the 'devil one knew'. Romance, love and marriage were in her view, sex, whose temperature had risen and burst into flames.

She needn't have thought about Juanito, as the man to trigger the hoisting of her flag of surrender and the lowering of her panties. He was out of the picture, riddled with guilt over the life he was living; he felt he was destined to burn in hell. He had resigned his post as pilot and in January would enter a Spanish seminary to train as a Jesuit priest. Hopefully, a life devoted to God would cleanse him of his sins. Coventry was not to know this now, or ever, nor was she ever to see or hear from him again. Nor was she to learn of his exploits in landing on the Isle of Man. That piece of news had escaped her in the crossfire of events at the time.

Jose del valle de la Rosa, who had killed Jack Kennedy and Martin Luther King was dead, pushed in front of a moving train by Enda McShane. Now McShane was dead, pushed from a speeding train headed for Belfast in Northern Ireland. Were the pushers the IRA, or was the hand of Fidel Castro involved? In the years to come, the American 'powers that be' would continue to insist that Lee Harvey Oswald had acted alone in the slaying of JFK. That was the conclusion of the Warren Report after Kennedy's death, but the report was a libido for the America public. Oswald was a fall guy. Now, in late 1969, those 'powers that be' knew for sure that Kennedy's real killer was the Cuban whose name was Jose del valle de la Rosa.

Jeremy Jones was back in the Kremlin saddle. Little by little, he was assuring Brezhnev and the Communist Party Committee that Nixon's trip to China was not a threat to their country, and that Chairman Mao himself had pushed for the meeting to take place. Within fourteen months, Nixon would make his trip to China and relations between America and that country would improve. Irrespective of all this, the USSR would remain suspicious. The trip was a chance that Nixon would seize because human rights, nuclear proliferation and Taiwan were issues on his agenda. Thanks to Jones, the Russians would give way and Nixon's trip would go ahead.

As for the Aberfan mining tragedy, Prime Minister Jones was out of the woods. Against a tide of opposition from the Tories, the newspapers and Parliament, he had placed the most damming aspects of the tragedy's report under the thirty-year rule. These facts would not be known for years, and by then the negligence of his government would no longer be subject to reprisals. Whether Jones knew or was in any way involved with the death of Yearwood was unknown, and if he knew, that fact would go with him to his grave. One thing was certain,

Jones was aware of the file the FBI was keeping on him and leaking around the world.

Whether he knew that Yearwood had a copy, or that *The London Evening View* had one too, that was another matter. Something else was also certain, Jones was very friendly with the Conservative Peer Lord Baxter, the chairman and owner of *The London Evening View*. From that fact, many in Britain had already drawn conclusions.

On the very day Coventry and her father met for lunch at the Athenaeum, Tina, Tanya and Tatiana Bolschekov had taken a daring step. They had planned it for ages, just as Willie Sutton had planned his escape from jail under cover of a snowstorm in 1951. Only it wasn't a snowstorm the three women were waiting for, but a tour of France by the Russian Ballet, where in Paris they would defect and seek political asylum. France was the only Western Europe country where asylum was sure to be granted. KGB operatives were always attached to cultural tours, which is why Tina and Tanya were involved; the defection was their idea. The three women were fed-up with the stifling nature of Communism, and when the iron was hot, they struck and were free, although always looking over their shoulders. The defection of Russia's Prima Ballerina was a coup for the West, but a nightmare for George Bolchekov. His sister's defection was world news but bad news for him. Freedom, however, was not to be the fate of good-natured Olga. She was still in Moscow haunting the corridors of the Ukraine Hotel with her ring of heavy keys and the twin-pocket apron round her waist. Celia and Charlotte couldn't wait to reach New York. Neither could their father and Coventry. They were eager for a bite of the Big Apple, while, at the same time, Willie Sutton was hungry for a taste of freedom and a life without mice and crooks that used bad language.

FORTY-ONE

They would spend two weeks in New York – they were in their aircraft, ready to depart. John, Coventry, Celia and Charlotte sat waiting for the plane's engines to start.

"Christmas in New York is next," said Charlotte who was seated with her sister.

"Yes," replied Celia. There sat the four of them, each one with similar eyes, the right one blue, and the left one brown. The cabin steward who had shown them to their seats was in a twirl in the galley of the plane, whispering to his colleague about the four passengers in his care.

The Trevelyan clan were flying First Class. Their carrier was a slim-line Viscount – a British Airways VC-10 with two engines at the back. The First Class section was exclusive indeed, twelve seats only, two abreast, and three rows deep.

Except for them, only one other person was in First Class, a famous Hollywood actress who was fast asleep with her mouth wide open, on the brink of a very masculine snore. Her seat was behind Charlotte and Celia. The glamorous goddess of the screen was recovering from the night before and the twins who were trying hard not to giggle.

"In my opinion she's lost all her blinking dignity," whispered Celia to Charlotte. John and Coventry muzzled their grins after a quick glance behind them.

The mood throughout the aircraft was a happy one. The symbols of Christmas adorned the cabins and Coventry's mind flashed back to her childhood and all the happy Christmases she had spent with family and friends, who now were mostly dead. Sitting by her side, John's mind was also on thoughts of yesterdays with his wife, who was dead. Each in their way, John and Coventry were at ease with the season, though the doors of loved ones had closed, another had opened, and sitting by their side was the one that had walked in. By the time the engines had started and the plane had taxied to position, John and his brood were itching to go. Now what? Some delay was holding up their take-off, so there was nothing to do but wait. There were many planes ahead of their Viscount, so they had to wait. All this waiting was a drag, just like the morning Coventry flew to Moscow.

At last the waiting was over and one by one the planes roared down the runway and thundered upwards. It was the Viscount's turn next, so with nothing to keep it, the jet roared down the runway and into the sky. After the roaring and the thundering were over and the Viscount had reached altitude, the captain announced that the flight-time to New York was seven hours and that the number on board was an even one hundred and fifty.

The twin's eyes were bulging, looking all around, looking up the isle, looking towards the cockpit, their eyes aglow. The girls had flown before, but that was small-time, within Europe, where the hops were short, but this flight was across the Atlantic to the Big Apple, to New York, to the US of A, to the land of the free, and of the brave, and of the crooks in jail, like Willie Sutton.

The day before, Willie's Sutton's eyes were bulging too, from a mixture of emotions. His lady lawyer had been to Attica to give him the news. Later in the day the warden had personally appeared at Willie's cell with papers for him to sign that confirmed the date of his release. So if Willie's eyes were bulging, they were bulging for good reason; only the rotten New York Governor and the stinking penal system couldn't show compassion when they set the old man free. They had to make it hard on him, had to bring him grief just a little longer. He was to be released on the 24th of December, Christmas Eve, and then flown to LaGuardia Airport in Flushing, Queens. This was a sneaky time of the year to avoid the media because Willie was news; the press knew his release was imminent, but they were foxed as to when it would be. They never for a moment would guess that his freedom would come hours before Christ's birthday.

Willie had asked his lawyer for a favour. On the 22nd, she would call the Plaza Hotel and leave a message for Miss Calvert on behalf of Mr. Warren. The message was that Warren would be free on December 24th and he would call her at some point on Christmas Day.

"Yes, Willie," said his lawyer, "will do."

The Viscount landed in New York at 11am. JFK Airport was buzzing from the increased activity of holiday traffic. The twins couldn't wait to exit the plane and see New York. They were on their feet even before the Viscount rolled to a stop. They knew nothing about Willie Sutton or the plans Coventry and their father had to meet him. At the top of their voices, the girls were singing the lyrics to a song from the film 'On the Town' the movie with Gene Kelly and Frank Sinatra.

"New York, New York, a wonderful town, the Bronx is up and the battery's down, the people ride in a hole in the ground, New York, New Yoooooooork…"

"Settle down, girls, settle down," said their father. Coventry could not contain a laugh and John's eyes lifted upwards.

Their 'Yellow Cab' driver was not New Yorker – yellow being the operative word – a slippery Korean from Da Nang with a tale that claimed not to know his way to Manhattan. Naturally, the petty-thief, a leech on the make, was lying through his yellow teeth. When he heard the twins chattering, he thought to himself, here are four naive Brits, I'll take them for a ride in more ways that one, and bump up the price on the meter. He was barking up the wrong yellow brick road. Coventry had sussed him out. Here was one of those immigrant hustlers, the type she objected to, but that America now welcomed

223

with stupidly open arms. The oily driver was nothing like the crisp Scotsman, the 'Black Cab' driver that had taken her to Heathrow the morning she flew to Moscow. Coventry leaned forward to get close to the driver.

"Listen here," she said in a sharp tone. "You know your way to Manhattan. I wasn't born yesterday, I was born in New York, not Saigon; head towards Manhattan and the Williamsburg Bridge, cross it, then go north on Madison to 59th Street. Make a left on 59th and you can't miss the Plaza. Got it?"

"Yes, lady," said the driver, who visibly shrank in his seat. There was silence in the taxi after that.

Trevelyan and his twins had seen a side of Coventry they hadn't seen before – she could not be taken for a ride. On their way to Manhattan everyone took in the sights and as the taxi crossed the Williamsburg to Manhattan, the twins grew increasingly excited. All this was new to them. They had seen New York in the movies, but this was the real thing.

The Plaza Hotel was everything anyone could hope for and a world away from the cloak and dagger atmosphere of the Ukraine Hotel. It was top shelf, smart, swanky but subdued, nothing like the brashness Brits attribute to America. There was nothing vulgar in the wealth to be seen. The lobby and its guests smelled of old money, the kind of wealth so familiar in the life of Trevelyan and his twins. While checking in, Celia and Charlotte nearly lost control when the British born Cary Grant – whose name was then Archie Leach – strolled by, wearing a smart suit and a camel-haired coat that looked a picture of perfection. At the front desk, Coventry was swiftly given the message from Mr. Warren. She read it and then put it away. Her dad would be informed when the two were alone.

Coventry had booked three suites on an upper floor of the Plaza. They were spotless and grand and each – as Coventry had requested – overlooked Central Park, Fifth Avenue, and all the surrounding Manhattan views in the region of Central Park South.

It was now the 20th of December and Willie Sutton would be free in four days. Coventry had a list of places she thought would be of interest for her guests to see. As a born New Yorker, she knew the nooks and crannies that were not always seen by visitors – places like Cobble Hill in Brooklyn and the Federal Reserve Bank in lower Manhattan. Washington Heights was also on her list. The latter was of special interest to John because that's where Coventry had grown up and had been schooled. The twins were keen to see Rockerfeller Centre, the Empire State Building, Radio City Music Hall and Macy's – they couldn't wait to visit Macy's and shop. They were keen to ice skate at Rockerfeller Centre and maybe Central Park too.

Coventry had booked at 'El Cijote' in Manhattan for their Christmas Eve meal, and 'Tavern on the Green' in Central Park for Christmas Day. So they were set. The next thing to do was to see the sights, hope for snow, and enjoy New York. For the next few days, this is what they did, blessed by weather that was crisp and clear. With Coventry leading the way, they saw many places of interest. They shopped at Macy's, saw the museums, walked up and down Fifth Avenue and zoomed to the top of the Empire State Building in an elevator. From its peak, to the horizon, they saw all that the eye could see – five boroughs of the city, as well as the shoreline and more of New Jersey across the Hudson.

Next in line for a visit came Washington Heights and for this a full day was needed. It was to be the highlight of the trip for John because most of what he had seen so far he had seen on other trips to New York. At Riverside Drive, John was impressed by the undulating curvature of the building's facades, tall, powerful apartment dwellings that stood shoulder-to-shoulder facing the Hudson River.

He enjoyed those moments when Coventry would say, "Look, John, I had a friend who lived there and another who lived there."

He enjoyed looking at the counterparts that comprised the Height's Riverside Drive. The spot at 149th Street where steep, stone steps swept down from Riverside Drive to join handball courts, baseball fields, basketball courts and swings for children to play on very near the river.

"And look, John" said Coventry pointing. "Mother would push me as I sat on that swing." John enjoyed these moments and so did Celia and Charlotte.

From where they stood by the river, across the Hudson were the palisades of New Jersey. Looking right, there stood the George Washington Bridge – the bridge a frozen, hungry Willie Sutton had crossed with the help of a black man, who had given him a five dollar bill – a man named Yearwood whose death remained a mystery.

From Washington Heights, they hopped a taxi and sped uptown to the Cloisters where Coventry had gone to school. When they entered the doors of the Convent and enquired about Margaret-Mary, the nun at the desk said that Margaret-Mary was still at Mother Cabrini, still teaching, a little older, but as bright as ever, and that the bell would soon ring, and that Sister would be passing the nun's desk very soon. When the class bell rang and Margaret-Mary appeared, there were hugs and greeting and touches of tears. Just as of old, there was little that escaped the eyes of Margaret-Mary.

"And who might these nice people be with eyes just like yours?" the old nun asked Coventry.

When Coventry explained, Margaret-Mary was not nearly as surprised as Coventry thought the nun would be, but she was happy at hearing the news, and just as in the past, Margaret-Mary's eyes twinkled because little escaped them.

Christmas Eve dinner at 'El Cijote' was a Paella bonanza. When they had finished and so much uneaten food remained, the twins – who were ready with a request – struck. John had paid the bill and the waiter was clearing their table.

"May we have a doggie-bag please?" Celia and Charlotte asked.

"Como no," said the waiter with a smile. 'Certainly'. The girls had heard about American doggie-bags and were intrigued by the custom. In England no one would have made a request for uneaten food they had paid for. Such a thing would have been out of line, taken to be greedy, grasping, not cricket, but this was New York, the US of A, the land of the free, and of the brave, and of restaurants that gave doggie-bags in neat cardboard cartons and with grace to boot. Their Christmas meal at Tavern on the Green was also a lavish affair, turkey with all the trimming. The meal was just like America, too much, too generous, so easy to misjudge, so fetching nonetheless. Even for the twins, withdrawing from the table was a chore. When the waiter suggested doggie-bags, the twins said, "No Thanks."

Coventry's phone was ringing when she entered her Plaza suite. The lady at reception said: "A Mr. Warren is on the line." It was Willie. He sounded weary.

"Where are you?" asked Coventry.

"LaGuardia Airport, the Holiday Inn."

"Are you free to talk?" Coventry asked.

The twins had yet to ice skate and the following day would be a good one because a date to meet Willie had been arranged by Coventry.

Charlotte and Celia were old enough to walk down Fifth Avenue to Rockerfeller Centre and make their way back. They weren't fools. Before calling the Plaza, Willie had checked the Queens yellow pages to see if The Venice Restaurant was still in business. He didn't know if it still existed. After seventeen years in prison, all sorts of changes had taken place in the outside world, so he checked. They were still in business, so he suggested to Coventry that the Venice was the place for them to meet; it was near Maine Street in Flushing, not far from LaGuardia Airport. Willie knew Flushing well. He once had digs there that he would use as a hideout when on the run from the law. By taxi from LaGuardia to Flushing wasn't far for him to travel. Coventry took down the address of the Venice and the time of the reunion, which was 1pm.

Willie was at the Venice when Coventry and John arrived. He was sitting in a booth at the back of the restaurant, almost out of sight. The Venice was the type of place where everyone minded his or her own business. The smell of good Italian cooking was everywhere and bottles of Chianti were on each and every table. Over the years, The Venice had changed hardly at all. Most of its dozen male patrons looked typically Italian, heavy-set and rough around the edges – the types you wouldn't want to borrow money from.

Coventry and John looked around the restaurant and when a waving arm rose from the rear, at the end of the arm, slunk in the booth, was the legendary Sutton, who once robbed banks because in addition to the money, he felt alive when robbing them. John and Coventry approached him. Sutton was smoking; the years in jail had taken their toll. He was wrinkled and his breathing was laboured.

"How you doing, doll?" asked Willie. Old and wrinkled he may have been, but there was still the twinkle in his eyes, life in old crook yet. Coventry slipped into his side of the booth and kissed him on the cheek. Willie lowered his eyes. He had forgotten what a kiss felt like. John sat opposite him.

"Willie, I'd like you to meet John Trevelyan, my dad from England."

"Hiya John," said Willie.

"A pleasure, Mr. Sutton" said John.

"Call me Willie," said Sutton, a bit embarrassed at being called Mr. Sutton. They shook hands.

Willie's hand felt like the skin of an alligator. For an awkward spell the conversation hung suspended. Coventry and John looked at Willie and Willie looked at them. It was like when Coventry met her father at the Athenaeum, but in this case, two people were drinking in the third, while the third was looking at them. When talk began, the words at first were tiny steps, but after a while their strides grew longer. When the food they ordered had been placed before them, the words began to gallop. Willie spoke of his plans for the future and of the book he would co-write. He said he would soon fly to Florida, and be joined there by his co-writer.

They would work on the book at the home of Willie's sister – which is where Willie would live out his days. Then Coventry told Willie all about her life in England, about her work, her trip to Moscow, and about how John had found her while she was trying to learn his fate in the war. Willie was delighted to hear all this and John listened quietly, a pleasant smile on his face.

"And how did you like Moscow?" Willie asked. Sutton had no knowledge of her secret mission.

All Coventry had told him in her letters was that the trip dealt with Russian cultural matters.

"It was a bit stressful, she replied. "The weather was dreadful, terrible snow and wind at one point."

"And what did you think of Ben Yearwood?" asked Willie.

Coventry was stunned. How on earth did he know about Yearwood, she thought. John was in the dark. He had no idea to whom they referred. Like Willie, John knew nothing of her secret mission, but if Willie knew about Yearwood, he had to have known of her mission, Willie did not know.

Coventry's mind was in a twirl.

"How do you know about Yearwood?" she asked. Willie laughed a deep belly laugh. When he pulled himself together, he leant forward. His head was over the centre of the table, as were those of John and Coventry – all three were up close. Willie replied almost in a whisper.

"Remember what I told you on one of your visits to Attica, about the time I broke out of jail, when I walked through the snow and was looking for a ride over the bridge – remember?"

"Yes," said Coventry, her eyes the size of silver dollars.

"Remember how I said a Negro in a truck stopped and gave me a lift."

"Yes."

Willie Continued. "I thought he didn't know who I was but he did know, and he didn't turn me in. He could have got a big reward, but didn't turn me in. Well that Negro was Ben Yearwood."

The revelation was just like the moment Tiplady had told Coventry that Yearwood was dead, the moment her mother confessed her indiscretion at the Café de Paris. Her mouth fell open. She had no idea of the link between Sutton and Yearwood.

After a drag on his cigarette, Willie continued. "A few years after I was caught and went to Attica, he came to see me. We've been corresponding ever since, coded stuff like what you and I use. Ben's a clever guy. His last letter said he had met an American journalist who worked for a London newspaper, that she had one brown and one blue eye. I knew you were in Moscow, so I put two and two together and knew it was you."

Coventry was speechless.

"How is Ben? Willie asked. Coventry hesitated before answering.

"Willie," she said in a low voice. "I'm sorry to say that Ben is dead.

When Coventry returned to London, she was surprised to find mail from New York, in a brown envelope. It was from her mother's lawyer. Inside there was a letter from the lawyer as well as a sealed white envelope on which her mother had written Coventry's name. According to the lawyer's letter, at her mother's instructions, the sealed envelope was to be sent to Coventry two years after her mother's death. When Coventry opened it she got a shock as great as Sutton's revelation about Yearwood. About a year after Coventry was born in December 1941, and before meeting Coventry's stepfather, her mother had entered into an affair with a man from which twins girls resulted – Claire and Mary. The letter didn't say who the father was, but it gave Claire's address as Table Top Road, Broken Bow, Texas, and Mary's at Ashfield Lane, Bella Vista, Arkansas. The date on her mother's letter was January 1958, ten years before she died, when her health was sound. Again, Coventry's mouth fell open; all she could do was think that life was wheels within wheels – things that take place when you are planning something else. Where before she had no siblings, now Coventry had four.

Life progressed well for Coventry. She married and had twins with the chap she told her father that was 'not for her'. Sex had caught fire and she was now Mrs. Harry R. Halfpenny. Her affair with Harry began in Cornwall when she was feeling frisky in her father's home and the two of them withdrew to suitable surroundings for a mutually urgent encounter. By then, Coventry's thirty-first year, her nest was like a dragon in need of slaying, so its surrender was inevitable. What followed was a hot bolt of passion – all else according to Allah was written. Her dad was her best friend; she eventually met her American siblings Claire and Mary, but Celia and Charlotte were her favourite sisters. The question of who was the father of her sisters in America was no longer a mystery for Coventry. As was the case with her Godfather, Aden McAvoy, Claire and Mary were tall, heavy set and each had moles above their upper lips. As far as the production of twins were concerned, Coventry was not found wanting. She produced two halfpennies of her own, named Paula and Pauline.

Willie Sutton went on to co-author the book about his life. It was called 'I Was Where the Money Was'. Despite his fragile health, Willie's last years were relatively happy. So engrained was he in the public's mind, that 'Town & Country', an up-market magazine aimed at the wealthy of America, ran a full-page add in the New York Times with Sutton's photo, which concluded by saying "If Willie had been this well informed, he would never have had to rob banks."

He died at the age of seventy-nine in Spring Hill Florida on the 7th of November 1980.

There were only four people at his funeral – his sister, his daughter Jean, Coventry and John Trevelyan.

Willie Sutton's remains rest in an unmarked grave in the state of Florida, USA.